I'LL BE HERE ALL WEEK

I'LL BE HERE ALL WEEK

WARD ANDERSON

KENSINGTON BOOKS
www.kensingtonbooks.com

For Laura

1

Spence turns the volume up on his laptop because the girl in the bathroom is being so loud. She's talking about comedians she thinks are funny, but he's watching clips of himself on YouTube and wondering when she's finally going to take the hint and leave. On the screen he's watching a set he did once on *The Late Late Show with Craig Kilborn*. At the time it seemed like a really big deal. Now it just depresses him. He still can't help but watch it from time to time, even though it never makes him feel very good.

"Do you like Dane Cook?" Brandy or Mandy or whatever her name is says while fixing her hair in the mirror. He chuckles at the thought of her putting in so much effort just to make the walk of shame out of his hotel room in a few minutes. All the primping in the world isn't going to erase the "just sexed" look she has.

"Sure," he says back, even though he didn't even hear the question.

"What about Daniel Tosh? You like Daniel Tosh?"

"Yeah." He nods. He pauses the clip and realizes for the first time that he still owns the shirt he wore on the TV show. It was eight years ago. It might be time to change things up a bit. He wonders if there's an outlet mall or something nearby that he can stop at when he heads out of town. His wardrobe has consisted of the same five shirts and pairs of jeans for so long, he doesn't remember the last time he tried something new.

"I think Dane Cook is hilarious." She emerges from the bathroom, still wearing nothing but her panties. In this light, he can see how poorly done the tattoo of the kitten just below her navel really is. Last night he thought it was Pac-Man.

"Don't you think he's funny?" she asks. "Dane Cook?"

"Sure." He goes back to watching the video of himself.

She sits down on the corner of the bed just behind where he is sitting at the tiny hotel desk. She's pushing thirty and talks like she's fifteen. Everything she says sounds like a question, even when it isn't one. She twirls her hair around her index finger while she talks and bobs her foot up and down to whatever song is in her head. He looks down at her toes and thinks it's kind of cute that her feet sort of look like hands.

"That you?" she says and points at the laptop screen.

"Yeah."

"From TV?"

"Yeah."

"What show was it? *The Tonight Show*?"

I wish, he thinks.

"*The Late Late Show*," he says.

"Oh, yeah. With that guy that was on, like, that Drew Carey show."

"Craig Ferguson."

"Yeah. That guy. He's funny, too."

"This was when it was hosted by Craig Kilborn."

"Who's that?"

"Some other guy."

"Is he like the guest host or something?" she asks.

"No, he was the guy who used to host it before the guy doing it now," he says.

"Oh," she says, "when was that?"

"Eight years ago."

"Oh," she says. "Wow."

"Yeah."

"So," she says and then sits in silence for thirty seconds.

"Dane Cook is probably my favorite comedian of all time. Daniel Tosh, too, but Dane Cook is better. He's, like, the funniest comedian I've ever seen."

He pauses the video and looks at her over his shoulder.

"What?" she asks and looks confused.

"Really?" he asks.

"Oh," she says, "you're funny, too. I mean, I just think, like, Dane Cook is awesome, you know? He's like my all-time fave. But I still think you're funny, too."

"I slept with a chick in Florida once who was absolutely gorgeous. She had the most amazing body I've ever seen. I've never been with a woman as gorgeous as she was. She was amazing. But you're pretty good, too." He raises his eyebrows. She has stopped playing with her hair and has her lips stuck out like she's pouting.

"What the hell is wrong with you?" she asks.

"Nothing," he says.

"That wasn't very nice."

"Tell it to Dane Cook."

She rolls her eyes and then stretches out across the bed. He's kind of surprised she didn't just get up and leave, but he guesses she's smarter than he gave her credit for at first. Maybe she got the point. Either way, she doesn't seem too upset by it and isn't leaving. He goes back to watching the video.

He killed that night, eight years ago, in front of the studio audience and in front of everyone watching it at home. It was an incredible set and, for a while, he used the TV recording as a demo tape. For the first couple of years after it aired, he got a good bit of work. He killed last night, too, right there in Enid, Oklahoma. Eight years ago he was on TV and hoping to be headlining Vegas within the year. Now it's 2010 and he's at the Electric Pony bar in Enid. There's even a mechanical bull next to the stage.

Welcome to Hollywood, baby, he thinks. *Could be worse.*

At least the audience was good to him and at least he got laid last night. He's been treated worse in better cities and had worse looking women than Mandy or Brandy or whatever her name is shoot him down. He reassures himself that there are worse places to be. They like him here, so he should consider himself lucky.

They treated him like a TV star. From the moment he set foot onstage, they treated him as if he were Steve Martin making his triumphant return to stand-up comedy. For a brief moment, he forgot that he was unknown and broke and actually felt like a celebrity. The bright lights shining in his face hid the fact that he was performing in a shitty bar and not an A-list comedy club. Those same lights also hid the fact that the place was half empty. They loved him so much, they sent drinks to the stage and bought him shots of liquor after his set that made Enid *feel* like Vegas. Or at least like Reno.

He looks around the hotel room and sighs. It isn't dirty as much as it's small and musty. The bedspread is frayed and a bit worn out, even though it smells like it's pretty clean. He hates places that only give you a single bar of soap and no other toiletries. He's got at least six little bottles of shampoo in his suitcase, but that's not the point. He just likes to have them available even if he has no intention of using them. He also likes hotel rooms that have two double beds. That way he can have sex in one and sleep in the other when What's-Her-Name finally leaves. Feeling like a celebrity wears off very quickly when the sun comes up.

"Do you like Carlos Mencia?" She picks up the TV remote and starts flipping through the channels. He remembers an interview with Charlie Sheen in the nineties. He was asked why someone as rich and successful as he was felt the need to pay prostitutes for sex. Sheen told the reporter, "I don't pay them to have sex with me, I pay them to leave." It makes perfect sense now.

His cell phone rings on the corner table, and the caller ID reads that it's Rodney. He's tempted to let it go to voice mail because Rodney knows damned well that he's normally still asleep at this hour. The problem is that Rodney never calls this early unless there's something wrong, so he answers.

"You having fun out there, dumbass?" Rodney says. Rodney has never so much as had one drag off a cigarette, yet he sounds as if he's been smoking since he was three. His sinus medicine apparently sucks because it never seems to work.

"What do you mean?" Spence asks.

"I mean did you get laid last night?"

He looks at his laptop to see if the webcam is on. "Why do you ask?"

"Because I hear you had some broad hanging all over you, you filthy man-whore."

"I had fun. It was a good show," he says.

"Oh, I see," Rodney says. Rodney is easily fifty, but the way he talks makes it apparent no one ever told him that. "She's still there, isn't she?"

"Did you call for any other reason than to live vicariously through me?" Spence asks.

"Hey, screw you," Rodney says. "I've got better clients than you I could vicariously live through, you know. You think you're the only client I have that ever gets laid?"

"I'm the only one you're calling at nine a.m."

"You should be flattered."

"What's the problem?"

"How do you know there's a problem?" Rodney asks. "How do you know I'm not just calling to check up on you and see how you're doing?"

Spence sighs. "Because I know you, Rodney. What's the problem?"

"There was a complaint," Rodney says as he switches gears. It has become routine. Rodney always starts by building people up before he tears them down. It comes from something he read called *The One Minute Manager*. Ever since then, Rodney tosses out a few compliments before delivering really bad news. It would actually be pretty nice if it weren't so predictable.

"Where?" Spence asks.

"At the Pony."

"Jesus." Spence closes his laptop and gets up from the tiny hotel desk. "Already?"

"Yeah," Rodney says and pauses for no reason other than the fact that he's trying to do too many things at once. He's probably checking his e-mail, clipping his fingernails, and reading *Variety* all while doling out the bad news from the night before. "Somebody said you weren't that great or you said something offensive or pissed someone off or something."

"That's a little vague, don't you think?"

"I guess," Rodney says. "I'm just telling you that someone bitched about you so they called me."

"Who was it?"

"Who was what?"

"Who'd I piss off?"

"I dunno," Rodney says. "Some guy. Or some broad. They didn't tell me. Just said someone complained."

Spence looks in the mirror and frowns. It's not going to be a good day. He looks like shit. Like he hasn't slept in a couple of days or is hungover. The fact that he managed to get laid looking like this is somewhat of a miracle. "This is about one complaint?" he asks Rodney. "They had one complaint, and you're calling me at nine a.m. to gripe at me about it?"

"I'm just telling you what they told me," Rodney says. Spence pictures him sitting at his cluttered desk with his feet propped up, wearing the same ratty baseball cap he's been wearing for years. He thinks that the way Rodney dresses is lazy. The irony is not lost on him, since he hasn't worn a suit or even a tie onstage in years. Still, he thinks that an agent should dress the part more often. Rodney looks more like a drunken golf caddy.

"There were almost a hundred people there last night," Spence says. He remembers it well because he killed. That's what all that laughter was about. That's what the free drinks were all about. That's why Brandy or Mandy is now lying half naked on his bed and watching *Full House*.

"Yeah, but they're pretty big on not getting complaints," Rodney says.

"One freaking complaint? Jesus, Rodney. That's a bit much, don't you think? You'd think that a hundred people laughing would outweigh one jackass, right?"

"Hey, I'm just telling you what they told me."

"Oh, for Chrissakes."

Rodney pauses for a minute to finish whatever else he's doing and says, "Look, just go back there tonight and have a great show, and they'll forget whatever it was that pissed them off. I just wanted you to be aware of it."

"And you don't see how telling me this is going to make me paranoid now?" Spence asks. He's pacing around the front of the room now and starting to realize why he looks like hell. Too many early phone calls from Rodney that stress him out for the rest of the day.

"Not paranoid, just aware," Rodney says.

"I'm supposed to just walk in there and be all carefree and jolly or something?"

"Hey, today is a new day," Rodney says. "Just don't do whatever you did last night. I dunno."

"Don't do—" Spence bites his top lip and makes a fist. He wants to throw the phone against the wall, but it would only freak out the girl on the bed and he'd have to go out and buy a new phone later in the day. "I was doing my act. A hundred people loved it. How the hell should I know what pissed off one person?"

"It was probably more than one person," Rodney says.

"If it was less than a hundred, they lose," Spence says. "It's a goddamned comedy show, Rodney. Majority rules."

"And I'm on your side," Rodney says. "I'm just telling you what they told me. If you wanna get booked back, you need to take it easy on them tonight."

Sure, you're on my side, Spence thinks. *Fuck you, Rodney.*

"Do something different. Mix it up a bit," Rodney says.

"Oh, okay, I'll just write a whole new act today. A full hour of squeaky clean jokes for the one table of people who complained last night and won't be back tonight anyway."

"Did it ever occur to you that you'd work more if you could work clean?"

"Did it ever occur to you that I know more about being a stand-up comedian than you do?"

"Just trying to help you," Rodney says without skipping a beat. "You can't get on TV saying 'fuck.' "

"This isn't *Letterman*, Rodney," Spence says, "it's a cowboy bar. It's not even a real comedy club, for Chrissakes."

"Really?" Rodney says. "Because I could have sworn that you were working there last night and that you're a comedian."

"You know what I mean."

"You can call it whatever you want. They pay you the same as any other place," Rodney argues.

"Right, but I can't perform clean in front of a roomful of drunk rednecks, Rodney," Spence says. Rodney never understands this argument, and they've had it a dozen times already this year. "The drunk cowboys want the dirty jokes, whether the idiot running the place understands that or not."

"You could be clean if you wanted to be," Rodney says.

"No way. They would eat me alive."

"Please," Rodney says, "save the drama for your mama."

"Save the—" Spence rolls his eyes. "What are you, calling me from 1998?"

"Don't kill the messenger here. I'm just giving you the news. That's my job."

"Are you reading from a book of clichés?"

"Are you listening to me, you ass?" Rodney says. "I'm trying to help you."

Spence looks back in the mirror. He really looks awful. Two years ago he was thirty-five and looked twenty-nine. Now he looks fortysomething. When did that happen? He wonders if maybe he should go back to highlighting his hair.

"Just once," he says, "I'd like for you to call me with good news. I had a great show last night, Rodney. Do you understand what it feels like to have you shit all over it like this the next day? Any idea how awful that is?"

"Look, it sucks and I know it," Rodney says. "But that's business, my man. This is show *business*. And it may suck sometimes, but it's better than sitting in an office. Last I checked, you haven't had a day job for, what, ten years?"

"Nine."

"Nine. Whatever. If I were you, I would stop feeling sorry for myself, check my ego at the door, and just do what they ask. Plenty of clubs love you. This one will, too. Just lay low tonight."

Spence sighs. "Alright, fine."

"I'm serious," Rodney says. "Check your ego at the door."

"Fine."

"And be careful where you stick your tallywacker, will you? I think the broad you're with is the bartender's ex or something. That may be what started this whole thing."

"So that's what the complaint might be about? Not about the show but . . . you know," Spence looks over at What's-Her-Name. She's still watching *Full House* and doesn't seem to even notice that he's been about three seconds away from an aneurysm this entire time.

"Yeah, maybe," Rodney says.

Unbelievable, Spence thinks.

"Fine. Anything else?" he asks.

"Yeah, scratch Rockford, Illinois, off your schedule. The club went out of business."

"Aw, hell," Spence says. It was just a one-nighter in a bar, but he needed it. The gig paid four hundred bucks for one night and led right into a weekend of other gigs along the way. He booked it because the routing was perfect and gave him a hotel to stay in on his way east from a string of western gigs.

"Yeah, I know it sucks," Rodney says. "I'll try to fill it in with something else. Maybe Baltimore or Cleveland. I dunno."

"Lemme know, okay?"

"And send me more headshots. I'm all out of them."

"Already?"

"Yeah, send me at least a hundred."

"Alright."

"Now go tell that girl you're with you just gave her the clap."

Rodney hangs up before he's even finished with his zinger. It doesn't matter because it's essentially the same joke every time he calls. If it's not the clap, it's syphilis or herpes or genital warts.

Damn it, Spence thinks and stares at his phone.

Another call from Rodney to ruin a perfectly good day. It has become so predictable that it's almost a routine. A show will go great only to be followed eight hours later by a call from Rodney telling him that the club is pissed for some stupid reason. They hated the shirt he wore or didn't like his joke about epilepsy or thought that his act was too dirty. Or maybe someone just hated the fact that he got laid and the bartender didn't. It's always something, and it usually has nothing to do with stand-up comedy, which is supposed to be the job description.

He tosses his cell phone on the bed and looks at Mandy or Brandy as she's watching TV. He's tired and he's hungry, but he's also a bit horny and thinks he could probably have sex with her again. She just fixed her hair, though, so she might not be up for it.

"What's up?" she asks, and he realizes he's been staring at the wall behind her head. She's attractive, but she could stand to do a little less tanning. If she keeps it up, her face will be leathery by the time she hits thirty-five.

He clears his throat. "Nothing."

"You okay?" she asks.

"Yeah," he says. "I've just gotta get out of here."

"But you have another show tonight."

"I mean I have to get going. Out of the hotel. I have to do an interview for the radio."

"Which station?" she asks as she gets up from the bed and puts her jeans on. They're bedazzled and have writing on them, and he suddenly wonders if she realizes that she's not a teenager anymore.

"I don't know," he says. "The rock station."

"106.7 or 92.9?" She pulls her T-shirt over her head, and her bracelets get caught in her sleeve. She stumbles around for a second, stuck in the middle of her shirt. He almost laughs at the way she wrestles her way into her clothes, her head buried somewhere inside and her arms just two awkward stubs trying to poke their way through. He thinks she looks like a low-budget *Star Trek* alien.

"106.7, I think."

"Oh, I like that one. I'll have to tune in and listen to you."

"Yeah. I'll be on with the morning crew, I think," he says. "Or maybe they'll tape it and play it later."

"*The Cubby in the Morning Show*?"

"I guess so," he says. All of the radio shows are the same. Some "Morning Zoo Crew" sitting around pretending to laugh at each other while playing ZZ Top. He probably knows three DJs named "Cubby" at this point and has met at least six guys named after animals.

"That's pretty cool. You get to, like, hang out on the radio all day and then, like, do shows at night."

"Something like that, yeah."

"Better than having a job," she says. He cracks a smile and tosses her a pair of tiny pink socks he found on the floor. He has had this same conversation so many times, it's almost as routine as the one he just had with Rodney.

Spence puts on his jeans and a sweater and checks out his hair in the mirror. He keeps wondering if maybe he should go back to highlighting it. He grabs his sunglasses off the small hotel desk because he's certain he won't be able to stand the sun when it hits him in the face. The one good thing this fleabag hotel has going for it is the blackout curtains. He opens the door, and the cold hits him at the same time as the bright sunlight. Neither feels very good, and he instantly wishes he was back in bed.

What's-Her-Name drives a Jeep. She followed him to the

hotel and parked it right beside him. She must've been drunker than he remembers because her parking job sucks, and she has taken up two spaces next to his old Toyota Camry. She throws her purse into the passenger seat and then leans up against the door with her thumbs in the belt loops of her jeans. She must be at least twenty-nine but, just like Rodney, she's having a hard time accepting her age.

"I had a great time." She bites her lower lip and looks up at him. The eyes she's making remind him of why he brought her back here in the first place, and part of him is tempted to just take her back inside and have sex with her again. But then she'd probably never leave and wind up sticking around the rest of the day.

"Drop me an e-mail or something," he says and unlocks his car. As he opens the door, she leans in and puts her lips on his. He puts one hand around her waist and lets her tongue slip into his mouth for only a second. Before she can really connect with the kiss, he pulls away.

"I had fun," he says and slips into his car. He rolls down the window and leans out.

"Me too." She gets into her Jeep and sits there with the door open. "You're gonna, like, be famous one day. You know that? I bet you will. I believe it. You're really funny."

"From your mouth to God's ears," he says as he starts the car.

"One day, I'll tell people I knew you when."

It's more likely you'll tell them that you slept with me when, he thinks.

"I hope so," he says.

She shuts her car door and starts the Jeep at the same time. He doesn't say anything, but he smiles at her and gives her a wink. She's probably a pretty cool girl, and he realizes he'd probably like her if he wasn't in such a foul mood.

Thanks for nothing, Rodney.

"See you later," she says. She waves at him as she pulls out and drives away. He sits in his car for a minute, screwing around with the rearview mirror. Maybe later today he'll get some highlights. Then he won't look quite as old. Maybe there's a hair salon and an outlet mall nearby. He can kill two birds with one stone.

When she has pulled out of the parking lot, he shuts off his engine. He sits there for a minute, then goes back inside his hotel room and goes back to bed.

2

Another night in Oklahoma and another show at the Electric Pony. Spence arrives at the bar about a half hour before showtime, which Rodney has specified in all of his contracts. Like most contracts Rodney handles, it says nothing about anything he needs from the club, but everything that the club expects from him. One of those things is that he always arrives at the venue with enough time to sit around and do nothing.

He walks straight up to the bar and looks around. The Pony is only a comedy club on Fridays and Saturdays. The rest of the week, it's a country western bar and that's exactly what it will become again the minute he leaves the stage. The lights will come up, the dance floor will fill, and people will start line dancing to Toby Keith or Kenny Chesney or whatever it is that country music people listen to these days. He doesn't know.

"Drink?" one of the two bartenders says to him as he sits down in the corner seat. This particular bartender is not the one that used to date Mandy or Brandy or whatever her name is, so the guy is being pretty friendly.

The other bartender across the room is giving him dirty looks, so he can only assume that what Rodney heard is true. This makes him happy. There are few things greater than knowing that you slept with a woman that made another man extremely jealous. He got laid and the bartender didn't, and now he's walking on thin ice for it. People rarely hate comedians for the laughs they get, but often hate them for the attention that comes with it after the show.

"Whiskey, neat," Spence says. The bartender nods and pours whatever is on the rail into a glass. He likes it when the bartenders don't measure out the booze and simply pour it straight out of the bottle. It's always annoying when he wants to have a glass of whiskey and they give him the equivalent of a shot in a rocks glass. He's always wondered who the hell sips a tiny shot of liquor. He tries to imagine Dean Martin sipping a shot of Scotch onstage and just how stupid it would have looked.

He used to not drink before shows. It was always a rule to keep his energy up, keep the show running smoothly, and keep things professional. It's not a good idea to be slurring through the show, especially not when there's the chance that people in the audience might start sending shots to the stage midway through. Now that he can do his act pretty much in his sleep, he doesn't worry too much about having a little something before the gig. Besides, he's got plenty of time to kill. The MC will go up and do at least twenty minutes of material and the show won't even start on time. That leaves him with almost an hour with nothing to do but hang.

The place is about as full as it was last night, which makes it about half empty by the looks of it. Still, it's at least a hundred people, which is good for some of these makeshift comedy shows that he's gotten used to doing. Some hotel in Lakeland, Florida, once made him perform for six people. That sucked. A hundred people in a room that seats two hundred isn't so bad when he remembers that gig in Lakeland.

"There's the funny man." The club manager walks over and pats him a little too hard on the back. His name is Billy, although he's old enough to simply go by Bill at this point. There's something about country guys that they always keep their kid names even once they hit their fifties. Billy has a scraggly gray beard and a belly that likely hangs over an unseen, huge belt buckle. He looks like a redneck version of Santa Claus.

"Having a little hair of the dog?" Billy says as he sits down on the nearest barstool and thumbs mindlessly at a Zippo lighter in his hand, flicking it open and then closed over and over again.

"Nah," Spence says, "just having a drink to loosen my tongue a little bit. Take the edge off."

"Take the edge off?" Billy says. "Shit, a pro like you should be able to do this show blindfolded."

"You'd be surprised."

Billy laughs and flicks his Zippo open and then shut again. "Listen, you know to take it kinda easy tonight, right? Don't hit 'em too hard like you did last night, and all."

"I'm not sure what you mean."

"Just go a little easy, is all."

"How did I hit them too hard?" Spence asks. "Do you mean the language?"

"Naw, it ain't nothing like that." Billy leans in, as if he's telling him a secret. "Just watch some of the racier content. You know, the controversial stuff. No one cares if you say 'shit' or even 'fuck' or anything. Just try to keep it light on some of the topics."

"Like what?" Spence asks. It's annoying enough when people want to tell him what to say. It's even more annoying when they are vague while doing it.

"Well, you did some joke last night about Jesus or God or something," Billy finally admits. "You might want to leave that one out."

"A joke about Jesus?"

"That's what someone said, yeah."

"I don't know what they're talking about. I don't have any jokes about religion."

Billy flicks his lighter. "Well, something got somebody fired up. They said you were making fun of Jesus or something like that."

"Well, I can assure you that won't happen again," Spence says, "since I have no idea what they're talking about."

"Did you say *GD*?" Billy asks. " 'Cause sometimes that's enough to piss people off around here."

"GD?"

"You know," Billy says and looks around, as if he's violating national security, "goddamnit."

"I don't know. Maybe."

"Well, that might be it. Best to steer clear of that tonight then."

"So no jokes about Jesus."

"No. Nothing making fun of religion or God or anything like that."

"How about Jews?" Spence asks. "Can I make fun of Jews?"

Billy shrugs. "I don't see why not."

"And the jokes about sex and drugs and pedophilia and incest and death . . . all of that's still okay?"

"Fine by me."

"Just no jokes about Jesus and don't say *goddamnit.*"

"You got it," Billy says.

Unbelievable, Spence thinks.

"No problem," he says.

"So we're clear?" Billy asks him.

"Crystal."

Billy pats him on the back again and laughs for no real reason, then flicks his lighter open and closed a few more times. After a moment of silence passes between the two of them, Billy gets up without saying anything and walks away, wheezing his way back into his office around the corner.

When Billy is out of sight, Spence goes back to drinking his whiskey in silence. He tries to remember a single joke in his act about Jesus but can't recall one. Across the room, one of the bartenders smiles and the other one glares at him. He sips his whiskey and wonders if this is the glamorous side of show business he always heard about when he was a kid.

Goddamn, he thinks to himself, smiles, and looks back down at his glass.

At least in the next thirty or so minutes he gets to take the stage and all will be right in the world. Club owners and bartenders and agents and managers always try to humble the comedians as much as possible when they are offstage. He knows this is just because none of them have the talent or balls to actually get up in front of the audience themselves. He has learned to shrug it off, since he knows that everything changes once the lights come up and he grabs the microphone.

"Hey, boss," a young kid, no more than twenty-three, calls and suddenly appears next to him. The kid is too young to be a manager and too nerdy to be a bartender. Skinny, wearing a Spider-Man T-shirt and a corduroy blazer, he's apparently trying to grow a lumberjack beard. It's obvious that the kid is an amateur comedian. He fits the profile.

"How's it going?" Spence nods at the kid and raises his glass in salute.

"I'm Marshall," the kid says, "the MC for the night."

"Where's the kid who was here last night?" Spence asks. He liked the kid from last night.

"He's in the kitchen," the kid says.

"Eating?"

"Working. He's the line cook."

"Really?

"Yeah." Marshall nods. "Billy lets us do the show one night a week if we agree to work in the kitchen the other night."

"So last night," Spence starts.

"I was the line cook," Marshall finishes.

"Right." Spence extends his hand. "Nice to meet you."

Marshall takes Spence's hand and shakes it. "Listen, I was wondering if you had anything you want me to say about you when I introduce you. You know, like any TV credits or anything like that."

"Sure, just tell them I've been seen on *The Late Late Show*."

Marshall pulls out a cocktail napkin and starts writing on it with a ballpoint pen. "Great stuff. Was Craig Ferguson cool?"

"I never met him," Spence says. "I did it when Craig Kilborn was hosting."

"Who?" Marshall asks.

"The guy before Ferguson."

"I didn't know there was a guy before Ferguson."

"More than one, actually. He also was the first host of *The Daily Show.*"

"No shit?"

"Scout's honor."

"Before my time, I guess," Marshall says. "Well, we're gonna be starting in a bit. I'll do, like, ten minutes and then bring you up. Cool?"

Spence nods at Marshall and motions to the bartender for a refill.

There is no green room, so he sits at the bar, watches Marshall onstage, and waits for his name to be called. He remembers back to when he used to pace the back of the room, anxiously awaiting the sound of his name being called. He would strut through the audience as he made his way to the stage, ready to take on the world. These days, he just leans against the bar and waits.

Marshall is getting chuckles, but hardly making a dent in the audience. His material is perfect for a brand-new host at his age and is perfectly safe, even if it isn't at all groundbreaking. It's observational fluff, which is what most twentysomething comedians wind up doing before they've had any real life experiences to bring to the stage. It's exactly the kind of material Jerry Seinfeld would be doing had he never become Jerry Seinfeld.

At least he didn't say goddamnit, Spence thinks and takes the last sip of his drink.

Time flies by onstage, especially when a comic is still pretty new. Everyone imagines they speak much slower than they actually do, and they wind up with less material than they thought they had. The ten minutes Marshall was supposed to do suddenly becomes five as he winds down and gets ready to pass the microphone.

Please don't mispronounce my name, Spence thinks as he watches Marshall trying to deliver a big closing joke that winds up being a six instead of a ten. Marshall then reaches into his pocket and pulls out the napkin he was writing on. Apparently it was too hard to memorize the words "has been seen on *The Late Late Show.*"

"Are you ready for your headliner?" Marshall says as he looks down at the napkin in his hand. The audience applauds halfheartedly, which is often the case with half-drunk crowds in makeshift comedy clubs. Marshall makes no attempt to hide the fact that he's reading off his cheat sheet as he holds the napkin up to his face. "The comic coming to the stage is a very funny man. He has been seen on *Late Night with David Letterman. . . .*"

Idiot, Spence thinks as he watches Marshall completely screw up the intro and then mispronounce his name. *How hard is it to remember which stupid TV show I was on?*

The smattering of applause leads him to the stage and, as he takes the microphone from Marshall, everything is reset and he is a brand-new man. He is all smiles and thrilled to stand in front of this room full of cowboys and rednecks. Just an hour earlier he was some guy sitting in the room. Now he's the star of the show.

It's under these lights and on this stage that he feels the most comfortable. It's here that nothing else matters. The glare is too bright for him to see Billy or the bartenders, and the lights darken everything in the background to where all he can focus on is doing his act. At the bar, he has to be social when he'd just as soon be alone, but onstage he's everyone's best friend. Onstage he's not some guy leaning on the bar drinking whiskey; he's the star of the show. Onstage he's charming and he's beloved by the audience. They love to laugh at him and he loves to hear it.

He kills. They love him. They laugh and they applaud. When it's like this and everything is right on, forty-five minutes feels like ten. Before he knows it, he's on his closing bit and bringing the show home. In a matter of minutes, he'll be back at the bar, soaking up the free drinks being sent his way and waiting to see if there's another Mandy or Brandy waiting to get to know him a little better. Even if he doesn't want to get laid or just wants to be alone tonight, it's nice to know that he has options. And, when the show goes this well, he always has options.

He was twenty-one the first time he had this feeling. He went to an open mic night at the Comedy Corner in Baltimore when he was home for Christmas. He signed up and watched the other amateurs try their jokes. Most of them sucked. A few were good. When he did it and people laughed, he knew he had to have more. He had to do it again. He wasn't even very good. Back then, he would have killed to get work at the Electric Pony in Oklahoma. Back then he would gladly work for free. Now he does it for a living and feels like he's being robbed.

But he still loves being onstage.

"You guys have been great," Spence says as he puts the final touches on some mindless joke about masturbating penguins. He knows better, but he leans in on the microphone and decides to go for broke. "Really, you've been the best goddamned audience I've had all week. Thank you, good night!"

The applause is thunderous, and a half-full cowboy bar sounds like Carnegie Hall in his head. He doesn't walk offstage so much as he swaggers. His adrenaline is up, the ego he checked at the door has returned, and the smile on his face is bigger than his already oversized head. He's probably going to be in trouble, but at the moment he just doesn't care. That applause is exactly why he got into this business in the first place. It's one of the reasons he stays in it. It might as well be a needle in his arm. He takes a moment and lets himself enjoy it.

Billy's desk is cluttered with paperwork, random stacks of money and cash register drawers, and an ashtray that needs to be emptied. On the wall is a poster of Elvira, Mistress of the Dark, holding a beer bottle near her breasts and looking surprised. The poster reminds you to have a great Halloween five years ago. On another wall hangs a calendar that hasn't been changed in two months. Billy is counting money out loud while watching ESPN half-assed over his shoulder.

Sitting and waiting for Billy to pay him, Spence pretends to be checking his cell phone for text messages. Out in the bar he can hear "Friends in Low Places" being played, and he guesses the bar will wind down before too long. It's pushing one a.m., and he figures they won't go past two, even in a place that parties as hard as this one. The drunks will tire of line dancing and eventually find somewhere to pass out or screw or both.

"Not bad, son," Billy says to him after throwing a rubber band around a stack of money and tossing it into a safe next to his desk, "even if you did do exactly what I told you not to do."

"What's that?" Spence says. He gives his best impression of someone who has no clue about what Billy is talking about and tries to look innocent. He's not good at it.

"I heard you say *GD*," Billy says.

"I did?"

Billy nods.

"I didn't realize I said it again," Spence lies.

"I got what you were doing."

"Just doing my show."

Billy smirks at him, takes a long pull off a bottle of beer he has sitting on his desk, and swivels around in his chair. It makes a tired, groaning squeak from under his weight and sounds like it could collapse at any moment. Looking up at Elvira, Billy sighs and rubs his eyes. He's one of those fat men who always breathes too loudly, even when he's just sitting still. He's probably awful to sit next to in a movie theater or on a plane, since he constantly sounds like he's a few breaths away from dying.

"Ever since we started doing comedy here on weekends, people started calling and bitching about shit. It's always something," Billy says.

"How many complaints do you normally get?"

"I dunno," Billy says. "Maybe six calls a week. Sometimes more. Sometimes less."

"There were over a hundred people at both shows," Spence tells Billy. "They all had a good time. That should easily outweigh any complaints. I'd say it's way better to make a hundred people laugh and piss off seven people than the other way around."

"That hundred people laugh and go home. The six or seven call me on the phone and bitch me out for an hour."

"You can't please everybody."

Billy snorts and shrugs his shoulders and makes a sound that might be an agreement or might be gas.

"Did you see the movie *Transformers?*" Spence asks.

"Sure."

"Did you like it?"

"Didn't care, really."

"Millions of people loved that movie," Spence says, "and people will remember that long after they remember that critics thought it sucked. You just can't please everyone. That's comedy. If you please the crowd, mission accomplished. It's a true democracy. Majority rules."

"I guess," Billy says, "but it sure as hell is a pain in my ass. Doesn't even bring in that much money for us."

Spence hears this and immediately does the math in his head. Each person that walked through the door that night paid ten dollars plus a two-drink minimum. About half of them stayed around and drank for another two hours after the show. The numbers he comes up with turn out to be better than the average comedy club, where people watch a show for a couple of hours and then immediately leave. At least the Electric Pony has dancing. It's now one a.m. and the place still has people there, buying drinks and trying to hook up.

"Do you normally have more than a hundred people in here at eight o'clock?" he asks.

Billy shrugs. "Well, we used to bring in this hypnotist every few months. That was one funny dude. He'd sell out, every single time. Hell, we'd have to add chairs to the dance floor just to fit people in here."

Spence cringes when Billy tells him this and he takes a sip from his glass of whiskey. He's not a fan of hypnotists. They always pull audience members onstage and make them do silly tricks. People love them, and they always sell out because everyone wants to watch their friends act like idiots. They're all the same, and there's no real writing or stand-up to it. To him, it's like watching monkeys dance.

"You can't have a hypnotist every week," he says to Billy.

"Hell." Billy swivels around in his chair. "I would if I could. They sell out every single time."

Spence takes a sip of his whiskey and just nods. Strippers would sell out, too. So would midget wrestling. So would cock fighting. He wonders if Billy even likes stand-up comedy.

"Here you go," Billy says as he takes a stack of money, thumbs through it, and tosses it to him from across the desk.

Pay day at last, Spence thinks as he picks up the stack of cash. He takes off the rubber band and counts through it. He always counts the money immediately, just in case it winds up short. And in this case, it does.

"We're two hundred short," he says to Billy, holding up the stack of cash.

"That's because we canceled the Friday late show," Billy explains, lacing his hands together and putting them behind his head as he leans back in his noisy chair.

"Yeah, but I get paid by the night, not by the show."

"Not according to our paperwork," Billy says. "No show, no pay. We cleared that deal with your boy a couple of months ago."

Spence takes a deep breath, then leans back in his chair and polishes off the rest of the whiskey in his glass. Thankfully, it's way more than just a shot.

Fuck you, Rodney, he thinks.

"Alright," he says. There's no point in arguing if Rodney is the one who screwed up, but this really throws a monkey wrench in his plans. Two hundred less bucks means he's not going to get his hair highlighted and the outlet mall will have to wait another month. It also means he'll likely eat off the dollar menu at McDonald's the rest of the week. He runs through the numbers in his head for a few seconds and manages to budget out his travel expenses. He figures he can squeak by for the week. But he's not happy. He wants to fly to New York and punch Rodney in the face.

"There's one more thing." Billy hands him a long piece of cash register tape across the desk. "This is your bar tab."

"Whoa," Spence says to Billy as he takes the bill. "I thought drinks were free."

"Beer is free," Billy says, "but you drank whiskey all weekend."

Spence looks at the bill and wants to cut his own throat with it. "I thought you said you were going to take care of me," he says.

"And you thought that meant I was going to let you drink for free?"

"Something like that, yeah."

"Naw," Billy scoffs. "I meant that I was going to make sure you got everything you wanted."

"Great," Spence says. He feels his shoulders slump as he goes over his budget one more time in his head. He wonders if Billy would respect him less for curling up into fetal position right there on the floor. Instead, he counts out the money for his drinks and lays it on the desk.

Billy flicks his Zippo lighter open and shut and looks around for a pack of cigarettes lost somewhere in the clutter on his desk. "Tell you what, I'll buy you one for the road. How's that?"

Kiss my ass, Spence thinks.

"Thanks," he says.

"Don't forget to pay the bartender for your burger on the way out, okay?"

"Damn," Spence says, "is there anything I get for free?"

"Yeah," Billy says. "The hotel."

Some perk, Spence thinks. *The hotel is always free. That's the only part of the contract Rodney always gets right.*

He stands up and shakes Billy's hand, mostly just because it's customary. He starts doing the numbers in his head again, trying to figure out what the average person's check would be on a two-drink minimum and then adding that to the cover charge at the door. When his temples start to hurt, he just smiles and opens the office door. The music from the bar pours into the room.

"We'll have you back next year," Billy says to him, although he's probably lying.

"Maybe then you'll have a Friday late show," Spence says.

"The hypnotist sold out both shows."

"But that's not really stand-up comedy."

"Tell me again all that stuff about *Transformers*." Billy grins. *Checkmate.*

"Later," Spence says and starts to leave.

"Don't forget to pay for the food," Billy says as he finally finds his smokes and pulls one out of the soft pack. Lighting up, the fat, old cowboy turns around in his noisy chair and goes back to watching ESPN.

Spence leaves Billy's office and steps back out into the club. On his way out the door, he drops ten bucks on the bar. The bartender who hates his guts is standing there and, from the look on his face, the hatred hasn't passed.

"For my burger," he says to the bartender. "Tell Mandy I say hello."

"Who?" the bartender asks as he scoops the bills up and counts them out, frowning the entire time.

"That girl from last night. The one who drives the black Jeep."

"Cindy," the bartender says and looks at him from under his thick eyebrows.

Cindy, Spence thinks. *I knew it was something with an "e" sound at the end.*

"Yeah, her. The one with the tattoo right there," he says and points at his crotch. "She was something else. Really. Something. Else."

He doesn't stay to see the bartender's reaction. He's pretty sure it's just a meaner version of the same scowl the guy has had for the past two days anyway. The satisfaction of knowing that the kid will be miserable for the rest of the night is almost worth the price of the cheeseburger. Almost.

Spence steps out in the parking lot and looks around at the collection of trucks and cars that are much nicer than his. It's quiet outside, and the silence makes the entire night seem a little anticlimactic. An hour ago he was a celebrity. Now he's just the hired help quietly shuffling away for the night, just like the guy who washes the dishes in the kitchen. He's back at the hotel before he realizes that he left without having that free drink Billy offered.

The sun is bright and it looks like the middle of summer, despite the fact that it's February and still freezing out. From his window, Spence can't even see the snow plowed up around the corner of the hotel. He could've slept all night and thought he'd woken up in May had he just looked out the window when he got up at noon.

He likes to drive on sunny days like this. Just the right music on his radio and plenty of sunshine can make even a ten-hour drive that much easier. The one good thing about shows out in the middle of the country is that he rarely has to deal with the traffic and congestion that always hits him when he works in any of the major cities. Driving straight east for two days isn't so bad when there's a nearly empty highway the entire trip.

His cell phone rings and it's Rodney. He puts his imitation Wayfarers on and tosses his duffel bag in the backseat of his Camry as he answers.

"Gimme the good news," Spence says without saying hello.

"Asshole," Rodney says.

"I take it Leno's people didn't call?"

"The Electric Pony doesn't want you back," Rodney says.

"Already?" Spence asks. "It's only been a day. Not even twelve hours. Hell, it usually takes them at least a week before they call and have me banned."

"Guess you broke your own record."

"What was the reason? Because I said *goddamnit?*"

"Did you?"

"What'd they say?"

"Whatever," Rodney says. "Same thing anyone ever says: You're difficult. You're a prima donna. You're spoiled."

"Spoiled? How do you figure?" Spence asks. He looks at the fleabag hotel in front of him, then back at his car. There's an Aquafina bottle on the floorboard full of his own urine from when he was heading into Enid the other day and didn't want to pull over to leak. He wonders if Steve Martin ever had to pee in a bottle and if it made him feel spoiled.

"You complain too much," Rodney says.

"Oh, screw them."

"Screw them?" Rodney says. "Screw you. I get tired of having to clean up after your crap."

"Oh, please," Spence says, "this is always because of something stupid that should be handled before I get to town."

"Like what?"

"Since when do I not get paid by the night, Rodney? They shorted me two hundred bucks because they canceled the Friday late show."

"That was just for that one gig," Rodney says.

"Well, it was bullshit."

"You made that clear, yeah."

"Forty-plus weeks a year you get me paid by the night, and suddenly I'm paid by the show?"

"Hey," Rodney snaps. "It was either that or no gig at all. You'd rather have been unemployed this week?"

"No—"

"I could have sworn you even got lucky last night, right?"

"Just next time tell me you've made that deal before I make an ass out of myself to the guy running the show."

"You do that on your own," Rodney says. "Did you tell him something about how much you love *Transformers* or something?"

Spence has to take a minute to figure out what Rodney is talking about. When it dawns on him, he almost laughs despite being so pissed off.

"No," he says, "I was trying to make a point about popularity."

"How'd that work out for you?" Rodney asks.

"That jackass wanted to sit there and tell me how it's bullshit I don't sell the place out like a hypnotist. Tell him to advertise his own show and they'll sell more tickets."

"That's not the problem"

"Yeah? What's the problem, then?"

"The problem is you like to screw with people."

"I do not."

"Just do the shows and get paid," Rodney says. "Stop whining about what they tell you to do. If they want you to be clean, be clean. It's always a fight with you."

"If they want the show squeaky clean, they should hire a squeaky clean comic."

"You would make more money if you worked clean, you know," Rodney says.

This again? Spence thinks but instead says, "I'd also make more money if I were a hypnotist."

"Good idea."

"You'd probably like that. Then you wouldn't have to worry about how spoiled I am."

"You are your own worst enemy," Rodney says. "You always have been."

Spence winces when he hears that. It never feels good, mostly because it's true. He tries to count all the times he's been fired or banned from clubs simply because he couldn't keep his mouth shut. After he counts six in as many seconds, he shakes his head and kicks the ground. He used to be so good about just smiling and doing whatever he was told. Once he started working the saloon gigs and awful one-nighters he started talking back when he should have just learned to nod his head.

"I'm not wrong here, Rodney."

"Being right never got anyone work," Rodney says.

Spence kicks some more gravel and stares at his left shoe. He needs new shoes. He *wants* all kinds of stuff, but he *needs* new shoes. He can't remember how long he's had this pair, but he knows that it's only a matter of time before the sole comes off the left one.

"I had good shows," he mumbles quietly, "so I don't know what they're complaining about."

Rodney lets out a long sigh right into the phone. "Look you're not going to please everybody."

"That's what I told them."

"Next time, let me tell them. That's my job."

"No shit."

"Whatever," Rodney says. "They're probably going to quit having comedians anyway. They say they aren't making any money at it."

"Me neither," Spence says. He should be annoyed, but he just doesn't care. The money in Enid wasn't enough that losing the gig should even matter. Still, it would have been nice to get some new clothes or maybe get his car detailed. His car has seen better days. It has two hundred thousand miles on it, and he's hoping it can last at least another hundred. Just like him, the car looks older than it is. Again he wonders when he started looking fortysomething instead of twentysomething.

"Where you headed now?" Rodney asks.

"Your backyard. I'll be there in a few days."

"Alright. Bring me some headshots."

"Sure," Spence says.

"I told you Rockford is closed, right?"

"Yeah. Get me a date in Cleveland, okay?"

"I'll see what I can do," Rodney says and hangs up.

Spence tosses his cell phone onto the front seat of his car and lets out a long sigh. He runs his hands through his already messy hair and slaps his hand on the roof of his car, feeling the slight sting on his palm and hearing the hollow *thunk* when his hand hits the metal.

"*Damn it,*" he says to no one, but loud enough for anyone within a quarter mile to hear. A decade in, and the business never gets easier. Every shining moment onstage is met with a humbling dressing down offstage. Every standing ovation comes with a bar tab. Every night in the arms of a beautiful woman is rewarded with an angry wake-up call from his agent.

The only agent that will have me, he thinks, and feels that familiar throbbing start on the side of his forehead.

It's true about Rodney. There was a time when Spence could have left him and signed on with someone else. Someone who might have gotten him slightly better pay in slightly worse venues. Too many burned bridges later, and it seems that Rodney is the wife he doesn't remember marrying. Like it or not, they're stuck with each other, come death or *The Tonight Show.*

After a minute of staring at his worn-out shoes, the gravel on the ground, and his car with too many miles on it, he slips into the driver's seat and shuts the door. He tunes his satellite radio to some talk show. The host is talking about how high taxes are and how everyone without money is lazy and poor because they have no skills. Spence chuckles to himself, rolls down the window, and heads out.

Good-bye, Enid, Oklahoma, he thinks. Another city checked off his map. Places he never thought he'd visit have now become footnotes on his résumé. On his way out of town, he pulls into the parking lot of the Electric Pony and empties the bottle of urine all over the front door.

3

New Jersey sucks. He's never liked it, doesn't like going back to it, and really tries to avoid it as much as possible. All of this makes it harder for him to believe that he lived here for over a decade. He doesn't like the people any more than he likes the traffic, but the traffic makes him hate the people even more. That vicious circle goes around in his head until he feels like driving his car into a tollbooth—of which Jersey has hundreds—just like the one he's sitting at right now.

Spence smiles at the toll collector who looks at him as if he just canceled Christmas. He remembers a time when *The Sopranos* was big on TV and people in New Jersey complained about it and protested the show. They said that it depicted people in New Jersey as rude and boorish and wasn't realistic. He still laughs when he thinks about this. The first time he saw *The Sopranos,* he thought it was a documentary.

He's stuck in gridlocked traffic on the Garden State Parkway and feels almost as if he never moved away. He just paid one toll and is now sitting in traffic simply waiting to pay another. It's raining slightly, which makes his day even worse. New Jersey drivers are bad enough on a sunny day. When it rains, they drive their cars as if the sky is falling and they're being chased by demons. It's the only state he's ever been in where the people drive a hundred miles per hour in the snow and yet twelve miles per hour in the rain.

This isn't his home, but this is where his stuff is. After the divorce from Beth, he put all of his things in storage about five miles from his old condo. That's the hardest part about his hatred for this state: He has to keep coming back to it. If he wants warmer clothes, he needs to come to Jersey. If he needs to pick up old files or tax returns, he has to come to Jersey. If he just wants to look at the TV he owns and hasn't used in years, he has to come to Jersey. Most importantly, if he wants his mail, he has to come to Jersey.

The mail is at Beth's condo, which is coincidentally his old condo and Beth is coincidentally his ex-wife. The good part of remaining friendly with his ex is that it has allowed him to keep a formal address while not actually having a home. He hasn't had a house or apartment for two years, but Beth still collects his mail for him. Most of it is junk. It's not like any bank is crazy enough to give him a credit card, and he doesn't own enough of anything to get any real bills.

He's not too far outside New York City, but he might as well be in Florida. The entire Princeton area looks more suburban than the rest of the state and is actually quite pretty. It's one of the few things he liked about the area. Pulling up to his old apartment complex, he sees Beth's blue PT Cruiser in the parking lot. Right next to it is a slick black Audi and he knows this means that Evan is home.

Spence grits his teeth a bit and sighs. Evan is Beth's husband and not remotely someone he would call his pal. Beth was friends with Evan before the divorce. About a month after the split, that friendship "suddenly" became something more serious and he moved into the condo. The ink wasn't even dry on the divorce papers before he settled in and married Beth. Spence thinks that Evan is a douche. As it turns out, the feeling is mutual.

Spence gets out of his car and looks closely at the PT Cruiser. Beth has been taking care of it, and it still looks almost new. Much better than his car. The Cruiser is in his name, even though it's Beth's car and always has been. The payments were cheaper and, after the divorce, it seemed easier just to keep it that way until the thing was paid off. Like the agreement with the mail, this arrangement pisses Evan off big-time.

Spence had hoped that neither Beth nor Evan would be home and that he could just slip in, grab his mail, and slip out again. No such luck. He prepares himself and knocks on the door. He still has a key, but he knows that using it will just piss Evan off even more than he already will by just being there.

Beth looks surprised to see him, although he knows he told her he was coming. He smells food and realizes he caught her about to have dinner. Garlic hits his nose, and he knows it's toasted French bread. There's probably fresh veggies, too. He loves both of those things, and Beth cooks them well. Now he really despises the Big Mac he had an hour ago, and he feels it churn painfully in his stomach.

"You meant today," Beth says as she opens the door. "I thought you meant next week."

"Nope," Spence says. "Today."

"Well, shit," she says, more embarrassed than annoyed. "C'mon in."

She looks great. She's only a few years younger than he is, but she's holding on to her youth very well. Her hair has grown out since he last saw her. It looks as if she's letting it grow dark. They used to get their hair highlighted together, which always made him feel a little bit gay. He imagines Evan would agree. Beth looks the part of upper-class wife and she wears it well. He hates admitting it, but she and Evan look good together. Like Ken and Barbie dolls that walked out of a toy store and into the real world.

Spence follows Beth into the living room and sees Evan on the back patio, standing over the barbecue grill. There are several plates lined up on the kitchen counter, along with four glasses and an open bottle of wine.

"Having company, I take it," Spence says.

"Just grilling out some steaks," Beth says and walks over to a side table in the front hallway. She picks up a stack of mail as thick as a dictionary and starts sifting through it. Outside, Evan is drinking a beer and wearing an apron with "Kiss This" written on it and an arrow pointing to his crotch. He looks good for the thirtysomething age he is and comes off a bit younger. He's never been too removed from whatever fraternity he was in and it shows.

Spence looks around the living room. The place looks about the same as when he lived there and Evan did not. During their last few years together, Beth made way more money than he did and paid the bulk of the bills. It's for that reason that she kept most of the belongings when they split. It made sense anyway since he had nowhere to put it. He's fine without the paintings and random other things, but he does miss his favorite recliner. It sits a few feet away from him, looking as comfortable as ever. He tries not to think about the fact that Beth and Evan have probably had sex in it numerous times.

"Mostly junk, you know," Beth says, sorting the mail.

"I figured."

"You going over to the storage place?"

"Yeah."

"Think you could look and see if you have a box of my Christmas stuff in there? I can't find the stuff my grandmother left me. The glass ornaments from Italy."

"You know it's almost March, right?" Spence asks.

"Yes, smart-ass," she says. "I couldn't find them in December, and I don't want to wait until this Christmas and forget about them again."

"Fair enough," he says. "Who's coming to dinner? Anyone I know?"

"Russ and Debbie," she says. Russ and Debbie were the couple they hung out with when he and Beth were still married. He lost them in the divorce and, like his favorite recliner, they now belong to Evan.

"Tell them I said hello," he says.

"They always ask how you're doing."

He holds out his hands as if to say "ta-da."

"Your hair is looking a little gray," Beth says. "You should go back to highlighting it."

"Thanks," he says.

"Are you still using that wrinkle cream on your face?"

"Yeah, why?"

"You look tired, is all."

"Thanks."

"Try using it twice a day."

"And with that, I'm outta here." Spence rolls his eyes. Beth always has a way of making him feel old. Maybe because she looks so good.

"Look for the Christmas stuff, please?"

"Sure. I'm getting warmer clothes, so I'll look in the back while I'm there."

"Warmer clothes?" she asks. "You know it's almost March, right?"

"Funny," he says. "I'm going to Canada."

"Canada? Moving up in the world, huh?"

"Yeah, literally."

"Vancouver?"

"Montreal."

"How'd you manage that?"

"Got a call from a guy there," he says, "said he saw the clip from the Kilborn show."

"See?" she says. "That show does still pay off."

"Sometimes," he says.

"Rodney get the gig for you?"

"Nope. Got it myself."

"God forbid Rodney find you any real work," she says. Beth has always hated Rodney. She thinks he's an idiot, not just a bad agent.

The sliding glass door opens and in walks Evan, a plateful of steaks in his hand. The smell of heavenly red meat fills the room and is a slap in the face to the one person who won't be having any. There is a low grumbling noise coming from a stomach that doesn't belong to Evan or Beth, but to someone who will wind up eating at McDonald's again later that day.

"Ooh, those look great, babe," Beth says as her husband steps into the kitchen and pours himself a glass of wine.

Bloody hell, Spence thinks as he watches Evan walk into the room. He was so close to getting out of there without talking to the guy at all. Evan raises his eyebrows in a way that's supposed to be a greeting as he walks over without saying a word and puts an arm around Beth. Spence chuckles to himself. Pulling out his penis and actually peeing on her would probably be taking it a bit far but, given the chance, Evan would probably do just that.

"Hi, Evan." Spence raises a hand and waves. Evan just nods and half smiles. There is an uncomfortable pause that probably lasts three seconds but feels as if it's at least three minutes.

"Oh," Beth blurts out, breaking the awkward silence, "I have something for you."

She hurries out of the room, leaving Spence there to stare at Evan and for Evan to simply look straight through him. Gunfighters meeting at high noon were probably friendlier with each other.

Douche, Spence thinks as he looks at Evan.

Deadbeat, Evan probably thinks as he looks back.

Evan thinks that being a stand-up comedian is a stupid way to make a living. This despite the fact that they met when Beth brought Evan to one of his shows. Evan went on and on about how great the show was and how much he laughed, but now he calls it a childish career decision. Not enough money in it, so it's stupid. Evan thinks it's wrong when men make less money than their wives do. Spence just thinks Evan is an ass.

"I need to talk to you about something," Evan says and puts his glass of wine down on the dining table.

"You want to just whip 'em out and compare right now?" Spence says. " 'Cause I'm pretty sure you've got me beat."

Evan ignores him. "We got a bill in the mail from the county. The registration and inspection fees are due on the PT Cruiser."

"Beth's car."

"Yes."

"I mean that's your answer. It's Beth's car."

"What are you talking about?"

"You were just about to ask me to pay the fees on the PT Cruiser, and I'm telling you that it's Beth's car," Spence says.

"No." Evan rolls his eyes and places a hand on his hip. He's pouting, and it looks a little feminine, which is actually funny to see from a guy over six feet tall who tries as hard to be as masculine as Evan does. "I was going to ask you to pay half. We'll pay the other half."

"Cool," Spence says. "Same answer, though. It's Beth's car."

"It's in your name."

"Out of convenience. It's never been my car. I hardly even got to drive it. She makes the payments. She pays the insurance. It's always been hers."

"But the car is in your name."

"So?" Spence almost laughs. "My name is still on the mortgage to this condo. Doesn't mean I pay rent."

"Maybe you should, since you still get your mail here."

Spence rolls his eyes. "You want my random bills and envelopes to pay a portion of the rent, Evan? Really?"

"I'm just saying."

"Is it really that big an inconvenience, Evan? You just toss it in a basket and hand it to me every few months."

"It's not about whether or not it's inconvenient," Evan says. "It's about responsibility. You're irresponsible, and we have to pick up the slack because of it. All the time."

"How am I irresponsible?"

"Because you chose to be homeless," Evan says. "Who *does* that?"

"Doesn't really make sense to pay rent on an apartment I'm never in, does it?"

"Especially not when you've got us to fall back on."

"I fall back on you?"

"Well, we're sitting here giving you your mail," Evan says.

"And you got to keep my favorite recliner," Spence counters. "Everybody wins."

"It's Beth's recliner."

"No," Spence says, "it's my recliner. I didn't have any room for it in storage so I let her keep it."

"And now it belongs to us," Evan says.

"Right. Just like Beth's car," Spence says. "Checkmate."

The look on Evan's face tells Spence that he's about two seconds away from a punch in the face. That wouldn't be good. For one thing, it would piss Beth off and ruin his already shaky friendship with her. For another, Evan is bigger than he is and would likely throttle him pretty good. As luck would have it, Beth walks in about five seconds later.

"Here you go." She hands Spence a picture frame. It's his college diploma. Six months after getting a degree in communications, he was waiting tables at Joe's Crab Shack. He thinks of the irony that the frame is worth more than the paper inside it.

"Thanks," he says. "Where was this?"

"In the bedroom closet," Beth says. "We must've put it there when we moved in and never hung it up. It was way back in the back. I found it when I was looking for those missing decorations."

"Nice," Spence says. He remembers that he was out of college over five years before he finally got the diploma matted and framed. It's never been hung on a wall, just moved around from one apartment to the next. At one point, it leaned against his desk for four years.

"This too." She holds up a key and drops it in his hand.

"What's this?"

"The key to your storage place. My key."

"You should keep this here," Spence says. "Just in case."

"No." She smiles. It's an awkward smile. "You need to take it."

"But, what if—"

Beth holds up her hand. "It's time."

Spence looks at her and looks at Evan and then back at Beth. She doesn't look at Evan. Evan smirks—it's hard to see it, but he definitely smirks—turns and walks back to the kitchen table and takes a long sip of his wine. Spence realizes that Evan won this battle before he even got out of bed. Checkmate, indeed.

"And my mail?" Spence asks.

"Time to move on with that, too," she says. "It's been long enough, okay?"

"But what if I—"

"David," Beth says and looks at him sternly.

Spence hates it when she calls him by his middle name, and she knows it. But she only does it when she's letting him know she doesn't want to lose her temper. He shrugs and sighs. It would probably bother him if it were a surprise, but it isn't. He actually thought she was going to have this talk with him six months ago. He's lucky he got away with it this long. He looks over at Evan, who doesn't look back at him, but just keeps looking out the window, sipping on his wine. At least the douche didn't gloat.

"Alright," Spence concedes, "I'll change my address. Maybe get a PO box. Have it sent to my parents or something."

"Cool," she says.

"I'm off," Spence says and makes his way to the door.

"So long," Evan says and waves over his shoulder without looking at him.

At the front of the condo, Beth puts her hand on his shoulder as she opens the door. "Christmas decorations, okay?" she asks.

"Sure."

She leans in the doorway for a second, looking around the breezeway. Spence tucks the picture frame under his arm and pulls out his car keys. He fumbles with the key ring for a minute and finally gets Beth's house key loose. He hands it to her, and she puts it in her pocket.

"You okay?" she asks.

"Yeah, I'm fine," he says. There's a second where Beth starts to walk back into the condo, but she stays in the doorway instead. They smile politely at each other for a few seconds, and he shrugs.

"You need a girlfriend," she says.

"I'm okay in that department," he says.

"No, I know you're getting laid," she gives him a tsk-tsk look and furrows her eyebrows, "I mean you need a girlfriend. A date. Someone else to talk to."

"I talk plenty. All I do is talk. I talk for a living," he says.

"You know what I mean," she says.

He laughs. "Sure. That's what every woman wants to date, right? A homeless, broke comedian."

"Women love comedians. I did, remember?"

"How'd that work out for you?"

"Not fair."

"Sorry."

Spence sighs deeply and runs his free hand through his hair. He's never understood Beth's fascination with whether or not he's dating. Part of him guesses that she feels a little bit guilty for replacing him with Evan so quickly after the divorce. He finds it odd that she always seems eager for him to find someone else to never be home with.

"You're doing better than you were this time last year," she says. "You're still working. That says something about you, right?"

"My last gig was at a place in Oklahoma with a mechanical bull next to the stage."

Beth laughs. He cringes from it, but he knows just how ridiculous it must sound.

"Hey, you're the one that wanted this life," she says. "You could've stayed right here and waited tables or been a bartender or done all kinds of things to pay the rent. You chose to live on the road, remember?"

She's right. It really seemed like a good idea at the time. The idea of not having a day job and being able to make money doing only stand-up was tempting. When Rodney started finding him work, he said yes to every single job. That meant he was never in one place for very long. Next thing he knew, he was never home. Not long after that, he didn't even have one.

"You're the one who hated to be alone, remember?" he says.

"And I always was."

He looks over her shoulder at Evan, back on the patio and

scraping off the grill. "Not anymore," he says. It's a quick jab, but he knows it's not fair. He would have done the same thing had he been her.

At least now, he and Beth get along fairly well and speak to each other without losing their minds. The last two years they were married it was outright chaos. She was happy to see him getting so much work and then crying to him on the phone every night that he was never home. At first she was sad all the time. Then she got angry and the screaming kicked in. After a while, they argued when he was away and kept arguing when he was home. The fact that the divorce was so easy was hard to believe. That they managed to somehow have the shell of a friendship left over was a miracle.

"I'm glad you guys are doing so well," Spence says and knows how phony it sounds. The chuckle Beth gives back lets him know he's right.

"Oh, sure." She smiles and rolls her eyes. Every once in a while, he sees what everyone else does. She's beautiful, and everyone he knew envied him for being with her. When they did get along, they laughed a lot. She was a great sounding board, and always knew which bits he was working on would be great additions to his act and which ones would fail. He wonders if she laughs a lot with Evan.

"You look good," she says.

"I thought I looked tired," he says.

"Well, yeah."

"You're a bad liar."

Beth rolls her eyes again, but this time it doesn't feel quite as friendly. "Just look for the decorations, okay?" she says and starts to close the door.

"Okay," he says.

"And you need to fire Rodney," she tells him. "He's sending you to redneck bars? That's bullshit."

"Mechanical bullshit." He grins. Rim shot.

The door closes, and Spence walks out into the parking lot. He stands there for a minute and looks around at the rest of the condo complex and all the cars parked in a neat little row.

Evan's Audi really is very nice. He probably gets it detailed regularly and changes the tires even when he doesn't have to. It probably still has that "new car" smell and always will.

Putting on his fake Wayfarers, Spence tosses the stack of mail into the backseat of his car. He sits there for a second and looks at the different condos in the complex. This really is the only part of New Jersey he ever liked. A minute later, he sees Russ and Debbie climbing out of their Honda Accord. He scratches his temple and pretends not to see them when they wave at him as he drives away.

4

Rodney used to have an office in downtown Manhattan, but now uses some dump in Brooklyn. There's no telling where Rodney's actual home is. It has never even come up in conversation or been mentioned. There have been times when Spence has called there at two a.m. only to have Rodney pick up the phone. The guy is not that efficient an agent, so there's no way he'd be doing work at that hour. It seems more likely that the sofa pulls out into a bed and Rodney lives in that little room around the clock.

"What's up, you filthy man-whore?" Rodney yells at him when he walks in the door. The place is a mess. There isn't a single place to sit down since every corner is covered with paper, trash, headshots, and videotapes. The videotapes stand out the most. Rodney still uses a VCR to copy the videos of comics that he sends out to clubs. While the rest of the world is watching clips online or, at the very least, on DVD, Rodney is still lamenting the death of Betamax.

"Love what you've done with the place," Spence says to Rodney as he climbs over the remains of other comedians' careers.

"The cleaning lady comes tomorrow," Rodney says. The phone is on his shoulder, but he isn't talking to anyone, so he must be on hold. Some teenager is sitting on the floor, sorting through papers.

"Intern?" Spence asks, tilting his head toward the kid doing all the work. Rodney nods, holds up his index finger, and swivels around in his chair. Rodney has a new intern every month. They work for school credit, hoping to leave NYU and get a job at the William Morris Agency or with Gersh. Most of them will wind up in Brooklyn, just like Rodney, or in Jersey, where the rent is cheaper. Also like Rodney, they'll all become D-list agents, managing the careers of comedians climbing or falling back down the show business ladder.

Agents like Rodney are everywhere, and they're surprisingly in demand. In both New York and LA, there are hundreds of comedians, actors, musicians, jugglers, magicians, and even balloon artists desperately seeking someone to desperately find them work. The only thing more amazing about how many talent agents there are is how difficult it is to get one. Every working comedian knows that having one gets you more work, and you don't ever fire your agent until a better one finds you first. Spence can't remember the last time another agent returned his phone calls.

Rodney looks like he slept in his clothes, which answers the question about where his home is. The ratty baseball cap covers a bald head that would probably still be bald even if Rodney didn't shave it. The remnants of an ill-conceived goatee cover his round chin, and he looks as if he hasn't gotten any sun in about four years. And he's wearing shorts. He wears shorts year-round, even when visiting the Christmas tree in Rockefeller Center.

Spence waves a friendly hand to greet the intern as Rodney goes back to talking to no one on the phone. Stepping over more clutter, he walks over to the filing cabinet in a corner of the room and opens it to his own file, marked under *S*. Right there, in a manila folder, are about two hundred of his headshots. He rolls his eyes and lets out a long, dramatic sigh. The filing cabinet is perfectly alphabetized, which is probably why Rodney can't seem to figure it out. Spence takes the photos out of the cabinet and tosses them on Rodney's desk.

"Thanks," Rodney says when the photos land in front of him, "where'd you find 'em?"

"The first place I looked," Spence says.

"Right."

"You have a check for me?"

"For what?"

"That casino in Syracuse, New York. Two months ago."

"Oh, yeah," Rodney says, still on hold, "that gig. I think I do have a check, yeah." He reaches into his desk drawer and takes out a stack of envelopes bound together with a rubber band. Then he flips through them, finds the right one, and tosses it across the desk.

"Thanks," Spence says as he picks it up and checks the balance. It's exactly what it should be. No deductions for drinks or food or postage stamps. Just his money minus the usual cut Rodney takes for booking the gig. He puts the envelope into the breast pocket of his coat.

"Any news about Cleveland?" he asks.

"What about it?" Rodney asks.

"You were going to see about getting me a gig there to make up for Rockford."

"What do you mean 'make up for Rockford'?"

"You told me the club in Rockford closed."

"It did?"

"Oh, for Chrissakes, Rodney."

"Oh, Rockford, Illinois." Rodney nods and puts the phone down. "I was thinking something different. Yeah, that club's closed. Scratch it off your schedule."

"Yeah, I did that," Spence says. "How about getting me booked in Cleveland instead?"

"Good idea," Rodney says. "I'll look into that. Maybe Baltimore."

Spence shakes his head and then looks down at the intern sitting on the floor. The intern gives him the same look back. The kid will change his major in three weeks and wind up going into computers.

"What are you doing here, anyway?" Rodney asks.

"I told you I was coming," Spence says.

"You did?"

"Yeah, three days ago."

"Right, after you screwed up in Oklahoma."

"Bite me."

"So why are you here?"

"I needed to get my mail," Spence says, "and warmer clothes, remember?"

"What for?" Rodney asks, absolutely clueless.

"The gig in Key West. You got me that gig at the resort."

"Oh, yeah, yeah, yeah. The beach gig," Rodney says. "Enjoy that. That should be a lot of fun."

Unbelievable, Spence thinks.

"You are such an ass," he says instead.

"What?" Rodney asks.

"You don't keep track of my schedule at all, do you?"

"What are you talking about?"

"You arrange the thing, and you really don't pay attention to it at all."

"I do too."

"Why would I need warmer clothes if I'm going to Key West?"

"Beats the hell outta me," Rodney says.

"I'm going to Canada, Rodney," Spence says.

"Canada?"

"Yeah, you know, moose and beavers and snow."

"That's this week?"

"Yeah, that's this week," Spence says. "I'm driving up tomorrow."

"I thought it was next month."

"Christ."

"Hey, you know how many assholes just like you I have to deal with?" Rodney asks. "You think I can memorize everything you do? You can't even keep track of it yourself. Imagine having to keep track of a couple dozen guys at once. That's what I gotta do."

"Yeah, yeah," he says to Rodney, "cry me a river."

"I mean it," Rodney says. "I've got to deal with you, a bunch of other guys out there on the road, and people right here in the city every single day."

He's telling the truth. Rodney has more clients than he knows what to do with. Besides booking comedians, he also represents actors and musicians and dancers. If there's the possibility of making a few dollars from it, Rodney will represent it. There are rumors that Rodney has booked everything from children's parties to singing telegrams to mimes on street corners. Somehow the fifteen percent commission on all of these jobs manages to add up to a livable wage.

"It's your job to keep track for all of us. Maybe you're spreading yourself too thin," Spence says.

"Shit. You wish I had the time to only worry about you," Rodney says. "You don't make me enough money."

"Whose fault is that?" Spence asks.

Rodney gives him the finger. "So when are you going to Key West?"

"There really is a job there?"

"You've never worked it?"

"I didn't even know it existed."

"That was a bluff?" Rodney asks, raising his eyebrows and slowly nodding his head. "Touché."

"I'll go there next week if I can get it," Spence says. "Hell, there are plenty of holes in my schedule. Make that gig happen."

"I'll work on it," Rodney says.

"I'll hold my breath."

Spence often wonders just how many sweet gigs like Key West are being kept from him. There's probably six weeks of work in Cancún that he doesn't even know about. Right after the Kilborn show, Rodney got him all sorts of A-room work. There were some resorts and some casinos. There was even a two-week stretch at the Improv in Houston. When more TV offers didn't happen, the gigs became B- and C-list. Five years ago, he never would have been booked at a dump like the Electric Pony. Five years ago, he thought *The Late Late Show* wouldn't be his only TV credit.

"You know what you can do?" he says to Rodney. "You can get me a showcase at Gotham."

"Gotham, huh?"

"I think the time is right, yeah."

Gotham Comedy Club is an A-list room in downtown Manhattan. It's a beautiful club, and one of the few spots in the city where comics can showcase for *Letterman* and sometimes Comedy Central. There was a time when Rodney could get him seen by TV bookers by arranging quick local sets and making a few phone calls. That's how he got the Kilborn gig years ago, and Gotham would be where it could happen again.

"I'll see what I can do," Rodney says, "I don't know if you're ready for it."

"What do you mean by that?" Spence asks.

"I mean you're still kinda new, is all. We're talking the big leagues. The TV guys might not be ready for you."

"Well, I'm ready for them. And I'm not new."

"That's what every comic says. A few years in, and everyone thinks they're a seasoned vet," Rodney says.

Listening to Rodney call him "new" after more than a decade of work and eight full years of nonstop touring makes Spence want to puke all over the desk. There is an old saying that it takes ten years to become an overnight success. Some comedians get discovered young while others troll around in the business for decades trying to scratch their way up. He thinks it's quite possibly because the industry is run by people exactly like Rodney.

Spence glances down at the intern, who is cramming comedians' headshots and demo tapes into large manila envelopes, putting together promo packages to send to comedy clubs. For a brief second, he swears that he sees the kid stuffing an envelope with the photo and résumé of a comedian who has been dead for three years. He thinks it's likely that a corpse is getting more work from Rodney than he is. While he's begging for a gig in Cleveland, the dead guy is probably booked in Key West that month.

"Please, just get me a showcase," he says to Rodney. "Get me in front of Letterman's guy or something."

"Maybe," Rodney says. "Can you work clean?"

"I can work clean for ten minutes, sure."

" 'Cause I don't want to put you in front of them and have you saying 'fuck' and making me look like an asshole."

"I've been working on some clean stuff just for showcasing to TV people," Spence says.

"Have you ever done TV before?"

Spence wonders for a brief moment if Rodney is able to tie his shoes or if there's an intern that does it for him. "You are unbelievable," he says as he rubs the back of his neck with his right hand. He can feel a migraine coming on, working its way up from the top of his shoulders.

"Why? What are you talking about?" Rodney asks.

"I did *The Late Late Show*."

"With Ferguson?"

"With Kilborn."

"When did you do that?"

"Almost nine years ago," Spence says. "Jesus."

"How'd you get that?" Rodney asks.

Spence says nothing and just stares at Rodney for at least ten seconds. "You got me a showcase for them," he says finally. He wonders how long it would take the police to find Rodney's body if he choked him as soon as the intern left the room. Then he wonders if the intern would help.

"I got you the audition?" Rodney asks.

"Yep."

"Oh. Oh, yeah. Now I remember."

Spence stands up and lets out a long, frustrated sigh. "I've gotta go," he says. "If I stay here any longer, I'm liable to kill all three of us."

It's at that moment he feels a throbbing pain beginning behind his left eye. In the back of his mind, he knew it would be this way, and yet he came anyway. He decides that next time he'll come with a bottle of aspirin in his pocket. Or at least a flask full of whiskey. He raises a hand in salute as he starts climbing over the mess that leads to the door. Anyone who ever said that society would soon go paperless has never been in Rodney's office.

"Have fun in Canada." Rodney waves and goes back to leaning on his phone.

"Get me Key West," Spence says.

"I'll see what I can do," Rodney says. "How much are they paying you up in the Great White North?"

"A grand."

"Canadian or American?"

"French."

"Really?"

"Idiot," Spence says. The intern on the floor laughs and tries to hide it from Rodney.

"Just make sure you send me my fifteen," Rodney calls out just before Spence makes it to the door.

"Your what?" Spence asks.

"My commission," Rodney says. "I get fifteen percent, remember?"

"You didn't get me the gig. I got it myself," Spence says. He doesn't know why he's bothering to argue; Rodney will likely forget he was even there. He wonders if Rodney even remembers that he just gave him a check for the casino gig. He briefly considers asking again just to find out. "The club owner called me directly."

"Doesn't work that way," Rodney says. "I still get commission, even when you book the gig without me."

"Since when?"

"Read the contract."

"What contract?"

"I'm sure we had one at some point."

"Screw you," Spence says.

"Kiss my ass," Rodney says.

The door closes behind him, and Spence waits for the elevator for a couple of minutes. As usual, he has left Rodney's office and feels as if he got absolutely nothing done. The only consolation he has is knowing that Rodney will forget all about the Canadian gig in about ten minutes, and that includes the commission he thinks he's owed. The sound of Spence's blood pumping through his brain slowly starts to get quieter and the pain lessens just before the teenage intern comes running out into the hallway.

Almost got away, he thinks. *Should have taken the stairs.*

"He says he needs you real quick," the intern says. The poor kid looks exhausted. Maybe he sleeps there, too.

"What for?" Spence asks. He tries to think if there's commission he owes Rodney that he's somehow forgotten that Rodney has somehow remembered.

"I don't know." The intern shrugs and shuffles back into Rodney's office.

Spence follows the intern back into the cluttered room and knocks a stack of papers over as he opens the door. Rodney doesn't seem to notice or care. It was probably just a stack of contracts for sitcoms that never made their way into his hands. Or obituaries for another dead comic still somehow making six figures per year. No big deal.

"What?" he asks Rodney as he tries not to fall down.

"Dude," Rodney says. "It's a good thing you didn't leave. I have something for you."

"Is it Key West?"

"Better. It's a TV commercial."

"Commercial for what?"

"A body spray ad. They need a funny guy who fits your description. That's what I was on hold waiting to hear about," Rodney says.

"When is it?" Spence asks.

"In a couple of hours," Rodney says. "Can you do it?"

"I dunno. I guess so."

"I'm telling you this is perfect for you. You're the first person I thought of when they told me about it. It's you, man. It's totally you."

"You always say that."

"And I mean it when I say it," Rodney says. "I wouldn't send you out there if I didn't think it was perfect for you."

"Oh, bullshit," Spence says.

"What?" Rodney says.

"The Sprite commercial ring a bell?"

Spence reminds Rodney that the last audition he sent him on was some TV commercial for Sprite. Rodney went on and on about how perfect he was for it. It was going to change his career for the better. It was a great gig; a national spot that could lead to a spokesperson role. He got excited by the way Rodney praised him and, when he showed up, the room was full of black guys. They wanted black men in their forties, and Rodney sent a thirtysomething white dude. When he retells the story to Rodney, he looks out the corner of his eye and sees the intern laugh.

"If you'd have gotten that commercial, you would've made ten grand," Rodney says.

"For the love of—"

"Look at this!" Rodney holds up a call sheet. "It says right here they want late twenties to mid-thirties. Comedic types preferred. That's you, asshole. Is it not?"

Spence looks at the call sheet. It is, indeed, him. The audition is actually calling for wacky, comedic men just like him. Even better, it pays five thousand dollars.

He sighs. "It's in two hours?"

"I'll make the call," Rodney says.

"Alright, I'll head over there."

"Sweet," Rodney says. "This will be perfect. You were the first person that popped into my head, too. How perfect is it that you were already here? That's fate, man."

"I haven't even gotten the part," Spence says. "Calm down."

"Well, you're gonna get the part," Rodney says. "This is you, baby."

Spence is on the subway before he even realizes that he meant to talk to Rodney about getting him better gigs at better venues. Of course, he knows that landing this audition will get Rodney to pay more attention to him. He also knows that landing a national TV commercial can up his pay on the road. A guy on a soap opera makes a fortune. A guy in a toothpaste commercial can make pretty good cash, too.

What any of that has to do with actual stand-up comedy is

anyone's guess, but that's how it works. The more credits a comic has, the more money he can make, even if the credit has nothing to do with stand-up comedy. Some guy from Omaha that used to open for him went from being an MC to being a high-paid headliner simply because he was "The 'Okie Dokie' Guy" in a series of commercials for Miller Lite. A few silly beer ads, and the kid was pulling in six figures at A-list comedy clubs. He didn't even have an hour's worth of material, and he was closing shows and raking in serious coin.

If only I'd been a black forty-year-old, he thinks. *I could've been the Sprite guy.*

After wandering around the same block for way too long, he arrives at the audition about five minutes early. Even if the audition is a bust, he's not so annoyed being there. He loves being in the middle of the city. Too many months on the road in the middle of nowhere makes him miss the big buildings and having everything a walk away. It feels nice to not be in the car for a change and to actually get out and walk somewhere.

The last time he was this close to Broadway was when Rodney sent him to some musical audition. Rodney told him it was for some new southern musical and that he was perfect for the show. When he got there, he found out it was to play Huck Finn in a Broadway tour. He was thirtysomething years old at the time, and they were auditioning teens. Needless to say, he didn't get the part. It was another brilliant move by Rodney.

He walks into the room and straight to the receptionist at the casting agency. Like most receptionists in most casting agencies, she's bored and barely looks at him when he says hello. She hands him a clipboard with the usual questionnaire attached to it asking all the usual questions. He fills out the audition waiver and hands it back to her, along with a copy of his résumé and a headshot. She tells him to wait around the corner with the other actors and then goes back to being bored.

He steps into the waiting room and finds himself surrounded by eight guys who look almost exactly like him. He laughs. The poor guys each look like a smaller or taller version of each other. A few of them have their hair highlighted. It looks like an awkward family reunion.

He sits down next to the guy who looks the least like him. The guy is reading *Entertainment Weekly* and picking mindlessly at the buckle on his boot. Watching the guy as he reads the magazine, Spence thinks to himself that they're really nice boots. This only reminds him that he needs new shoes.

"I suppose you're wondering why I called you all here today," he says to the group. A few of them chuckle. The others don't really pay attention. He sits quietly for a moment, looking at the doppelganger next to him. He wishes he had brought something to read. Sitting and waiting for an audition is both brutal and boring. It's a combination of nervous anticipation and complete indifference.

"So how'd you get this audition?" Spence asks.

"My agent set it up," the guy says.

"Yeah? Who are you with?"

"Rodney Carnes," the guy says.

"No shit," Spence says. "So am I."

"Me too," the guy on the opposite side of him says.

Spence looks around the room at the remaining six guys. Each of them has the same realization on their faces. It only takes him a second to put the pieces together. The pain in his neck suddenly returns.

"So," he says to the room, "anyone else here represented by Rodney Carnes?"

Every guy in the room raises his hand.

Fuck you, Rodney.

5

Spence thinks that if you knocked him out, woke him up in Montreal, and told him he was in some part of Europe he might just believe it. It's an amazing city, and it doesn't look like anywhere else he's ever been in North America. The city is beautiful, everything is written in French, and he is surrounded by some of the most gorgeous women he's ever seen. Even the girl behind the counter at McDonald's looked like a lingerie model.

He's never been this cold at this time of year. Jersey is often cold in the early spring, but not like it is in Montreal today. He's wearing a turtleneck sweater, thick overcoat, and wool scarf, and he's still freezing. It's a good thing he stopped off at the storage unit after all. Coming up here in his lighter clothes would have been nuts.

He walks down Saint Catherine Street, only a few blocks from his hotel. He likes city life, and walking around the busy people as they crowd the sidewalks doesn't bother him like it does many people. It has a very cool feeling. His entire career is about standing out, so it feels good to blend in once in a while. He strolls slowly, watching the beautiful people coming in and out of random shops. He tries to figure out what the English translation is to the French billboards and storefronts. The menu at McDonald's was pretty easy.

For the first time, he is very aware of the fact that he knows almost nothing about Canada. How is it possible that he learned so little about it in all of his years at school? It's not just that he doesn't know anything about Canadian history; he doesn't even know anything about the culture. He had no idea things would be written in two languages everywhere. He had no idea that McDonald's has a maple leaf in the middle of the golden arches. He sees a billboard advertising a Canadian TV show and laughs to himself. He had no idea there was a TV show called *Canadian Idol.* In school the teachers always said Canada was pretty much like America. He has been here only a few hours, and already realizes that they were full of shit.

He hasn't even been to the Comedy Crib yet, but the people here are already treating him better than he's used to. The hotel is gorgeous and only a few blocks away from the club. Even though he can walk anywhere he needs to go, they have a cab company on call to take him anywhere he wants. And he has already been told that all of his drinks and meals at the club are free.

He thinks this is really how he should always be treated, but it feels special when it happens these days. For every club that treats him as well as the Comedy Crib, there are six just like the Electric Pony. Somewhere along the way, comedians became a dime a dozen. Most clubs treat him as if he should feel lucky just to get paid.

Supply and demand, he thinks.

He blames "The Boom." Comedians talk about it all the time. Back in the '80s, there was a boom in the comedy business, and clubs popped up everywhere. There were more clubs than there were comedians, and being a comedian was a hot job to have. The money was great, and people wanted stand-up comedy everywhere. Every network had a stand-up comedy show. Even mediocre comedians got their own TV deals. Getting on a talk show was a given. It wasn't a matter of if you would get a spot on *An Evening at the Improv* so much as when.

Then it all imploded. Too many comedians, too many comedy clubs. Places that had no business doing stand-up comedy hired people who had no business calling themselves comedians.

Bowling alleys had "Comedy Night" and brought in headlining comedians who were only amateur comedians a few weeks before. Agents like Rodney popped up left and right and crowded the market. Too many comedians' sitcoms tanked. Stand-up comedy lost its charm, and clubs closed one after another. That left way too many comedians and not enough work.

That's about the time he finally started to get paid. Bad timing, really. Just when the business was starting to tank, he was trying to make a career out of it. A few years earlier and that appearance on Kilborn would have guaranteed him A-list work for many more years. With hundreds of comedians willing to work for less money and plenty of clubs looking to save every buck they possibly could, that TV credit didn't have the same effect it used to.

On top of that, the money stayed the same. The pay was never adjusted for inflation. What was good money in 1987 pretty much sucks these days. Yet there are new comics out there willing to work for half what Spence thinks is terrible pay. Some are willing to put themselves up in hotels on their own dime. Some even offer to work the first time at no pay, just for the chance to audition.

No wonder the Electric Pony thought I was such a spoiled jerk, he thinks. *They probably talked other comics into cleaning the bathrooms.*

But there are always exceptions. Dane Cook is around the same age as Spence and a millionaire. All the late night talk shows are still showcasing comedians. There are still random TV shows and movie deals. Everyone still has a shot to make it. Everyone can still get noticed. It's just a matter of timing. The right place at the right time. The right routine and the one killer bit can put a comedian over the top. That and a truckload of luck. Deep down, every working comic out there is waiting for another "Boom."

He turns the corner on Saint Catherine and winds up standing in front of the Pepsi Forum. He stands on the street corner for a second and simply watches people walk by. In front of him is a nice little park, and he thinks about sitting there for a while. In one direction, taxis and cars crowd the streets and, in another, there's a quiet park bench with his name on it. It's so rare a sight that he just stops and enjoys where he is right at that moment.

A woman walks by and looks at him funny. She chuckles and then crosses the street. He looks over his shoulder and realizes that he's standing in front of a string of posters with his face on them. Just like when bands plaster their fliers all over anything they can in New York City, the comedy club there has posters of him randomly spread around Montreal. It's rare that he sees this sort of thing. Nowadays clubs post stuff all over the Internet. He wants to take a picture to remember this. He knows it will just be covered up by newer ads in a few days.

"Three Nights Only," the poster reads, with his ridiculous mug staring bug-eyed at the camera. His hair is lighter in the picture, and he looks a little thinner and a lot younger. The photo is only four years old.

The Comedy Crib seems to still treat comedians the way he always heard it was like during The Boom. That's a nice feeling and exactly what he needs after several weeks of one-star hotels and saloon gigs. Those jobs manage to pay the bills, but sometimes a guy needs to be pampered a bit. He just hopes the rest of the week in Montreal is as nice as the first few hours. He heard that Canadians were very nice. Thus far, it seems a fair assessment.

He laughs to himself and, deep in the pockets of his overcoat, crosses his fingers.

Marcus is one of the friendliest club managers Spence has ever met. He has to wonder if this is as unusual for Canadian clubs as it is for the clubs in the States. It's more than just being generous or treating him well; Marcus seems to really *love* stand-up comedy. And comedians.

It's so easy to hate comedians. Just like any other job, running a comedy club can be a pain in the ass. When your employees are often bitter narcissists that come in and out every week, a person can get downright pissed. Comedians are known for being social misfits. The average bar has a dozen employees. Add fifty or so comedians who change every week to that roster and the fact that Marcus seems so jolly is understandably rare.

"This guy is hilarious," Marcus points at a framed headshot on the wall of the Comedy Crib. Then he points to another one. "So is this guy. Oh, and this guy is one of my all-time favorites."

Marcus can't be older than forty or so, but his thick glasses make him look a little older. They look like welding goggles and are clearly too big for his small head. His hair is salt-and-pepper and almost shoulder length. The guy would probably be a very handsome man if not for the thick glasses, the hippie haircut, and the fact that he is hardly over five feet tall.

Many of the comedians that Marcus is pointing out are pretty familiar. Spence recognizes several of them. Some are friends. There are several that he has never heard of before, and Marcus points out that they're all Canadian comics. Some are very popular in Quebec but not elsewhere because their shows are completely in French.

"We do one French week per month," Marcus says.

"All French comics?" Spence asks.

"And customers," Marcus says.

"I thought everyone here was bilingual."

"You'd be surprised."

"Will they get all of my American references here?" Spence asks, suddenly wondering if he should have learned how to say "fuck" in French before rolling into town.

"Of course," Marcus says, "except anything having to do with American TV, movies, sports, or current events."

Spence feels his heart shoot into his throat. "Really?" he asks.

"I'm just messing with you," Marcus says.

"Jesus. I was about to sneak out of here before being run out of town."

"You'll be fine," Marcus says. "But, seriously, don't say you're American. They'll boo you and throw things."

"Really?"

Marcus winks at him and walks away.

Nervousness is nothing new to Spence but, this time, it feels different. His first time onstage in a new venue can sometimes be a little nerve-racking, but this is his first time onstage in a completely different *country*. Sure, people can assume Canada is just like the United States all they want, but he suddenly doesn't feel like he's simply performing a little north from home. Mostly, he doesn't want to screw up onstage in a place that already has treated him pretty well.

The lights go down, and he stands in the back of the room, watching the local comedians perform. There are four of them, each of varying ages, and each of them completely different. There's the low-key monologist who drones on about Canadian politics. After him, a young hipster takes the stage and essentially reminds the audience that he's cooler than they are. At one point, an impressionist does what must be excellent impressions of Canadian celebrities and, of course, Arnold Schwarzenegger.

There's an energy in this place that he immediately loves. The audience seems to hang on every word. Even when they don't laugh, they smile. They nod when they don't outright applaud. It's often quiet and yet friendly. The comics onstage seem to be pals with the audience instead of just paid performers. Even when the language onstage gets vulgar, it all seems very easygoing. Of course, with all he knows, this is because the audience barely speaks English and they're just smiling while they try to figure it out. Maybe he got booked on one of those French nights and no one bothered to point it out?

The MC calls his name, and Spence steps onstage as if he owns the place. He's not a stranger in a strange land here. He's not a foreigner and certainly not just the ugly American. On this five-foot-by-four-foot block of wood, he is in charge. This is his home. This is where he lives. He is throwing the party; everyone else is invited to come along.

The sound of that first wave of laughter after the first joke in a set is amazing. It's the greatest feeling, and it always follows the same nervous anxiety. He hopes they will laugh. They always have before. There's no reason to think they won't. But sometimes they simply don't go where he wants to take them. Sometimes something is off. Sometimes it's him. Usually it's them. He just doesn't know until he delivers that opening line. When he sells it just right, he can tell in the first two minutes how the rest of the night will go.

"That's why I only date Asian women," he says. The laughter hits him, and he knows that everything will be just fine. They will like him, and he will like them. They will go where he leads them. He will have fun taking them there.

Part of it is easy. They give him the benefit of the doubt before he takes the stage. After all, he's paid to be there. He must be funny, right? He must know what he's doing, or he wouldn't be on a poster in the lobby. They wouldn't give him a microphone if he didn't know how to use it. The audience is his before he takes the stage. It's up to him to lose them. They want to laugh. They want to be friends. After that first laugh fades and he leads them into the second one, he knows that they will be.

"Fucking brilliant." Marcus nearly spills his beer because he's leaning in so close. Music is playing in the background, and Marcus is yelling in his ear as if it's much louder than it really is. Ten or so blocks from the Comedy Crib, sitting in an Irish pub with several French Canadians, all is right in the world. Marcus puts an arm around him and pats him on the back at the same time.

Spence smiles and takes a long sip of his beer. He had a pretty good show, but Marcus is treating him as if it was the best thing he's ever seen. A couple of hours and several drinks later, it's all they've talked about. It's the same set that got him into trouble at the Electric Pony, yet here almost got him elected mayor. He doesn't think it was that great a set, really. It was fine, but not nearly the best he's ever done. Still, Marcus loved it, and he's the guy who signs the check at the end of the week.

Spence laughs to himself. *Last week I'm a spoiled baby, and this week I'm a star.*

He enjoyed the show, despite the fact that he felt the crowd was a bit more politically correct than he normally likes. It wasn't the language they were hesitant with as much as the more controversial topics. He wonders if that's part of the Canadian politeness he has always heard about. Maybe it extends into comedy as well.

"When you did the bit about shitting your pants in the bar, I almost shit mine right there in the club," Marcus says. It's an odd and yet appropriate compliment.

"I'm glad you enjoyed it," Spence says. He takes a long gulp from his Canadian beer. He's never had it before, but it's yummy. He holds two fingers up to the bartender and orders another round.

"This one's on me," Marcus says and tosses several coins down on the bar.

Spence is thrown off whenever he sees people using Canadian currency. He had no idea they use one-dollar and two-dollar coins. Before today he never knew what a "loonie" or a "toonie" were. Now he has a stack of them in his pocket. It feels like he robbed a pirate ship.

"You bought the last one," he says to Marcus. "This one is on me."

"No way," Marcus says.

"I insist," Spence says.

"Okay, but I get the next round," Marcus says.

Spence can't even believe there will *be* another round. He's already nursing a nice buzz and can't imagine having too many more drinks, yet everyone around him has been pounding shots and beers without a second thought. He's always heard that the Irish know how to knock back the booze. At the moment he thinks the exact same thing about Canadians. It seems hard to believe that he's only a day's drive away from where he used to live. It might as well be Paris.

"You know who this is?" Marcus is talking to a pair of gorgeous women who have sat next to them at the bar. "This guy here is the headliner this week at the Comedy Crib. He's fucking hilarious, eh?"

It's the first time Spence has heard Marcus say "eh" at the end of a sentence. In fact, it's the first time he's heard anyone in Canada say "eh" at all, despite the fact that he has spoken with dozens of people all day. He wonders if it's just something Marcus does when he drinks. Some people are mean drunks, and some are sloppy. Marcus apparently gets drunk and becomes a Canadian stereotype.

"This guy is a star, eh?" Marcus says. There it is again.

The girls smile politely but honestly couldn't care less. Spence knows that, if he were them, he'd feel the same way. At the comedy club he's a star; in this pub he's just another half-drunken jackass. Marcus has no problem promoting him regardless. Maybe he thinks it will somehow help them both get laid. Or maybe he just wants to promote the show. Either way, it's met with indifference by the two beauty pageant winners sitting next to them.

"I can't get over how hot all the women are in this city," Spence says.

Marcus shrugs. "They're okay, sure."

"You're spoiled. I was in Jersey yesterday. Trust me, these women are amazing."

"You saying the women in Jersey are ugly?" Marcus asks.

"Just the ones with facial hair."

Marcus laughs and spits a little of his beer. "That bad, eh?"

"No, but it's not like here." Spence shrugs and gives the room a once-over. "Even the homeless women are hot here."

Marcus laughs. "And bilingual."

"Shit, I didn't even think about that."

"Yeah," Marcus says, "they'll ask you for spare change in French and then ask you again in English."

"They speak two languages and they're unemployed?" Spence asks. "Hell, I'm an idiot and even I could get a job at Starbucks."

Marcus laughs again and takes a gulp from his beer so big

that it runs down the corners of his mouth. The girls sitting next to them vacate their barstools and smile politely on the way out. In their place, two equally beautiful women come and sit down. Both tall and both with short hair, the new ladies smile and nod hello as they take their seats.

Spence has always had such a thing for women with short hair and glasses. The woman sitting next to him has both, and he can't help but smile. Her dark blond hair sits just above her ears. Her horn-rimmed glasses would look nerdy on most people, but she's beautiful. She's taller than he normally goes for, but everything else is just his style. It's only a matter of minutes before he talks to her. The only question now is how many he will wait before he does. He counts the sips of his beer as if each one is part of a countdown to a missile launch.

One sip, she laughs with her friend.

I've never been to Canada before. How about showing me around?

A second sip, she twirls the straw in her glass and nods her head.

That's a stupid line. Don't say that to her.

A third sip, she looks right at him.

"You're staring." She turns to him and speaks. "So you might as well introduce yourself."

Spence feels the hairs on the back of his neck stand up and realizes that he indeed had his eyes locked right on her face the entire time. He searches for a clock on the wall behind her, hoping he can use that as an excuse for what he was looking at. A person with a funny hat nearby, the Bee Gees sitting in the corner, anything. No such luck.

"Was I staring?" he says.

"For a few minutes, yeah. I figured you were trying to think of what to say," she says.

He's caught and he knows it. Now his only chance is to be charming or get up and leave. Marcus is singing along with a song on the radio and appears to be on cloud nine. Both of their beers are half full. He's not going anywhere.

"I have this way of getting tongue-tied when I see beautiful women," he says.

"But with me you just use bullshit?" she says.

"I . . ." he tries to say. He waits for something clever to pop out of his mouth, but it never does. It's embarrassing. He gets paid to be quicker than this.

"You're going to have to drop the cheesy lines if you wanna talk to me, okay?" she says and stirs her drink with her straw.

"Cheesy lines?" he asks. "I was being serious."

"Mm-hmm." She nods slowly.

"Really," he says. "People don't tell you that you're beautiful?"

She sighs, and he knows that he's lost her. There will be no rendezvous in Paris, and they'll never frolic together on the beach. He's ready for her to turn away when she swivels on the barstool and faces him.

"I saw you earlier," she says.

"At my show?" he says.

"Here," she says, "for the past hour."

"Oh yeah?" He's almost embarrassed. It's a common comedian pickup tactic to try and drop your profession in order to impress women. Unless the woman in question has already seen you perform, the tactic normally has the effect of making you look like a douche. This time is no exception.

"Yeah, and you're going to have to cut the act if you wanna sit here and talk to me," she says.

"Act?" he asks. "I was acting?"

"Yeah, you and your friend," she says.

"How so?"

"Telling jokes, talking to girls, giving everyone the finger guns."

"I have never given anyone the finger guns in my life," he lies.

She laughs. It's not a pretty or seductive chuckle like some women have. It's actually kind of nerdy. It belts out of her almost like she's coming up for air after swimming underwater. It would normally be off-putting but, on her, it's adorable. It doesn't fit her look whatsoever, which only makes him even more attracted to her.

"Yes, you have," she says. "You were doing it right here." She mimics making a gun with her hand and pulling an imaginary trigger.

Over her shoulder, Spence sees her friend watching the entire exchange. To his relief, the friend is smiling. In these kind of situations he just never knows. Sometimes the friend is a willing participant and sometimes the friend is a buzzkill. Sometimes he's so busy trying to fend off a girl's bodyguard BFF that he can't get a word in edgewise. Maybe it's a Canadian thing, but the friend is being, well, friendly.

"I think you have me confused with someone else," he lies again. "I'm not a finger gun kinda guy."

She looks back at her friend. The friend says, "She's right. You were doing it for the past hour."

Checkmate, Spence thinks.

"You win," he says, and throws up his hands in surrender.

She smirks and takes a sip of her drink. It's some concoction he's never seen before that he finds out later is called a Caesar. He wonders when Bloody Marys got replaced with this thing. He'd never even heard of Clamato juice before arriving in Canada.

"So if you wanna sit and talk," she says, "you'll have to drop the act."

"Well, I'm a comedian," he says, like an idiot.

"Yeah, I know."

"How?"

"Because your friend has been telling everyone in the bar all night long," she says.

He's embarrassed and wants to smack Marcus, but Marcus is already on the other side of the bar, talking to the BFF. Marcus would probably be a good wingman if he weren't such an obnoxious drunk. As luck would have it, the friend is patient and mildly amused. Either that or she's also a terrible drunk. Either way, it's helpful.

"He's the manager of the comedy club," he says, and nods toward Marcus.

"Yeah, he's been saying that all night, too," she says.

"Really?"

"He gave out his business cards when you were in the washroom earlier," she tells him.

Spence laughs and shakes his head. So much for trying to be charming. He'll be lucky if he just manages to leave not looking like a complete jackass.

"My point is that I'm not intentionally funny," he says. "It just comes naturally."

She rolls her eyes. He gives her a toothy smile, to which she gives him a halfhearted laugh.

"Well, drop the funny and just be you," she says. "I'd like to talk to you. But just you; not some act. Can you do that? Can you just be you?"

"I am being me," he says.

" 'You' is this awkward?"

"Often, yeah"

"Then we'll get along fine," she says, and extends her hand. "I'm Sam. That's Claudia."

Behind her, Claudia waves and goes back to nodding her head and humoring Marcus. How they've hit it off so quickly is anyone's guess, but Marcus is doing great. There are no sparks flying, but at least they're keeping busy. Claudia smiling and nodding is much better than her tossing a drink in Marcus's face and storming out.

"Sam as in 'Samantha'?" he asks his dream girl as he shakes her hand.

"Very good," she says.

He can't remember the last time he talked to a woman after a show without bullshitting his way through it. Normally it's easy. Women who want to sleep with the comedian often seek out the comedian. It normally doesn't require much effort on his part. The hard work is already done onstage. Once he's made a woman in the audience laugh for an hour, the rest is cake. Meeting a girl in a bar who has never seen his show before is a different story. He hasn't tried this approach in years. He's not even sure if he likes it.

His first thought is to find a way out of the pub and back to the hotel. His second thought is just to say "what the hell." Maybe it's the booze that makes him stick around. She's not the first clever, attractive girl he's ever talked to. The fact that she doesn't seem to care what he thinks might be part of her appeal. There was a time when he loved this sort of challenge.

"From the States?" she asks.

"How did you know?"

"You act like it," she says, "and you have an accent."

"An accent?" Spence asks. He has never been told this before. Years of growing up in Maryland and he never heard it. Years of living in New Jersey and he never heard it. He has never heard it on the road, either, even when he was in the middle of the sticks, talking to rednecks.

"It's an American accent," she says. "You said *sorry* earlier, and I knew it. You pronounced it *saw-ree.*"

"That's right," he says. "How do you say it?"

She smiles and says it. It comes out *sore-ee.* It sounds like Marcus's drunken voice, which makes him laugh almost as nerdily as she did earlier.

"You're saying it all wrong," he says.

"Ah, and that's how you *act* American," she says.

"Yeah?"

"Yeah. You think that you Americans invented everything."

"Didn't we?"

"How about penicillin?"

"No thanks, I've got a beer."

"We invented penicillin," she says.

"I'm pretty sure that was the Dutch," he says.

"Canadians."

"Really?"

She nods. "And the zipper, and the pacemaker, and basketball."

"I use one of those things all the time."

"And we invented the snowblower," she says.

"That doesn't impress me," he says. "I would expect something like that to come from Canada. It snows ten months out of the year up here."

"Hey," she says defensively, "*nine* months out of the year."

"Oh, sorry." He pronounces it *sore-ee*.

"Credit where credit is due," she says.

"Well, I can now say I had a history lesson in Canada."

"There's more where that came from," she says.

"A fountain of useless knowledge, are you?"

"Something like that."

"Let me guess," he says, "your father was an encyclopedia salesman."

She shrugs. "Insurance, encyclopedias, heroin. Whatever."

He likes her. She makes him laugh but doesn't seem eager to get him to entertain her. Sometimes the hardest part of trying to spend time with a woman is that they want the guy who was onstage earlier to be the guy sitting with them at the bar all night. They want the show to go on forever. They can't imagine that the guy offstage might just want to chill and have a beer and maybe fool around. Sam seems to get it. She takes the cues, and he lets her be the funny one.

The bartender walks up and hands Sam another Caesar. Marcus and Claudia are talking about the movie *Sweeney Todd*. In another corner of the bar, people scream at a TV, and he gets to see for the first time how Canadians react when watching a hockey game. It's like watching people finding out that they just won World War II.

"What do you do for a living?" he asks when the excitement dies down.

"Retail sales," she says. "I work at the Gap."

"Yeah?" Spence says and shows her the label on his jeans. "Check that out."

"Gap jeans," she reads.

"You got it!"

"Must be fate," she says.

"Must be."

"Either that or millions of people buy Gap jeans every year."

"I prefer to think of it as tens of thousands," he says, "which still makes it better odds that our meeting was fate."

"Whatever you need to tell yourself," she says.

"Hey, I coulda been wearing Guess jeans."

"Blasphemy!" she yells.

"See?" he says. "Maybe you should just be thankful I'm brand loyal, huh?"

"Or that we make jeans that are cheaper than Guess."

"Checkmate."

She laughs again and, for the first time, he notices how big her eyes really are behind her plastic-framed glasses. She looks in one direction, closes her eyes and, when she reopens them, is looking right at him. It's either brilliantly cunning or completely unintentional, but it might as well be a fishing lure.

A familiar feeling hits him all of a sudden, and he chuckles to himself. It's awkward at first because he knows this feeling but doesn't normally have it when he's sitting at a bar having drinks. It's normally the feeling he gets when he's standing on-stage. Now he's getting it while sitting on this stool, talking with Sam. He's comfortable.

The time gets away from him. Beer and women have that effect. Out of nowhere it's two a.m. and the bar is closed. Before he knows what happens next, he's on the street next to the pub and saying good night to Sam in the freezing cold. He tries, but he can't remember the last time he did this and just said good night on the street and walked home. Or the last time he didn't try to push some girl out of his hotel room after lying his way into bed with her.

He thinks Sam is beautiful. He likes listening to her talk (he normally likes the sound of his own voice too much to listen to anyone else), but he can't imagine asking her back to his room. Ending it here seems oddly more appropriate. He likes himself more when he doesn't feel as if he's just being a horny toad.

"You wanna come see my show?" Spence asks, and puts an arm around her waist. He's afraid she'll back away, but she doesn't. She responds by doing the same and rests her hand on the top of his Gap jeans. It feels right. It doesn't even feel new.

"Tomorrow night?" she asks.

He nods. "I can put you on my guest list."

"Sure," she says. "Just don't put me in the front row."

"Never," Spence says. He wouldn't want that, either. It's hard enough to perform when someone he knows is watching the show. It's the only time he ever really gets nervous onstage. Being able to see them four feet in front of him is even worse. It's like being sent by Rodney to a bad Broadway audition.

"Okay," she says. "But I mean it. No front row. I don't want you heckling me."

"It doesn't work that way," he says. "The audience heckles the comic. The comic doesn't heckle the audience."

"Same difference," she says.

"How do you figure?"

"Look," she huffs, "I don't tell you that the way you fold your pants is all wrong, so don't tell me when I screw up your comedian lingo. Got it?"

"Fair enough," he says.

He leans in and kisses her. It's quick and it's sweet. It's not at all the drunken make-out session that more than a few of his recent nights have ended with. It's a change of pace, but he likes it. She smells good, and her lips are soft. He wants to stay there for about a year.

"Tomorrow then?" she says into his ear. He can feel her breath on his skin, and the hairs on his neck stand up when she speaks.

"I hope so," he says.

Five seconds later and she's gone. She walks in one direction while he heads the opposite way. Somewhere in a cab, Marcus is probably trying not to pass out or puke or both. Sam walks with Claudia and hopefully talks about the nice guy she talked to all night long. Claudia hopefully has his back and tells Sam she must go to his show tomorrow night.

Spence turns the corner on Saint Catherine and starts walking toward his hotel. He's freezing, but he doesn't button his coat. He doesn't even pay attention to the cold as it pierces through the buttons on his shirt. He's alone, but he really likes it. He thinks that this must be what it feels like to walk with a skip in his step. There are people on the street, but he only hears the cold wind in his ears. He smiles and, for once, enjoys the sound of nothing.

6

Spence taps at his laptop, checking his bank account online. Not having an apartment anymore was supposed to save him a ton of money, but he hardly sees it. His expenses are still too high. With the price of gas more than double what it was when he started touring, it costs him too much to get to some of his gigs. It's almost cheaper to fly. He wonders when that happened and if it's going to be like that for good.

His computer chimes a binging sound that lets him know he has an e-mail from Rodney:

Rockford is closed. Scratch it off your schedule.

Idiot, he thinks.

The phone on the nightstand rings, and he nearly falls off the bed trying to get to it. It's always jarring to him when the phone in a hotel room rings since he takes most calls on his cell phone and never expects anyone to know where he is. Usually it's just the front desk asking if he needs housekeeping or towels. In this case, he's pleased when it's Sam.

"Do I have the right room this time?" she asks.

"Why?" Spence asks. "Did you call here earlier or something?"

"They gave me the wrong room twice," she says. "I almost gave up and asked some old man out to lunch instead of you."

"Lucky guy."

"Tell me about it," she says. "I'm good company."

"No argument here."

"Did I wake you?" she asks.

"No, I've been up for hours," he lies. He's barely been up for thirty minutes. He checked his bank account online the minute he woke up as an incentive to go back to sleep for another hour or two. He would have done exactly that if she hadn't called.

"Well, I'm bored and not working," she says, "so I figured I could get out for a while and you might want to explore the city a bit."

"I do like to explore," he lies again. He's been to South Dakota, a few times and has never seen Mount Rushmore. He only saw the Saint Louis arch because he looked out the window of his car as he drove past it. He's seen more shopping malls than landmarks.

"Does this mean you're free?" she asks.

"I'm available, but I'm never free."

"Blech," she says. "Forget I asked."

"I thought it was clever." He smiles.

"You were wrong."

"Ouch."

"Despite that, I'm still asking you to lunch," she says.

"I will again consider myself lucky," he says.

"What do you say to fifteen minutes in front of your hotel?"

"I only get fifteen minutes with you?" He grins like an idiot, as if she can see him through the phone. "That's not much of a lunch date."

She sighs dramatically. "I mean that we will meet in fifteen minutes, not *for* fifteen minutes."

"Ah, I see my mistake."

"I think you were smarter last night."

"I'm the anti-drunk," he says. "Alcohol makes me smarter."

"Fifteen minutes, weirdo?"

"Easy."

"See you then," she says and hangs up.

Now he's in trouble. He's not remotely ready. He's lying dirty in the hotel bed in his boxer briefs with his laptop on his stomach. He's unshowered and unshaven. He looks like the kind of person who sleeps until after noon every day, which is what he is. But he wants to see her and he wants it to be soon. He can't remember the last time he showered, shaved, and brushed his teeth at the same time, but he'll remember from now on.

On the corner, Sam meets him dressed in a long green overcoat and very sexy black boots. That's three for three with him; he likes short hair, glasses, and boots. She's just getting better every minute. She's wearing a dark scarf wrapped up to her chin, and her short, pretty hair is hidden underneath a knitted hat that matches the scarf.

"Cute hat," Spence says as he leans in to hug her. She offers her cheek, and he kisses it as he takes in the smell of her perfume. It could just be her shampoo or skin cream for all he knows; he's never been one to tell the difference. Whatever it is, he likes it.

"It's called a 'toque,' " she says.

"A what?"

"A toque," she says again. "That's what we call hats here."

"Really?"

"You didn't know that?" she asks.

This makes him smile. Every Christmas he hears "The Twelve Days of Christmas" on the radio. It's a Canadian novelty song that he's heard since he was a kid. It was recorded by Rick Moranis and Dave Thomas from *SCTV*. They mention "toques" in the song, and it always threw him off. He never knew what the hell a toque was until now. It's nice to have the mystery solved.

"See?" he says. "Two minutes into the day and you're already teaching me stuff about Canada I never would have learned otherwise. I wouldn't have even thought to ask."

"That's what you're impressed with? Finding out what a toque is?"

"Pretty much, yeah."

"Nothing about Canadian history or politics," she says. "You just want to know what we call things."

"Works for me."

She holds up her hand. "This is a glove," she says.

"Alright, smart-ass," he says, "where are we going to eat?"

"I figured I'd leave that up to you," she says.

"McDonald's it is."

"Such a charmer."

"Only the best for you."

"Alright," she says, "lunch is on me."

"Shit." He smiles. "In that case, take me to the most expensive place in this city. Nothing's too good for us, I say."

"Burger King it is," she says.

"I prefer McDonald's."

It's the middle of the afternoon, and people are everywhere. As dozens of people scurry past them, no one seems to notice the shaggy-haired guy talking to the bespectacled woman bundled up in front of him. Even wearing a sweater and heavy overcoat, he looks underdressed compared to everyone else walking by. At least the locals are better prepared for the weather than he is. He's still freezing.

"Okay, more Canada," Spence says.

"The first prime minister of Canada was John A. Macdonald," she says.

"Screw that," he says. "I told you, no history. Just tell me what they call a quarter pounder with cheese here."

"It's called a quarter pounder with cheese."

"Really?" he asks. "I thought it was called a royale with cheese. Like in *Pulp Fiction*."

"That's France."

"But Montreal is French, right?"

She raises an eyebrow at him. "You really don't know anything about Canada, do you?"

"Nope. That's why you're not allowed to give me any history lessons. I like to be as ignorant about Canada as possible. You know, just like the rest of America is."

"Mission accomplished," she says.

She takes his arm and leads him while making it seem like he's doing the leading. They walk down the street that way for a couple of blocks. It's odd to him that it doesn't feel odd to him. He likes walking with her and likes her on his arm. He also likes her near him because her body helps shield him from the wind. No one told him Montreal was so windy.

"It just hit me," she says and comes to a stop. "We're going to eat at Manny's."

"What kind of place is it?" he asks.

"Well, it's kinda like any other sandwich place, but we're going to get you some poutine."

"Pou-what?" he says. The name sounds like an accident.

"*Poo-TEEN,*" she says slowly. "It's food."

"It sounds like an intestinal problem."

"It's one hundred percent Canadian, and it's yummy. The perfect lunch lesson for you today, Mister American-Who-Has-Never-Been-to-Canada."

"Oh, yeah?" he says. "Well, if it will further my lesson of learning Canada without having to actually learn anything about Canada, I'm all for it."

"You sure? Because poutine is made from moose hooves."

"Get the hell outta here," he scoffs. "Really?"

She rolls her eyes.

A half hour later the two of them are sitting at Manny's, and he discovers that poutine is french fries covered with cheese curds and gravy. It's a huge plate with huge fries, full of starch and fat. It's so messy and so greasy that he has to eat it with a large fork and shovel it into his mouth in enormous gulps. It's too much, and it's a ridiculous thing for him to be stuffing into his face. It is, without question, delicious.

"Did you know that we call the Gap "le Gap" here?" she asks.

"Now you're just fucking with me," he says.

"No, really. That's what the French Canadians call it."

"I'm not that stupid. 'Le Gap' just means 'the Gap' in French."

"Very good."

"Did you know that 'La Bamba' is Spanish for 'The Bamba'?" he asks.

"I did not."

"See?" He shovels a mouthful of carbohydrates into his face. "Now you've learned the only Spanish I know."

"I know that *agua* means 'water,' " she says, "from watching *Sesame Street*."

"They have *Sesame Street* here?" he says, and she kicks him under the table.

Spence watches her eating, mesmerized by the way she shovels food into her mouth and yet manages to make it look cute. She's beautiful, but not like the statuesque women he sees littered all over the streets of Montreal. He still can't help but find her sexy. Her long legs and short, curvy frame make her just as tempting as any other woman he's been with for as long as he can remember. But she's quirky, and he finds that adorable. She's funny and quick. He thinks that in high school she was probably a very attractive geek.

"So how's Canada treating you thus far?" she asks, while trying to hide the fact that she just dropped food on her lap.

"So far I love it," he says, and immediately blushes. He's normally better at not showing all of his cards at once.

"Yeah?" she says. "Do you wanna see Parliament?"

"Nice try, but I know that's not in Montreal."

"Very good."

"Isn't it in Toronto?"

She rolls her eyes. "Ottawa."

"I knew that," he lies.

"Just checking," she says.

Canada is different enough that he's aware he's in a different country, even though most of the things he is familiar with at home he finds right here in Montreal. Sure, the money is different and, yes, everything being printed in two languages is strikingly noticeable. But he expected that. It's the subtle things that he stumbles across that really stand out in his head.

"Like what?" she asks, and he realizes that he's been rambling, mostly thinking aloud.

"Well, like little things on television," he tells her. He recalls the *Canadian Idol* billboard he saw the day before.

"That was canceled a while back," she says. "You must've seen an old ad that hasn't been taken down."

"That's a shame," he says. "I would've liked to have seen it."

"Trust me, you didn't miss anything."

"I'll take your word for it." He shrugs and realizes that he's never even seen an episode of *American Idol,* so he doesn't know why he'd ever watch the Canadian one.

"We have all the American shows, too," she says.

"Yeah, but check this out. Yesterday on TV here I saw a commercial that had two men together as a couple shopping in a grocery store. Holding hands and everything."

"Yeah, so?" she asks.

"That's just it," he says. "Two gay men shopping. It was wild. I don't think you'll see a commercial like that in the United States for years, if ever."

"Really? You don't have commercials like that?"

"Not at all. Just the occasional print ad, and those are always controversial."

"That surprises me."

"It's stupid," he says. "It should be just like it is here: No big deal. But people are still really nuts about gay people. Even people who don't think they're homophobic get weird about it."

"That just seems silly," she says.

"It is."

"Maybe you should move to Canada."

"If the rest of Canada treats me as well as Montreal has, I just might have to consider it," he says and winks.

"The Comedy Crib," she says. "Do they treat you really well?"

"They do," he says and then checks himself. "That is, they treat me the way comedians should be treated, but usually are not."

She raises one eyebrow. It's a neat trick.

"Let's just say my job isn't nearly as glamorous as people think it is," he says and shrugs his shoulders. In the background he can hear some band whose name he can't remember playing on the radio and tries to remember if it's a Canadian group. He wonders how many Canadian bands he could name if he tried. Rush is one.

"Where do you want to go from here?" she asks.

"After all this poutine, I could use a nap," he says. He remembers that Bryan Adams is Canadian, too.

"No, jackass," she says. "I meant with your career."

"Ah." He winks. "Good question. As soon as I figure it out, I'll let you know."

"Really?" she asks. "No big plans? No talk show in your future? No big movies?"

"Oh, sure, I'll just make a few phone calls and make it happen." She thumps his arm with her index finger. "No, seriously," she says.

"I want all of that," he says. He's pretty sure Alanis Morissette is Canadian.

"Everything?"

"Everything."

"The whole nine yards?"

"Well." He takes a long sip from his Diet Coke. "I used to think that, anyway. Now I'm not so sure. My plans seem to keep changing, whether I like it or not. For a while there, everything seemed to be going along just like it was supposed to. I got an agent, did the Kilborn show, started getting regular gigs. That's the way it's supposed to happen and that's what I was doing. Then everything just kinda leveled out."

"What do you mean?" she asks and eats a forkful of fries.

"I don't know," he says. "I sometimes think that maybe I've reached a point that I'm not going to cross. That maybe this is where I'm at and where I'm going to stay. And it took a long time to get this far. I mean, I'm working, so that's cool. But I think sometimes that I already peaked."

"Nah," she says. "I'm sure this is only the beginning. You're probably ready to break out at any time."

"You haven't even seen me perform yet. For all you know, I could really suck."

"Don't think it didn't cross my mind."

Spence puts his fork down and makes the decision to stop eating. He could probably finish what's in front of him and still go back for seconds, but he thinks it's best not to push it. Outside it looks like it's absolutely freezing, so the thought does cross his mind to keep stuffing himself with comfort food. When Sam speaks again, it surprises him. He doesn't even realize that he's been staring off into space, thinking to himself for a couple of minutes. He was busy trying to remember whether or not Joni Mitchell is Canadian.

"If you're working full-time and you're always on tour, why do you feel that you're not going anywhere?" she asks.

"I'm working, but I'm not advancing."

"You mean not getting promoted?"

He nods. "It's the curse of every comedian at my level. Not enough of a following or enough TV credits to play bigger rooms and make more money. I did *The Late Late Show*, but that's not enough anymore."

"No?" She seems surprised.

"Not with too many comedians and not enough work. There's a bottleneck at the top. People get in the industry and never get out. Comedians don't retire. We quit or we die. There are guys thirty years older than me who are still out there working the same clubs I'm working. Then there are guys ten years younger than me trying to work there, too. There's just not enough work unless you find a way to stand out or get noticed."

"Jesus," she says, "that sounds awful."

"It honestly can be," he says. He remembers that Nickelback is a Canadian band.

"So why do you still do it?"

"Because I love it."

She raises her eyebrow again. "Do you?"

He pauses for a second. No one has ever second-guessed that line before. "Sometimes. I still love being onstage, let me put it that way. I still love to make people laugh."

"No offense," she says, "but it seems like a big pain in the ass."

"Oh, it is," he admits. "Trust me, there are parts of the job I absolutely detest. My agent is an idiot. The constant driving sucks."

"You ever think about quitting?"

"I won't lie to you, but yeah."

"What stops you?"

"I don't know what else I would do," he says. "I've been doing nothing but stand-up comedy for ten years. That's a long time to be doing the same job and suddenly look for a new one when you're forty. I wouldn't know what other jobs I could get at this point. And, really, I'd always wonder 'what if.' "

"What if what?" she asks.

"Well, I'd sit around wondering, 'What if I never quit?' Or, 'What if I was weeks away from something bigger and better?' "

"What if you went back to doing it part-time?"

"That's still assuming I can find some kind of job to do full-time."

"Hey, the Gap is hiring!" She smiles.

"Don't think I've never thought of that," he says. "Know anyone who can get me an interview there?" He can't help but smile back, even though the thought of working retail sends a cold shiver down his back. He worked in retail all throughout high school. It's probably one reason he can barely stand shopping now. Too many flashbacks of working Christmas seasons at the mall. It's also probably a good reason why he thinks most people suck. Working at the Gap would probably cause him to go postal.

She reaches across the table and holds both of his hands in hers. He can tell that she bites her nails. Her hands are smooth, just like the skin on her face, but her nails look like they were clipped with a pocketknife. He likes the way she looks at him over the top of her glasses. When she smiles with just one corner of her mouth, he realizes that he's been doing all of the talking.

"And what's your story?" He switches gears and smiles.

"There's not much to say," she says. "Not all of us live the exciting life of a traveling comedian."

"If only."

"I don't know what I want to do with my life, either."

"You mean the Gap isn't your final destination?"

"Maybe," she says. "Maybe it is and I just don't know it yet. It started as a job I was going to do for a few months after I got out of university. That was six years ago."

"Do you like it?"

"Sometimes."

"So why do you still do it?" He winks.

She smirks and looks long and hard at him as she pushes her glasses back up the bridge of her nose.

"Because I don't know what else I would do," she says and, for a moment, they both smile without saying anything. Spence likes the way it feels to just sit there and watch her for a second. She looks at him in a way that tells him she's thinking the same thing.

Just before it becomes awkward, Sam lets out a tiny sigh and clenches his hands a little harder than before. "At some point, doing this comedy thing you do, you had a real passion for it."

"Yeah, sure," he says.

"Yeah, well, I've never had that."

"What do you mean?"

"No passion for what I do. Nothing about my job that I love or adore or moves me forward or any of that."

"What?" He pretends to have a heart attack, clutching his chest and gasping. "Retail sales doesn't motivate and inspire you to greatness?"

"Not at all," she says. "But I'm good at it."

"So you keep doing it."

"So I keep doing it."

"You've never had a hobby?" he asks. "Something you do on the side you'd love to make into a career?"

"Nope." She shrugs. "I'm good at managing people. So I imagine I'll keep doing that."

"Nothing else you've ever wanted to be?"

"Yes, but I'm not allowed to tell you that."

"Aw, come on!" He pokes her in the shoulder. "You gotta now!"

"No way," she says. "Bad luck."

"Please?" He does his best impression of a basset hound. "Tell me what you wanna be when you grow up."

She pushes a strand of hair out of her eyes as she rolls them and lets out a long sigh. Shaking her head, she grins slowly. "Okay, but you're not going to like it," she says.

"Lay it on me," he says.

"Wife and mother."

The mock heart attack instantly returns. Making a huge display, clutching his chest and gasping for air, Spence coughs loudly and collapses onto the table. Sam reaches over and thumps him on the back of the head.

The check is paid and, both feeling huge in the stomach, they trudge out into the cold. Sam walks him back to his hotel, holding his hand the entire way. He likes the way it feels to walk next to her. He's never been one for public affection. He barely knows this woman. Yet none of that even crosses his mind. Something about being with her is just . . . easy.

"Nine o'clock," Spence says, reminding her of showtime.

"Nine it is," she says. "Then we get to see the artist at work."

"Stay out of the front row."

"I promise."

"I'm going to hold you to that."

"Believe you me—I don't wanna be in that front row. If you suck, I'm going to wanna sneak out of there before you have a chance to see me."

"You'd better not," he says.

"Then you'd better not suck."

With that, she kisses him and disappears around the corner. In another few hours he gets to see her again at the show, but she's only gone thirty minutes before he feels the urge to call her. It's very different. He's not even sure he likes feeling that way. Then he realizes that he's just had his first real date in seven years. He's had one-night stands. There have been plenty of women. But this is a first for him: an actual date.

Christ, he thinks, *what the hell am I gonna do with a girl in Canada?*

7

Spence is pacing. For the first time in years, he's actually pacing. He tried sitting on the sofa in the green room, but that didn't last very long. After reading the same paragraph in some magazine six or seven times, he finally gave up and just started wandering back and forth from the green room to the bar and back again. He's on trip number six and drink number two by the time Marcus steps in his path.

"What the hell is wrong with you?" Marcus grins as he says this, showing that he's not really worried about Spence so much as giving him a hard time. He already knows the answer.

"What do you mean?" Spence asks. "I'm fine."

"No, you're not," Marcus says. "You're all over the place like you're coked up or something. You're not, are you?"

"Of course not," Spence says. He doesn't like cocaine one bit. Too many comedians live on it.

"Kidding." Marcus chuckles and punches him lightly on the shoulder. "Man, this girl really has you all wound up, eh?"

"What are you talking about?" Spence takes a sip off his glass of Scotch and does his best impression of a man without a care in the world. He's never been good at impressions.

"I'm talking about I'm a grown man and I know what it looks like when a guy has a girl on his mind."

"Trust me, I'm fine."

Behind them, at the front of the club, customers are slowly filing in and are being seated throughout the showroom. A young employee shows people to their tables as waitresses scurry about, quickly taking drink orders and getting people nice and buzzed before the show starts. It's looking like the show is going to sell out, and the mood in the room is already high and exciting.

Sam is nowhere to be found. When it was forty-five minutes before showtime and the first few customers came through the door, Spence thought nothing about it. Thirty minutes before showtime and he expected that she'd be there any minute. Now there's only five minutes to go, and Spence isn't feeling quite as confident as he was an hour ago. Part of him wonders if he's been had. The other part hates himself for thinking like that.

"I'm sure she'll be here," Marcus says, completely seeing through Spence's bad acting.

"I'm sure she will," Spence lies. "I'm not worried about it."

But you are worried about it, he thinks to himself. *What the hell is that all about?*

He can't remember the last time he was this nervous before a show, and it drives him nuts. Mostly, it drives him nuts because he realizes that the butterflies in his stomach have nothing to do with going onstage and telling jokes. The punch in the gut he's feeling is because he wants to see Sam. An hour ago he was nervous about her seeing him perform, which was already not like him at all. Now he's nervous that he'll never see her again.

"There's plenty of other women here, mate." Marcus pats him on the shoulder again.

"Always," Spence says and raises his glass, but he knows Marcus is only trying to make him feel better.

He walks back into the green room and collapses onto the sofa. In the span of thirty seconds, he goes from reassuring himself that she's just late to telling himself he'll probably never see her again anyway. She's just another girl in another city. And he's seen plenty of both. This is nothing different.

But isn't everything here different? he thinks to himself and then shakes his head so he won't again.

Spence wonders why he would let himself care like this. The show is going on whether she's there or not. By the time he's onstage, he'll forget he was waiting for her at all. He'll forget everything except his act, the audience, and getting the job done. He always does. He doesn't take anything with him on-stage except what he's about to say into the microphone.

It's for this reason he's avoided having a girlfriend for so many years. It's just one more stress in his life that he doesn't need. The minute things went sour with Beth, he knew he wouldn't be in another serious relationship for years, if ever again. His career ruined his marriage, so the least he could do is make his loyalty to it the only real commitment in his life. Besides, who would want to be seriously involved with a man a few weeks away from homelessness whose only roots are the dark ones on his head he keeps meaning to get highlighted? The last thing he wants is to repeat everything that made his marriage fail.

Yet he sits in the green room and realizes something he doesn't want to admit, which is that he really likes this woman. He likes being with her, likes thinking about her, and likes the man he is when he's with her. Still, in the back of his mind, a nagging voice reminds him that there is nothing remotely convenient about any of it. It's the same nagging voice that keeps telling him that all of this worrying probably means nothing, since Sam isn't here and probably isn't going to show up anyway.

"You ready?" Marcus peeks his head into the green room and gives Spence an "okay" sign.

"You bet."

"You cool? Not still worried about her, are you?"

"I'm fine," he lies.

"Cool. Just making sure," Marcus says.

"I take it she didn't show up?"

"I don't know," Marcus says. "I've been running around, helping the bartender."

"No big deal."

"Have a good show, eh?"

"Thanks," Spence says and gets up off the sofa. He checks himself in the enormous dressing room mirror directly in front of him and suddenly is back to thinking he looks older than he should. Sam is almost a decade younger than him. If he realizes it, she must have realized it, too. He suddenly remembers that Celine Dion is married to some guy who is much older than she is. Then he remembers that Celine Dion is Canadian.

He straightens his blazer, pushes his hair back, and walks to the bar again. He surveys the crowd and—again—sees that Sam is nowhere to be found. The nagging voice in his head is gone, but he doesn't feel very good. Music fills the room as the lights come down. A hush comes over the room as a recorded announcement welcomes everyone to the Comedy Crib and tells them to turn off their cell phones and not talk during the show. Spence decides to walk back to the green room when a waitress stands in his path.

"Here," she says, holding out a basket of fries covered in cheese curds and gravy. It's poutine.

"What's this?"

"Poutine."

"Yes, I know. But why are you handing it to me?"

"It's yours." The waitress looks at him like he's high.

"No," Spence says slowly. "I didn't order it. I don't eat before I go onstage."

"Someone bought it for you." The waitress hands him a napkin and the basket of poutine. "Read the note."

Spence stands there holding the hot bowl of food as the waitress walks away. He looks down at the napkin she handed him and notices that there's writing on it.

DON'T SUCK!

—S

He laughs out loud and instantly feels his face go flush. A couple of people sitting nearby look over to see what the noise is when no one is even onstage yet. His eyes dart around the room, to the front door, and back to the bar. He scans the audience and looks for some kind of sign of her, but it's too dark now that the lights have gone down.

Where the hell is she?

The preshow music ends, and the stage lights go up. The MC takes the stage to applause and cheers from the audience, and the show is off and running. Spence stands in the same spot, holding a bowl of poutine, ignoring everything else while searching through the darkness. Then, after what is probably ten seconds but feels like ten minutes, he sees her.

She's sitting in the front row.

Sam kisses the back of his neck as he fumbles with his hotel room key. So far, he has inserted the tiny plastic card into the door lock three different ways, but each of them has somehow been wrong. A red light on the door handle keeps blinking at him to let him know he's not having any luck getting into his room.

"You may be good at comedy, but you suck at opening doors," Sam says and squeezes his arm while giggling a little too close to his right ear.

"Hey, shaddup," Spence says. "This is high-tech stuff."

"Yes, I could see a man your age being confused by such advanced technology like a hotel key."

"Ouch. She hits below the belt."

"Relax, I don't like boys my own age anyway."

"Thanks," Spence says and makes it sound like a question. The key card is inserted into the door lock one more time. A green light flashes, and the door unlocks. "Success!"

"My hero."

Spence puts his arm around her waist as he opens the door with his other hand. Sam practically twirls into the room, taking him with her as they both laugh. More than one drink has been consumed, as well as a bit more poutine just to help soak it all up. The door has barely closed before she has her mouth on his and has pushed him against the door. He loves the way her hair smells as it falls in front of his nose.

"You want a drink? I have some whiskey here." He stops kissing her long enough to motion to the bottle of Crown Royal sitting on the nightstand. He never realized that Crown Royal is Canadian before today.

"Blech." Sam scrunches up every part of her face.

"Or not," Spence says.

"*Agua.*"

"You learned that on *Sesame Street,* I know."

"Bring me water."

"Your wish is my command." He pulls free of her embrace and walks into the bathroom. He pours her a glass from the tap and looks at himself in the mirror.

"*I don't like boys my own age anyway?*" Spence thinks to himself. *What the hell is that supposed to mean?*

At this moment, he doesn't feel old. He doesn't even think he looks old, which makes this the first time he's thought that in weeks. He feels pretty damned good. An amazing show followed by food and drinks and laughs. Now the pretty girl with the short hair and glasses is back in his hotel room and everything is going according to plan. Everything is perfect.

Everything being perfect is exactly the reason Spence can't figure out why something is eating at him. Everything feels amazing. It feels like this is exactly where he wants to be and he's with who he wants to be with. But something about it all seems a bit off. He's not sure what, since he's been right here dozens of times before.

He walks back around the corner. There, Sam is already lying on the bed. The remote control is in her hand. She's fully dressed, although she has pulled back the blankets and sheets and has propped up the pillows behind her head.

"Now you see why you got me back here so easily." She looks up at him and grins. "Pay-per-view."

"You're not about to tell me you're into hotel porn, are you? Because that's the worst kind of porn there is."

"Don't be ridiculous. There's this invention called the Internet," she says. "No one pays for porn anymore."

"Good point. Guess we're stuck with action movies."

"Rom-coms," she says, "or I walk."

"You drive a hard bargain," he says. "You should be a talent agent."

"And give up the glamour that is retail sales? Forget it."

He hands her the glass of water, which she downs very quickly before reaching up and pulling him down onto the bed with her. She moves over so he can lie beside her, but doesn't do anything more than put her head on his chest as she flips through the channels. Spence kicks his shoes off and rests his chin on the top of her head.

"I'm so glad you were funny," she says. "I was totally going to sneak out if you sucked."

"Not after they sat you in the front row, you weren't."

"Yeah, what the hell was that all about?"

"Wasn't my idea, believe me."

"At least you were funny."

"That's what I thought about you," he says. It makes no sense, but she laughs anyway. Mission accomplished.

"You were worried I wasn't going to show up," she says and runs her right hand across his chest.

"Not at all," he lies.

"A little?" She holds her index finger and thumb up to show him a tiny amount.

"Maybe this much," he says and moves her finger closer to her thumb.

"Good enough," she says.

Better late than never, Spence thinks to himself. He didn't let on to Sam that he was worried she had stood him up. He made it seem like he didn't much notice that she wasn't there. He's pretty sure she can see through it.

The good performance he'd had the night before at the Comedy Crib was nothing compared to the show he put on tonight. Every beat was perfect and every punchline hit like it was supposed to. From the moment the microphone touched his hand, he spoke nothing but gold into it. As much as he tried not to make eye contact with Sam during the show, he couldn't help but occasionally glance over at her. She looked stunning when she laughed really hard.

"I think I'm your muse," she had told him when he walked offstage and had her brought back to the green room after the show.

"I think you may be on to something," he had said back, although he was being flattering. This wasn't the best show he'd ever done. But it certainly felt better than most.

Sam now tilts her head upward and kisses him. It's sweet and as if she knows he was just thinking about her. Spence leans down and touches the side of her face and returns the kiss. In just a few seconds, they are on top of one another, rolling over in the bed, pulling at each other's clothes while keeping their mouths locked together.

Sam pulls his sweater over his head as she whispers in his ear, "What's next?"

"What?" Spence is distracted and stops fumbling with her bra. He pulls his head back and runs his hand through his hair. "Oh, well, I think I'm going to Iowa next week. Or Indiana. I don't remember. Then it's Ohio and Illinois."

"No." Sam rolls her eyes and smirks at him. "I mean us. What's next?"

"What do you mean?"

"I mean I want this"—her eyes run up and down his body and back to his eyes—"but not if you're just going to kick me out afterward."

It hits Spence what felt odd this entire time, why he couldn't quite relax. Everything with Sam tonight *has* been amazing and perfect. It's also been typical. It's been what he has done so many times before. As much fun as she's having, even Sam can tell it's been his routine.

"I'm not going to kick you out," he says. "I want you to stay."

"Me too."

Spence kisses her again, softly, then puts his arms around her and squeezes her tightly against him. He loves the way she smells and the way her hair feels when it tickles his bare shoulder. She pulls her head sideways and kisses his neck. He rolls over onto his back and holds her against him.

Isn't everything different here?

Spence leans in for one more kiss, this time looking in her

eyes. He runs a hand through her hair and smiles. "So tell me what movie you want to watch."

Sam kisses him on the cheek and wakes him from whatever he was dreaming. He turns over in the bed and sees that she's already dressed and fully made-up. She looks beautiful. How did he manage to sleep through her getting ready?

"You talk in your sleep," Sam says.

"Really?" Spence says. He's been known to sleepwalk in the past, but he didn't realize that he yammers when he snoozes.

"Yeah," she says. "You talk onstage. You talk in your sleep. It seems that you never shut up."

He chuckles and wipes his eyes. He hopes he didn't say anything incriminating. The last thing he wants is to call her by the wrong name while he's in Sandman Land.

"What was I saying?"

"Mostly gibberish," she says. "You were going on about how the motions need to be filed and how the account executives were falling behind."

"Really?"

"Yep."

"Like in an office?"

"Something like that."

"Damn." He stretches his hands and looks around the hotel room. "Other people dream they can fly, and I dream I actually have a job."

"Could be worse," she says and shows him her Gap name tag.

He rolls over and sits up in the bed. Putting his arms around her waist, he looks into her eyes. She really is beautiful. It's a different feeling for him to wake up and have this conversation. He's used to trying to kick women out of his hotel room as soon as possible. Looking at Sam on the edge of the bed, he just wants to sit here for a while longer. He doesn't want her to leave.

"I don't want to leave," Sam says. How appropriate. "But I've got to go to work."

"Those pants aren't going to fold themselves," he says.

"Don't I know it?"

"I have to leave town today," he says with a painful grimace.

"I know," she says. Her mood suddenly changes. She's still smiling, but her voice gets quiet. "Send me a text message before you head out, okay?"

"Sure will. You want me to stop by the Gap and see you?"

"You cruising for a new sweater?"

"Of course."

"Sounds like a plan to me," she says and kisses him. He gets out of the bed and puts his arms around her. She could probably call in sick, right? A Gap store doesn't need a manager to operate on a Sunday, does it? He wonders if begging her to stay would cause him to lose his cool exterior.

"You were great last night," she says.

"And what about my stand-up?" he jokes. She bites his shoulder, and he howls. He laughs and massages it as he puts on his clothes so he can walk her out.

He holds her again and stands there for a minute enjoying the silence. This was not at all what he expected. He figured a week in Canada would be about snow and starchy foods and people saying "eh." He thought maybe he'd get laid like he sometimes does and that maybe he'd enjoy entertaining some different audiences for a while. What he didn't expect was to wind up holding some woman from Montreal and hoping she could stick around for a few more days or decades.

"You've got my number, guy," Sam says after what feels like a year and yet not long enough.

"Yes, I do," he says.

"So"—she tosses her purse over her shoulder—"use it."

"I promise," he says and for the first time thinks it's quite possible that he isn't lying.

"Pinkie swear," she says and holds out her littlest finger for him to grab. When he does, he figures that now he actually has to call her. Breaking a pinkie swear is tantamount to blasphemy in the Vatican.

"Don't walk me out," she says. "I kind of like ending it here."

"It doesn't have to end here," he says before he realizes what is coming out of his mouth. "I'll call."

"Use the number, guy. Montreal ain't that far away."

She's nuts. It might as well be China.

A moment later she has kissed him, hugged him, and walked out the door. He stands there staring at the room for a few minutes before deciding it's time to pack up and move on. He looks out the window of the hotel at the people below, scurrying like ants down the sidewalk. They are off to eat French bread and French fries and buying French maid outfits or whatever people in Quebec do on Sunday afternoons. He wonders if he can see Sam down there if he surveys the crowd.

Then he remembers that Barenaked Ladies is a Canadian band.

8

Spence wakes up, and his head feels like he got into a fight the night before. He can't remember if he did or not, but if it happened, he definitely lost. This is by far the worst hangover he's had in a long time. It takes him a few minutes to realize the ringing in his head is actually the alarm clock on the nightstand. He slaps the top of it a few times before it finally turns off. He switches on the lamp next to the bed and takes a long look around the hotel room to get his bearings.

It looks like most hotel rooms he stays in. His clothes are in the same place as where he pulled them off last night. His laptop is still sitting in the middle of the desk. His suitcase is still where he left it. He's not sure why but, every day when he wakes, he looks around to see if everything is how he left it the night before. As if elves were going to come in while he slept and rearrange the furniture and put his computer in the bathtub.

He's lying in a huge king-sized bed and yet managed to wrap himself in the blankets like a burrito. The bad news is that his head is killing him and he has to actually get up and get dressed. The good news is that there isn't a strange woman lying next to him. He might have had a few too many drinks last night, but at least he went home alone.

It's six a.m. He puts his feet on the floor and sighs. He has to get dressed and drive over to the local radio station for an interview at six thirty. How long did he sleep? Three, maybe four hours? Not enough. When he started touring, three hours was enough sleep for him to drive the entire next day. Now he's going to need an entire pot of coffee just to get through the interview. He gets up and walks into the bathroom and turns on the light.

Fluorescent lights are evil. They offer no mercy. They show every flaw he's ever had on his skin. He even notices scars from pimples he had when he was a kid that he thought disappeared long ago. There is definitely gray on his temples now, and the drinking did not help his eyes look any younger. He thinks he has aged more in the past three years than he did in the previous ten.

He laughs. Two weeks and a thousand miles since he left Canada and he's right back to where he was before. For a brief hiccup, all seemed well in the world. Then he woke up this morning and realized nothing changed. Peoria has been good to him so far, but he still misses the way he was treated in Montreal. His hotel room is just as nice here as anywhere else, but he feels like something is missing. He's had two weeks of great shows and has been traveling to good clubs in good weather. But he doesn't feel right. Something is off, which is probably why he drank too much last night.

He puts on his jeans and the same shirt he wore onstage the night before. He pulls on his corduroy sports jacket, which is standard comedian issue. Then he messes up his already messed-up hair and looks at himself in the full-sized mirror next to the bed. Besides looking exhausted and a bit too old, he looks exactly like every comedian you've ever seen on TV. A quick brush of the teeth and half a bottle of Tylenol and he's ready to baffle the airwaves with his brilliance.

The sun is just barely starting to come up, but he's wearing his sunglasses anyway. Part of it is because even the glow from a cigarette lighter would hurt his eyes at this point and part of it is to hide the fact that he looks like a basset hound after this little sleep. He gets in his car and tunes the radio to the station he's going to be on. He thinks it's always good to know what kind of show he's getting ready to do.

Every morning radio show is pretty much the same. It's usually two or three hosts talking about local news and playing music. One host anchors the show and tends to be the name behind it. The other host is a wacky sidekick named after an animal or body part. The third host is almost always a woman, and her job is technically to tell the weather and traffic updates. More importantly, her job is to laugh at the other two hosts. If it's a two-host format, then the main host doubles as the wacky character and the woman is still on the show groaning at his antics. Easily ninety percent of radio morning shows are coed and just like this.

It doesn't matter that he's a bit hungover. He can do these interviews in his sleep. He often has it planned out and knows exactly what he's going to do. Some comedians simply come in and recite jokes they do onstage or recreate their acts on the air. He sometimes has bits that he does only on radio, but he doesn't really like to use jokes he plans on using that night at the club. Most times he just follows along with the hosts' lead.

At least he likes doing it. Some comedians hate doing morning radio because they can't hear the laughter on the other side of the radio. Some just think it's phony and forced. As true as that may be, he still enjoys it. The interaction with the DJs is often a lot of fun for him and lets him share the spotlight a bit instead of standing naked and alone onstage.

Sometimes the DJs hate him. It's not his fault; a lot of DJs hate comedians in general. Sometimes the morning host is a local celebrity and sees the comedian as competition. That guy might think that no one sets *him* up to be funny every morning, so why the hell should he do it for some traveling comic? But the radio station is usually paid ad money by the comedy club for that interview, so the DJ in question has no say in the matter. That only pisses them off more.

Spence once did an interview with a host who asked him in advance for the punchlines to the jokes he was planning to tell. That's pretty standard procedure; the DJ wants to know where you're going to take the bit. But this DJ took those punchlines and used them himself.

"That's why I only date Asian women," the DJ had said as he claimed the joke as his own.

Thanks, jerk, he remembers thinking to himself, *now I have nothing to say. Glad I could help you be funny this morning.*

Spence arrives at the radio station and checks in at the front desk. This is also pretty routine. Morning show hosts have as many death threats as politicians. There's always a ton of security to get past in order to get into the studio, no matter how small the town or how tiny the radio station. A young girl who couldn't be older than nineteen checks his driver's license and a guy who looks like a bouncer comes around the corner and has him sign a waiver about what he's allowed to say on the air. This is also standard procedure. Someone obviously said "fuck" on the air at some point and now the station has to cover its ass with everyone.

It's never as simple as just language usage. It used to be that he simply agreed not to use profanity over the airwaves. Nowadays everyone gets offended too easily, so the list of things he's not allowed to say or do is longer than it has ever been. At this station, he's not allowed to curse, talk about religion, talk about race, talk about politics, insult the local mascot, or say anything overtly sexist. He's essentially allowed to make fun of himself and anyone who looks just like him.

Walking into the studio, an obese man stuck behind a radio console reaches across the desk without standing up and extends his hand. "Hey, I'm Buzz," he says. This would make him Buzz Barker of "The Buzz Barker in the Morning Show." Buzz is wearing a baseball cap with the Van Halen logo on it, an enormous black T-shirt that stretches across his enormous belly, and jean shorts. He speaks with that DJ voice that they all seem to have and has a big smile on his face. This is comforting. It means that Buzz likes comedians.

"Spence," he says as he shakes Buzz's hand and looks around the studio. They are always so much smaller than people think. He remembers that "The Bob and Tom Show" has an enormous studio. So does Howard Stern. Both are exceptions to the rule. Most radio studios look like the inside of a Toyota Yaris.

"Nice to have you," Buzz says and points to a skinny guy in

the corner sitting next to a thirtysomething woman. "That's Monkey-Boy. And that's Sheila."

Spence waves to both of them. They both nod and go back to reading whatever papers are in front of them. Buzz relaxes back into his seat and offers him a pair of headphones to wear.

"So where do ya live?" Buzz asks him.

"The Toyota Camry outside," he deadpans.

Buzz laughs. "I'll bet. That's great."

I wasn't joking, Spence thinks.

"What'd you wanna talk about today?" Buzz asks.

"Anything is fine with me," he says. "I usually like to just wing it. I've been listening on the way here, so we can pick up where you guys left off."

"Cool," Buzz says, "I like that. We're in the middle of a block of songs. When we come back in four minutes, we'll go right to you."

"Sounds good." Spence holds up a thumb and puts the headphones over his head.

"One other thing," Buzz says.

"Shoot."

"I know you're supposed to be on the air for thirty minutes, but we're going to have to cut that down to about four."

"Really?" Spence asks.

"Yeah," Buzz says, "sorry about that. We have to do some giveaways and won't have time to keep you around."

Damn it, Spence thinks, *I'm glad I got up at six a.m. to be on the air for four goddamned minutes. I'll be forgotten before nine.*

"No problem," he lies. He smiles, and Buzz, Monkey-Boy, and Sheila all smile back. They barely speak to each other, and Buzz is the only one who seems actually happy. Spence wonders how long the team has worked together and if they even like each other anymore. Spend several years in a room the size of a closet with your best friend and you might want to push him in front of a train.

"Hey, where's the promo sheet for the Laff Shack?" Buzz asks Sheila.

"How the hell should I know?" Shelia responds, which an-

swers any doubt about whether or not she and Buzz actually
like each other.

"You'll have to excuse Sheila," Buzz says to him. "She's what
we in the industry refer to as a 'bitch.' " He makes finger quotes
in the air as he insults his cohost.

"Dick," Sheila says and, for a second, almost seems to smile.
Buzz comically grabs his crotch and tugs at it in her direction.
The entire confrontation is confusing, and it's hard to tell if the
two of them are about to come to blows or start kissing.

"I have all the info," Spence tells Buzz, but both he and Sheila
are too busy giving each other the finger to notice.

Someone brings Spence a cup of coffee and the rest of the
song block passes quickly. They all put on their headphones, put
down whatever they were doing before, and switch into character when it's time to go live. When the music was playing, the
three hosts had almost nothing to do with each other besides a
few random insults and obscene gestures. Once they go live on
the air, they all seem like the best of friends. Spence follows their
lead and goes from hungover to enthusiastic in a millisecond.
Listeners must think he's always up this early.

"Today's best music on 99.7, The Wave," Buzz cheers into
the microphone. "Just playing a little Green Day for you. Third
Eye Blind before that. It's Friday morning, and you know what
that means!"

The sounds of wacky music starts playing. Monkey-Boy
laughs for no reason, and Sheila groans. The sound of Bugs
Bunny saying something blares through Spence's headphones. A
recording of Homer Simpson goes, "D'oh!"

"Time for 'Friday Funnies.' " Buzz laughs, and it sounds like
he's hosting a game show. The sound of a spring going "boing"
is played and—again—Monkey-Boy laughs.

Buzz introduces Spence while playing a recording of fake applause. Spence rolls with it and does what he's always known to
do: He takes over the show. Whether he has four minutes or
forty-five, a comedian has to try and attract as many of the listeners as possible. He does this by taking over the microphone
and putting out as much energy as he can. Instead of waiting for

Buzz to set him up, he takes charge. He chooses the direction to go and doesn't wait for a cue. It's not what Buzz is used to, but it's obvious that he likes it.

"I'll be honest," Spence says as Buzz watches on eagerly. "I'm hungover and have barely slept."

"You seem okay to me," Buzz says.

"That's because I've had six cups of coffee and half a bottle of aspirin."

"You should be good for at least a few hours then."

"A few hours or until my kidneys fail, either way," Spence says. Buzz laughs. Monkey-Boy laughs. Sheila groans.

"Nice road construction you've got going on here in town," he says. When in doubt, he always takes a stab at the local road construction. It doesn't matter which city he's in, everyone hates it the same everywhere.

"You like it?" Buzz asks.

"What's your local mascot?"

"The Chiefs."

"Yeah?" he says. " 'Cause it should be an orange construction cone."

Buzz laughs. Monkey-Boy agrees. Sheila groans.

"I like that idea," Monkey-Boy chimes in.

"You could call him Coney," Spence says. He imitates the voice of a sportscaster, "Here comes Coney, everybody! Oh, the kids sure do love Coney!"

Buzz laughs and hits a button that makes a rim shot sound over the air waves. "So you're in town all week?"

"Until the warrants catch up with me, sure." Another rim shot.

"How do you like Peoria?" Sheila chimes in.

"From what I've seen of it, I like it," Spence says.

"What have you seen so far?" she asks.

"My hotel room," he says, "and I like it."

Buzz laughs. Monkey-Boy laughs. Sheila—surprisingly—laughs.

Just like when he's onstage, all is right in the world. Right here, he's not hungover. He's not worried about getting more sleep or what it reads on his bank statement. Right here, he knows that, on the other end of the radio, people are having fun with him. Here he can be friends with strangers. When the DJs laugh, it's real. That tells him that other people are laughing too, and that makes him smile. When he smiles, it's genuine, too.

"Are you married?" Buzz asks him.

"Divorced. But we still see each other," he says.

"Really?"

"Sort of," he says. "She doesn't see me. I hide outside and look at all the stuff I used to own."

"Work out well for you?"

"Sure," he says. "Why would I want to have financial security and a nice house with all kinds of great stuff when I can be in Peoria, Illinois, at seven a.m., talking to a guy named Monkey-Boy?"

All three of the hosts laugh, and Spence realizes that four minutes is never as long as it seems. He recognizes the routine of "laughing into the commercial break" that all morning shows are excellent at doing. When the laugh carries over longer than even the best joke deserves, he knows what it means. His time is up, and he feels like he barely got started.

"Buzz in the morning with the Friday Funnies," Buzz says into the microphone. He signals with his eyes to Monkey-Boy and Sheila, who seem to understand the look. "We'll be right back after this."

With that, all three of them go back to how they were before the show went live. Monkey-Boy checks his phone for text messages, his bangs hanging in his face in a way that makes it hard to tell if he can actually be reading anything. Sheila begins looking at her computer screen, reading the news or checking the weather or whatever the hell she does when she isn't groaning. Buzz pulls his headphones off his ears and leans in.

"Great stuff," Buzz says to him. "You're really good at this."

"Thanks," Spence says with a smile. People occasionally compliment him for what he does on the radio but, from Buzz, it sounds really sincere.

"You ever thought about getting into radio?" Buzz asks.

"Not once," Spence says and means it.

"You'd be good at it."

"That's what they said about stand-up comedy."

"Yeah"—Buzz laughs—"that's what they told me, too."

"Isn't radio a dead-end job?" Spence asks.

"Isn't stand-up comedy?"

"Ah, we're kindred spirits."

"Indeed we are." Buzz gives him a fist bump, and a huge smile spreads across his enormous face.

"You ever do stand-up?" Spence asks.

"A couple of times," Buzz says, "but I'm no better at being up at midnight than you are at being up at six."

"Fair enough."

"Listen"—Buzz looks at the clock on the wall—"screw the giveaways. We'll let you do them with us. It'll be funnier that way. Can you stick around for another hour?"

9

The Laff Shack is a beautiful comedy club. The room is exactly what comedians dream of performing in when they fantasize about all things stand-up comedy. The ceilings are low, which makes the laughter bounce all over the place. The room itself is tight, making that laughter enormous and powerful. The stage is spacious and well-lit, the seats are comfortable, and the owner obviously put serious money into the upkeep. Inside that club, it looks like 1987. That was the high point of The Boom. If a comedy club can be a time capsule, the Laff Shack is it.

Despite this fact, Spence can't help but be a little bit depressed. The room seats two hundred, but there's maybe twenty people sitting in the audience. A club this beautiful with this much money behind it shouldn't be this empty on a Friday night. The place should be jam-packed with people trying to get in. Something is wrong. There must be a championship basketball game in town or something. Leave it to a popular sporting event to crush the attendance at a comedy club every time.

He looks around the room and notices posters everywhere advertising some old comedian who is going to be there in a couple of weeks. This guy was very popular in the '70s and was on a hit TV show for years. He hasn't done much of anything since then and is now back to doing stand-up comedy. The posters are even emblazoned with the catchphrase he used on that sitcom thirty years ago: "okie-dokie-pokey." Every poster in the place practically screams it with a large, comical font.

Spence grimaces. Every comedian hopes to get a big TV show one day. No one ever thinks of what it might be like when that fame peaks and you're stuck right back doing small comedy clubs all over again. There are many comedians from twenty-five years ago, still working the same clubs they used to. Almost all of them milk a TV credit that's older than most of the audience. Whenever he sees a comedian touting an appearance on *An Evening at the Improv,* it makes him a little queasy. That show went off the air fourteen years ago. He likes to think that, in another ten years or so, he will have something more to show for himself than his Kilborn appearance.

"Gonna pack the place in," a voice comes from over his shoulder, and Spence turns around. Frank owns the club. They are around the same age, but Frank looks older because of his hair transplant. The plugs show a little bit, which doesn't help. Frank is short, probably about five foot five, and he dresses like a mobster. His suit is sharp and obviously expensive.

"Tonight?" he asks Frank.

"I wish," Frank says and points to the poster of the has-been. "You wouldn't believe the money I've dropped getting him here."

"Really?" Spence asks. He wonders how a guy who hasn't done anything in thirty years can be that expensive.

"Yup," Frank says.

"Who's his agent?"

"Rodney Carnes," Frank says.

Fuck you, Rodney, Spence thinks.

"Small world," he says.

"Plus, we've gone all out on advertising," Frank says. "Newspaper, radio, TV. You name it. Even doubled the ticket prices."

"All for him."

"Yup. Spent a shitload on the whole thing. That's one reason we're slow tonight."

"What do you mean?" Spence asks. It's not lost on him that his own headshot wasn't on display in the lobby. Three different posters of the has-been are there instead. In fact, if it weren't for all of the posters and signs promoting the has-been, there'd be no proof that *any* other comics perform there at all.

"Well, we normally do more PR and advertising," Frank says. "But we cut back on it this week and next week so we can promote the special event."

"But you said you're going to sell it out."

"We will," Frank says.

"Isn't he famous enough that you could've packed it anyway?" Spence asks. He wonders why they would spend all that money on advertising a sure thing.

Frank shrugs. "I'm not taking any chances. He cost us ten grand."

Spence almost swallows his own tongue. He's making eight hundred dollars for the week. He doesn't even have ten grand in savings. In fact, he doesn't even have a savings account.

"Couldn't you sell out every week if you spent half that on advertising and PR?" he asks.

"I dunno," Frank says. "We often do sell out."

"No matter who is onstage?"

"Yep."

Then why bring in the celebrity act at all? Spence thinks. *Don't you wind up making the same money after expenses?*

He can't say this because it will only get him in trouble. He knows that he can never tell a club owner that the guy has made a bad decision. It will just get him banned from the club for being a jerk. He has to let Frank believe that overspending is a good idea.

"I like bringing in the big names," Frank says with a big smile. "Hell, we're thinking about bringing in Gallagher."

Spence smiles and pretends to be impressed. He's not sure why club owners always expect him to be excited when they brag about other acts. Why would he want to hear about people getting paid a hundred times what he makes to work in the exact same place? He wonders what kind of career he needs in order to have his pay shoot up to ten grand a week. He suddenly finds himself a bit depressed that he didn't get the body spray commercial. The guy who got it looked exactly like him.

"C'mere"—Frank motions for him to follow—"I wanna show you something."

He follows Frank outside into the parking lot and turns to look at the club. He can't help but notice his name isn't on the marquee. Instead it promotes the has-been's show that isn't for another two weeks.

"Check it out," Frank says and extends his right hand. At the end of where his hand is pointing is a very new, very shiny, very expensive Corvette. It is red and gorgeous and easily cost more than most comedians will make in two years.

"Whad'ya think?" Frank stands in front of the car as if it's a child who just won the spelling bee.

"Nice!" Spence says, acting like he gives a damn. He should win an Oscar for being able to grin and bear it.

"Just a little toy I decided to get myself," Frank says.

"It's hot." Spence wonders again why he's only getting paid eight hundred dollars for the week. Frank can apparently afford ten grand for a comedian and five times that for a sports car.

"Yeah, I love it," Frank says, "Life is too short, my man. Sometimes you've gotta treat yourself. Know what I mean?"

"Hell, yes," Spence lies. The last thing he treated himself to was an extra night in a Days Inn instead of sleeping on what used to be his sofa at Beth's house. He looks at the car and the has-been's name on the marquee and wants to drag his car key across the Corvette's hood. "You deserve it."

He doesn't hear Frank yammering on about the car because he is still wondering what it must be like to make ten grand in a week. The best month he ever had in stand-up comedy, he made a little over five. That kind of ride dried up pretty quickly. But the shelf life on a '70s sitcom is apparently endless.

Inside the club, the twenty people in the audience are giving a very mild reception to the opening act. The kid is very white and yet seems to think he's black. He was probably raised in the suburbs but tries to play it as if he's from the streets. Every sentence ends with "knowwhatI'msaying" and begins with "fuck."

"All I'm saying is you girls gotta wash that shit every day," the kid says and points to his crotch. "That shit is nasty if you don't wash the shit outta it. KnowwhatI'msaying?"

The audience does know what he's saying. The problem is that what he's saying isn't funny. New comics often mistake profanity for real material. Just saying "fuck" doesn't necessarily make the joke funny. The kid onstage hasn't learned that yet.

"Fuck," the kid says, "all I'm saying is that if the bitch don't wash that shit, I ain't going anywhere near it. If I wanna eat tuna, I'll go get myself a foot-long at Subway."

Sitting down in a booth in the back of the club, Spence watches the new kid slowly dying onstage. He feels a headache coming on, knowing that he has to follow this train wreck. The audience isn't offended as much as insulted. Their response is tepid at best. The kid has two minutes left to bring them over to his side and close big. After that, it's all over. Going onstage after another comedian has bombed is like going up first; the show essentially has to start all over again cold. Going on after this kid is worse. It's like being in the band playing on the deck of the *Titanic*.

"You ever take a shit that smells like pussy?" the kid says and hammers the final nail in his own coffin. It's all over for him. Executions have ended better. His time is up, and he wasn't able to pull the crowd around, leaving an awkward silence hanging over the room like someone who just confessed at the dinner table to having an abortion.

Spence starts to feel uneasy and looks at his watch. This isn't good. It's been thirty minutes. The kid was supposed to do twenty minutes but is running long and no one seems to notice. He's still struggling to get chuckles, yet keeps hitting them with more alleged jokes. The audience isn't even lukewarm at this point and dangerously close to becoming hostile.

Spence looks around the club and looks down at his watch. Someone needs to give the kid a signal and let him know it's time to get offstage. It's hard enough to follow an act that bombed. It's even harder to follow one that ran too long and sucked all the life out of the audience. A root canal is easier.

Where the hell is Frank? he thinks to himself. *Outside with his penis in the tailpipe of his new car, actually trying to have sex with it?*

When forty minutes rolls round, a blind man could see that Spence is pissed off. The kid is still onstage and still eating it, yet still ranting away. Every comedian knows before he goes on-stage just how much time he's expected to do. Going over by a few minutes is usually forgivable. Doing double the time you were supposed to do is absolute bullshit. But since Frank is apparently masturbating all over his car, there's nothing to be done about it this time around.

What the hell are you doing? Spence wants to scream at the stage. *They aren't into this. Read the crowd, you idiot. Do they seem like they are remotely into this kind of crap?*

Just watching it makes him cringe. Every comic has a night that goes badly. Everyone knows what it's like to be bombing and wanting to turn it around. But there comes a time when you simply accept that you're never going to win them over. You do your time, cut your losses, and go home to lick your wounds. The only thing you do by digging the hole deeper is drag the next comedian down into it with you.

It used to be inexcusable and was the kind of behavior that got you banned from comedy clubs. At some point over the past several years, a trend started with young comics who find it more amusing to offend the audience than to make it laugh. Rather than adapt and try to read them a little better, young co-medians started going onstage almost daring audiences to laugh. The desire to shock the crowd is more important than making it laugh.

It's because of that kind of thinking that this kid onstage doesn't know he's digging himself into that hole. He doesn't see that he's bombing. The few awkward chuckles he's getting is the best response an audience has ever given him. To that kid on-stage, this is a good set.

"That's it for me, bitches." He finally wraps up the disaster that was his act. "Peace out, muthafuckas."

With that, the kid takes the microphone and slams it to the ground. The audience makes a noise that sounds like a mixture of mild amusement and disgust. A table of five people gets up and walks out of the club. That leaves only fifteen audience members left to watch a show that is now running almost thirty minutes behind.

"They're a rough crowd, yo," he says to Spence as he brushes past. Spence nods when what he really wants to do is punch the kid in the throat.

He is not looking forward to this. He's been more optimistic about getting a catheter inserted into his penis. He takes the stage with the same smile and high energy he gives when the club is packed. Taking the dented microphone into his hand, he goes straight into his first joke. He cannot see through the lights, but he feels himself slip right into the same persona he always does. Here is where he belongs. Here is where he lets everything that was bothering him go away for at least forty-five minutes. Here he doesn't think about Frank or the unfunny kid or the has-been who makes a truckload of money. Here he is ready to just enjoy himself. Here is where he is in charge. He is ready for them.

"And that's why I only date Asian women," he says.

Nothing happens. The audience doesn't laugh; they simply look at him. It's the same joke he has done a million times before. They don't go for it at all. He's had some jokes go over better than others, but his opening bit always kills. That's why he uses it. It gets the audience on his side right away. Not this time. He is shocked.

"When he said he was smacking the midget, I just assumed he was talking about masturbation," he says. Nothing again. He can't believe it. He wonders if the audience is too tired. Maybe that opening act pulled all the energy out of the room by going too long? Is everyone in the room an Asian midget and he somehow missed it and offended them all? It's bad enough to feel like he's not connecting with the audience, but now he's flat-out bombing. This hasn't happened in years.

"I'll tell you the best part of being divorced . . ." he says. He rolls into another surefire hit; an old joke about divorce that he pulls out of the cobwebs whenever he needs a quick fix to a dull show. Again, he is met with blank eyes and a silent room. The cold feeling of sweat down his back hits him. He hasn't felt it in years.

You did this to me. Spence imagines his opening act standing in front of him and wishes he could break the microphone over his head. The same microphone the kid threw to the ground when he strutted offstage. *You sucked the life out of this room.*

Now his mind is working a million thoughts per second. He's going through jokes in his head, trying to find random tracks on Spence's Greatest Hits in his mind and then toss them out to the handful of silent audience members. He's like a duck, looking calm on the surface while paddling furiously to stay afloat. Every great joke he's ever told in front of roaring applause is being met with . . . nothing.

The next twenty minutes creep by at a snail's pace. When things are going great, ten minutes can feel like one. When a comedian bombs, twenty minutes feels like hours. He feels as if he's been onstage all day. The flop sweat rolling down his forehead is just a reminder. At any second he could win this crowd and feel relief pass over his entire body. Or, at any second, he could burst into tears. It's a toss-up whichever happens first.

But there comes a time when you simply accept that you're never going to win them over. Spence hears his own advice coming back to haunt him. *You do your time, cut your losses, and go home to lick your wounds.*

His mouth is dry, and the sweat on his back suddenly feels cold. He is only a minute away from calling it quits. He knows it's over, and he isn't about to rebound.

"Next!" A voice comes from the darkness. A guy in the audience has made a buzzer sound like on a game show. The audience laughs at this, which only makes the jab sting even more. Having a heckler sucks. Having one the audience likes is murder.

"I've got it from here, thanks," Spence says to the heckler. He always starts nice. Hecklers don't always want to cause problems. Sometimes they actually think they're helping the show; they're just trying to have fun. It's for that reason he often leaves them alone. But sometimes they need to be put in their places.

"I don't think so," the heckler yells from the darkness. "You're losing it, buddy."

"Yeah, don't worry. I do this for a living, so let me do it without you."

"Not our fault you aren't funny," the heckler says. This is followed by oohs from the audience.

"But it is your fault you wore that shirt tonight," Spence responds. This actually gets a laugh. It also gets some more oohs. Seven people like him, and seven more think he's an asshole. Either way, it's not remotely the turnaround he needs on this show.

"This shirt cost more than you make in a week," the heckler yells.

"So does sex with your mom," Spence says. This gets a few more laughs.

"Who cares? Sex with your wife is free," the heckler says. The audience laughs. It makes Spence want to hang himself with the microphone cord, mostly because it's actually a pretty good comeback.

"Every time you open your mouth, I smell some other guy's cock," Spence says through his teeth. This normally gets a huge laugh, but it stalls. It's almost as if the audience hates him for actually trying to outwit the heckler. Hope is pretty much lost at this point. Once the audience has decided to side against the guy onstage, all bets are off.

"*Next!*" the voice calls again.

Stepping forward to the very front of the stage, Spence shields his eyes from the lights. Just like being stuck behind a bad driver in traffic, he has to know what this guy looks like. He can't leave the stage without knowing just who it was giving him hell while he was already having his worst set in years.

There, in the middle of the room, sits a short, old man. He's got a potbelly and is wearing an old golf shirt and he's leaning on a cane. He's at least seventy-five years old. It might as well be Santa Claus talking trash in the darkness.

"This is who is heckling me?" he says and points at the old man. "The dude from *Cocoon*?"

This gets mild laughter. Before the old man can speak, Spence goes right back at him.

"No, really," he says, "I'm up here trying to entertain you people, and I'm getting yelled at by freakin' Father Time."

Again, a little laughter. Some groans. Even the people laughing obviously don't like him very much at this point. Less than fifteen minutes to go and he can leave the stage. In the meantime, he's got to do something to kill the time and telling jokes apparently isn't working. He decides to keep going after the heckler because it's the only thing at this point keeping *him* entertained.

"I'm surprised you even know you're here," he says. "Shouldn't you be at home, changing your own diaper?"

The old man doesn't look pissed off, and he doesn't look like he's ready to come at Spence with another crack. He actually looks hurt.

"When you say 'next,' are you really just talking about when you're actually going to finally die?" Spence says. "Well, do everyone a favor and make it tonight."

He thinks it's funny, but he's alone in this thought. This is not the first time he's taken it too far with a heckler. It can be fun at first. Push it too hard and the audience will turn away. Sure, it's only fifteen people and they never found him that funny to begin with. Now they think he's a complete asshole. If he walked offstage right now, that wouldn't change. But he's so angry that he wants someone else to feel as bad as he does. The fact that it's the old man means nothing to him—just collateral damage.

"I know that's not new to you, hearing someone tell you that you should hurry up and die," he says to the old man, practically standing in the front row when he does it. "Your wife must say that every single day that she wakes up and you're still here."

"My wife is dead," the old man practically whispers.

Spence knows he should back off, but he's too pissed to stop. Instead, he delivers one last blow. "You call her dead. I call her lucky."

Checkmate. The old man slumps in his chair and has nothing to say. It's as close to retribution as a comic will ever have when staring down the double barrels of a failed show. There is no joy in this kind of victory. Spence knows he does not win by humiliating the old man. All he does is share the pain.

"Thank you, good night," he says and storms off the stage. He's out of the showroom and in the parking lot before he realizes what just happened. He wants to hit something. He wants to scream. He wants to choke his opening act and Frank and the CEO of whatever car company makes Corvettes. He wants to knock that old man's cane out from under him. And he wants a cigarette. He hasn't smoked in ten years.

SHITSHITSHITSHITSHITSHITSHITSHIT, he keeps repeating in his head, over and over again. He stretches his fingers out and then balls them back up into fists, over and over again. He walks around in circles. He stomps his feet on the pavement like a child who didn't get what he wanted at the toy store. He sulks, he curses to himself, and he generally lets himself fume for what feels like forever.

He waits until he is certain all fifteen people in the audience are gone before he walks back into the club. He can't even remember the last time he bombed. He does not want to be there anymore in the place where it happened. He just wants to get his coat and go back to his hotel for the night.

"You"—Frank comes storming around the corner and into the lobby—"my office. Now."

Being almost forty and spoken to like he's fourteen doesn't sit well with Spence. The waitstaff pretends to be looking the other way as he follows Frank into the office. Even there, the furniture costs more than most things he has ever owned. There's probably a joke there, but he's too upset to think about it. He knows that what's coming isn't good.

"I have never seen anything like what I just saw," Frank says.

"Really," Spence says. It's not a question because he knows that Frank is lying on two counts. First of all, he knows that what just happened isn't that outrageous. Comics bomb all the time, even famous pros. And second, Frank wasn't even in the room to see it. He was probably out back polishing his car with a diaper.

"Never," Frank says. "What the hell did you think you were doing?"

"Responding to a heckler," Spence says.

"You mean Earl?"

"What?"

"His name is Earl."

"How should I know what the hell his name is?"

"He's a regular here," Frank says. "Comes here every week and sits in that same place."

"How was I supposed to know that?"

"He's always here. Everyone loves him."

"If he's here every week," Spence says, "then he should know better than to be yelling shit at the stage."

"What did you do to provoke it?"

"Provoke what?" Spence has to remind himself not to yell. "Since when is it my fault if a guy in the audience won't keep his mouth shut? You're supposed to take care of that so I don't have to."

"You open your own comedy club and you can tell me how to run mine." Frank points an index finger in his face.

"You ever become a comedian and you can tell me how to do my act." He points back. He knows full well that Frank has never so much as set foot onstage.

"If I'm paying you, then I can tell you whatever the fuck I want," Frank says. In the end, he's right. It always comes down to the money.

"That was bullshit and you know it."

"What's bullshit is that you walked offstage ten minutes early," Frank says.

Spence looks at his watch. "The show ended when it was supposed to end. Nine thirty, just like you said. That idiot you put onstage before me ran over his time."

"So?"

"So what?"

"So what does that have to do with anything?" Frank says. "You were supposed to do forty-five minutes. You did thirty-five. What that kid did doesn't concern you."

"It certainly does," Spence says, "when I have to go onstage and mop up his mess."

"You were supposed to do forty-five minutes," Frank says.

"Which is it?"

"What are you talking about?"

"Are you pissed at me for bitching out your loyal customer or for running short on my time?"

"Both," Frank says.

"That's just stupid."

"You watch your mouth."

Spence wants to reach over and punch Frank in the face. He could do it easily and probably knock the man off his feet. It certainly would have a better outcome than arguing; no matter what he says now, he's already lost. There is no coming back from this. It's over. He might as well kiss Peoria good-bye right now. He wants to bitch Frank out and tell him exactly what he thinks of him, his Corvette, and his buddy Earl.

"It won't happen again," he says after thirty seconds of tense silence.

"You're absolutely right about that," Frank says. "You know goddamned well I could fire you right now."

"I know."

"I could get Rodney on the phone and tell him to send you packing," Frank says.

"I know."

"I'm cutting your pay in half," Frank says.

"What?" Spence turns around again and faces Frank. That cuts his pay down to four hundred dollars for a week of shows.

It comes out to fifty bucks per show at the end of the week; fifty bucks to be the closing act at a successful comedy club.

"You heard me," Frank says. "Half."

"For what?"

"For running short and getting out of hand onstage," Frank says.

"You can't be serious," Spence says.

"It's either that or you walk right now," Frank says.

This is the hard part. Spence could tell Frank to go straight to hell right now and walk right out the door. He'd never work there again, and Frank could easily replace him tomorrow. At least then he'd have his pride intact. But then he's got to put himself up in a hotel for the next seven days. He can't afford that. He can't afford to be without eight hundred dollars, but he certainly can't afford to leave with nothing. He practically lives week to week as it is. Losing the gig could cripple him.

"Fine," he says, "but that's really an overreaction."

"There have to be repercussions," Frank says.

"I had a terrible night," Spence says, "that should be punishment enough."

"But it's not," Frank says and sits behind his desk. He props his feet up and seems oddly comfortable despite what just went down.

Spence puts his hand on the back of his neck and rubs where the throbbing has started to grow. "If you were actually a comedian, you would understand."

"You comedians all think you're something unique," Frank says, "but you're all the same. We both know I could replace you tomorrow and no one would think a thing about it. There are a thousand guys out there who want this job."

Spence stands in the doorway and keeps his mouth shut. It's the best idea he's had all night.

"I'll see you later," he says.

"One more thing," Frank says, "don't think you're coming back here next year. Enjoy the rest of the week, but this is it for you."

"Yeah, I kinda figured," Spence says and walks out of the office. He grabs his coat out of the green room and makes his way back out to the lobby. He sees the bartender looking at him and walks over.

"Can I get a Scotch?" he says.

"Absolutely," the bartender says. It's obvious everyone in the club heard the screaming in the office. Spence can tell by the way the staff is tiptoeing around him and giving him sympathetic eyes. At least the bartender is on his side, even if Frank is not. He pours a good three fingers into a rocks glass and passes it across the bar.

"Thanks," Spence says and downs it as if it were just a single shot. "What do I owe you?"

"Nothing," the bartender says.

"Mighty kind of you." Spence stands up to leave.

"The comedians all drink free here," the bartender says.

"What?"

"Yeah"—the bartender nods—"that's the club policy. The comedians drink free and eat for free. We've got a full menu if you're hungry."

Spence sits back down on the barstool. "My drinks are free?" he asks.

"And your food." The bartender grins and slowly nods. He gets it.

"I'll have two steaks, medium rare," Spence says without looking at the menu. "What's the most expensive Scotch in this place?"

The bartender winks and reaches into a closed cabinet behind him. He pulls out a bottle of Johnnie Walker Blue.

"This is Frank's private stash," the bartender says with a sly little smirk.

"I'll have three fingers of that." Spence puts his glass down on the bar.

"How about four?" the bartender says and fills the glass.

"Perfect," Spence says. If he's going to get his pay shorted by four hundred bucks, he's going to eat and drink his money's worth. At least the bartender is thinking the same way.

"Hey, man, forget about that show." The bartender sets the bottle down next to Spence. "I heard you on the radio this morning. You kicked ass."

"Thanks." Spence shrugs his shoulders and turns away. He wants to cry. He can't remember the last time he did. He doesn't know what he feels more: anger or helplessness. He takes a long gulp from his Scotch and paces in the middle of the lobby, waiting for his food. He has no appetite. He'll throw it away if it will make Frank lose money. He'll do it again tomorrow night.

He steps outside and lets the air hit him. It's getting warmer. A few weeks ago, he was in Montreal and freezing, but it's unusually warm here in Peoria. Either that or the Scotch is kicking in very fast. He looks down at the clock on his cell phone. It's midnight. It's late. He knows he shouldn't call Sam, but he does it anyway.

"What's wrong?" she asks. He has talked to her several times since he left Montreal, but never this late.

"I fucked up," he says.

"What'd you do?" she asks quietly.

"Nothing," he says. "I mean, everything. It was just a shitty night. I didn't really do anything wrong. At least I don't think I did. I don't know."

"What happened?" she asks. He can tell she was asleep when he called. It's one more thing he feels bad about. He can feel the tears welling up in his eyes. How long has it been since he cried? He feels like such a pathetic loser right now, but he really doesn't care. He wonders if what he needs is one good tantrum to make him feel better.

"I don't know," he says. "I just can't keep going like this. Something has to change. Something's gotta give."

"The job?"

"Yeah, the job."

There's a long pause on the phone. He closes his eyes and waits for the feeling to pass where he doesn't think he's going to start bawling. He wants the booze to kick in and make him not give a damn. In the background, he can hear music still playing in the bar. He tries to think of Canadian bands and singers. Does he know this woman enough to spill his guts out like this? Sure, he spent a few days with her. Sure, he calls her from time to time. But does he know her well enough to show her this?

"I'm sorry," he says. "Are you still there?"

"I'm here," she says. "I'm listening."

10

Spence stands onstage, looking around the room. The club is completely empty, and he's standing under the lights, trying to see if anyone is coming in. He knows he's on time and he's supposed to be there, but he's the only person in the room. He's cold even though the lights are so bright he can't see past them without shielding his eyes. There's a drum being played offstage, but it's not a rim shot for his jokes and there's no other instruments. Just three beats, a pause, then three beats. Then it's "Shave and a Haircut, Two Bits"; five quick beats followed by two quick beats.

Spence opens his eyes and realizes that he's not standing onstage, but standing in the middle of his hotel room. Someone is knocking on the door, and he's standing in his underwear with the sheet draped over him like a cape. He's like a half-naked superhero in the middle of a Red Roof Inn. Here to rid the world of sleeping past checkout time. He tosses the sheet back onto the bed and rubs his eyes.

"Just a second," he yells through the door and looks around for his pants. This is not the first time he's woken up standing in the middle of the room. He does it every few months. Sometimes he wakes up sitting at the desk. He's always draped in the bedsheets or whatever he's thrown over himself in the night. Each time he wakes up and is unaware of where he is. By the time he puts on his jeans, he remembers that this time he's in Pittsburgh.

He opens the door and lets the sunlight burn his retina for a few seconds. He steps back into the darkness of the room and looks at the silhouette standing in the doorway as his eyes adjust to the light.

"You don't look like housekeeping," Spence says.

"I'm not." The silhouette chuckles. It's a young black man, about twenty-five or so, almost six feet tall, with a shaved head and thin beard only on his chin.

"Jehovah's Witness?"

"Nope."

"And you're not selling cookies."

"Not at all."

"Then you must be a comedian."

"Bingo," the kid says.

"C'mon in," Spence says and looks around for a shirt to put on. The kid walks in the room and closes the door behind him. "What's up?"

"I'm Jamie." The kid shakes his hand and looks around the small room. "Jamie Hernandez. Remember? We met last year at the Comedy Corner in Philly."

"Yeah, I remember," Spence lies. "How have you been?"

"Great, man," Jamie says. "Doing all right. How have you been?"

Spence extends his hands and shows off his hotel room. "The same."

Jamie nods. "Yeah. Keeping busy, I see."

"Always."

"So Rodney told me you're cool, right?"

"Cool with what?" Spence asks and wonders if he's in the middle of a drug deal and no one told him.

"About me tagging along to Toledo," Jamie says.

Spence has no idea what Jamie is talking about and he's certain Rodney never told him anything about it. This comes as no surprise whatsoever.

"Shit," Jamie says. "He was supposed to ask you if it was okay if I catch a ride with you to Toledo. I'm opening for you, but I don't have wheels. Rodney said you'd be cool giving me a ride there."

"Sure, I'm cool with that." Spence nods. This isn't the first time and probably won't be the last time he's had another comedian ride along to a gig. He did it himself when he was an opening act. There's no way Jamie is getting paid very well; opening act money is always awful. The least he can do is throw the kid a bone and make it a little easier.

"Great, man," Jamie says and pulls out the chair at the small table in the corner. "I really do appreciate it. And I'll chip in for gas."

Spence waves his hand dismissively. "I'm going there anyway. Don't worry about it."

"That's cool, man," Jamie says. "Thanks."

"You live here in Pittsburgh?" Spence says as he starts packing up his stuff. He would've slept another hour had Jamie not shown up, but he figures there's always time for a nap when they get to Toledo.

"Yeah," Jamie says. "Born and raised, man."

"Got your start at the Funny Bone, right?"

"You remember," Jamie says. He's wrong. All Pittsburgh comedians started at the Funny Bone. It's a safe assumption Jamie did, too, and was just a lucky guess.

"Getting out on the road, huh? Gonna start touring the country?"

"I hope so, man," Jamie says. "That would be amazing."

"Sure."

"I just wanna work as much as possible. Maybe get more work from Rodney, you know?"

"I do know," Spence says. He smells a T-shirt he found in his suitcase to see if it's the clean black one or the dirty black one. He thinks it's the clean one. He's not sure. He has several that all look the same. He puts it on. If he's going to be in the car all day, it doesn't really matter if it's clean or not.

"Can you drive a stick?" he asks Jamie.

"Naw, man," Jamie says. "Is your car a stick shift?"

"No, I was just curious."

"Really?" Jamie asks.

"What do you think?"

"Aw, man," Jamie says, "you can't mess with me like that. I'll fall for it every time, man."

"Get used to it," Spence says. "It's a long drive to Toledo. You ready?"

"You got it," Jamie says.

"Cool. Get my bags."

Jamie stands up and goes to grab the suitcase.

"Get the hell outta here." Spence laughs and brushes Jamie away from the luggage. "I'm kidding. Damn." He takes his suitcase and tosses the strap over his shoulder. Jamie shrugs and opens the door to the hotel. The light hits them both, and they each scramble for their sunglasses. Jamie grabs a duffel bag he left lying outside and tosses it into the Camry.

"You sure you don't want gas money?" Jamie asks as he plops into the passenger seat.

"I'm cool," Spence says. "Just remember it's my car. I get to control the radio."

"You got it, man," Jamie says. "I'm cool with pretty much anything."

"Good, because all I listen to is country music."

"For real?"

"Or talk radio," Spence says. "I like Rush Limbaugh the most. Whatever, as long as it's right-wing stuff."

"No shit, huh?" Jamie says.

Spence looks at Jamie and raises his eyebrows. He waits a second. After a beat, the kid catches on.

"Aw, man. You're screwing with me again. Shit," Jamie says. "I was worried for a minute there."

Spence starts the car. "Hope you like the eighties," Spence says. "And this time I'm not screwing with you."

He tunes his satellite radio to the channel that plays all eighties music and aims the car away from Pittsburgh and toward Toledo. It's nice weather for a drive, which is just what he needs.

He's been sitting in the Red Roof Inn for days, letting the rain make him miserable and lonely. Now he's feeling okay as he lets Rick Springfield lead him onto the Pennsylvania Turnpike.

"Hernandez?" he asks Jamie. "That your real last name?"

"Yeah, man. My dad is Mexican."

"Get the hell outta here."

"Yeah, man, it's true."

"And your mother is black?"

"What gave it away, man?"

Spence laughs. Jamie nods his head to the music and smiles. He's a charming kid. Women probably love him. He's probably still at that point in his career when he's happy to get work just because it gets him laid all the time. The money is an after-thought.

"That's cool," Spence says after a few minutes listening to the radio tell him about Jesse's girl. "Half black and half Mexican. I bet the material is endless."

"It's alright."

"You kidding? With that kind of heritage, you didn't have a choice. You had to become a comedian."

"You said it, man," Jamie says. "Or a boxer."

This makes Spence laugh again. The kid is lucky, in a way. Having a background like that probably gives him a ton of stories that he can turn into bits and milk them for God knows how long. TV people love that, too. They love having some kind of catchphrase or trait they can latch onto if they think it's marketable. A young, biracial comedian screams "hit sitcom."

Spence never had anything like that. He was never fat or awkward or beaten up. He has no childhood trauma he turned into jokes. He didn't have a weird family, and no one was drunk or abusive to him along the way. His parents are living in some nice retirement community in Florida. He has no emotional scars, and his nice suburban life ruined him for any real edgy stories or personal material. It's probably why he relies so heavily on dick jokes.

Ironic, he thinks. *Only comedians would see having a happy upbringing as a bad thing.*

It didn't start with dick jokes, of course. There was a time when Spence thought of himself as a social commentator. He went onstage and talked politics, religion, anything that was on his mind at the time. The problem was he was in his early twenties. The average audience member is over thirty-five. They don't want to hear a kid stand onstage and tell them about how the world works. When that didn't work so well, he moved on to jokes about dating. From there it was jokes about sex, then marriage. And then it was all about divorce. Somewhere along the way, he found himself going back to the dick jokes. People say it's love, but nothing is really as universal as sex . . . and jokes about penises.

"This is cool, man," Jamie says after about thirty minutes, right during the middle of A Flock of Seagulls.

"This song?"

"Nah, man. Being on the road like this. Going to a gig."

"We just left."

"Yeah, but it's cool just to be going there, man," Jamie says. "Getting paid to make people laugh. That's cool, man."

"Sure."

"No?" Jamie looks over at him.

"Of course it's cool to make people laugh."

"Then what's up?" Jamie says.

"Just talk to me after you've been in the car eight or nine hours," Spence says. "It can be a bit much, is all."

"For real. You drive a lot, huh?"

"That's the job."

"Yeah," Jamie says and looks out at the scenery. "Still sounds pretty cool."

"It can be." Spence nods. Sometimes the driving is the best part of his day. It's the one time he can escape everyone and not feel guilty about getting nothing else done. There are no e-mails to check when he's behind the wheel, and he doesn't talk on the phone when he's driving. Rodney isn't there to annoy him. All he has to do is sit back and listen to Men Without Hats.

"You don't have another job?" Jamie asks. "No day gig?"

"This is it."

"That's cool, man."

Spence smiles. "It can be."

"I work for a free newspaper," Jamie says. "Selling ads. That job sucks. I'd choke someone to be doing what you do."

"I understand how you feel," Spence says. Glass Tiger on the radio. It takes a second before he remembers that Glass Tiger is Canadian. He wonders what Sam is doing today. Probably working. He thinks about her folding pants and wonders if he should go to the Gap and buy new stage clothes.

"You ever done any TV?" Jamie asks.

Spence nods. "I did *The Late Late Show* once."

"Sweet," Jamie says. "With Craig Ferguson?"

"Craig Kilborn."

"That was a long time ago, huh?"

"Thanks," Spence says and gives Jamie an "eat me" look over the top of his fake Wayfarers.

"Anything else?" Jamie asks.

"Yeah." Spence rubs the back of his neck with this right hand while steering with his left. "I wrote some stuff for Keenen Ivory Wayans. I wasn't on the show, but I wrote some jokes for his opening monologue."

"In Living Color?" Jamie asks. He looks confused.

"No, his talk show."

"He had a talk show?"

"Briefly."

"When was that?"

"A long time ago."

"Like five years?"

"Forget it," Spence says and shakes his head. When did five years become a long time?

Jamie looks out the window. He taps his feet as Glass Tiger leads into Paul Hardcastle. Outside the car window, Pennsylvania passes by, but it could be anywhere in the country. This highway doesn't look much different than any other. Sixty-five thousand miles were put on the Camry last year, and each mile looked pretty much like the last one.

"I've never done any TV," Jamie says, "but I've been close. I almost did *I Love the 90s* on VH1. I had a friend who was an intern over there."

"Nice," Spence says. "Make more friends like that."

"Yeah, right?"

"It's true. Best advice I can ever give someone is to make friends anywhere you can in this business. It will help you out a lot down the road."

"I worked for a publicist once," Jamie says, "back when I was in college. I stay in touch with her."

"A publicist?" Spence says. "Stay in her good graces as long as possible."

"No shit."

"Well done, grasshopper."

"Got any more advice?" Jamie says. He's eager and sincere. It makes Spence smile, because he knows that attitude lasts for only a few years. "I'd love to know anything you can tell me, man."

"Get a reliable car," Spence says.

Jamie laughs. "For real. But right now I'd settle for any car."

"Good point."

The scenery flashes by them. For a while Spence thinks that Jamie is actually enjoying the eighties tunes. He saw him mouthing the words to "Electric Avenue." He looks slightly left out the window as Jamie looks slightly right. Spence remembers when he couldn't wait for the next gig. When each week was exciting and every gig stood apart from the last one. There was a time when it never felt like a job; he was thrilled to get paid to do what he used to do for free. He remembers when he was eager and sincere.

Jamie reaches down and pulls a notebook out from behind his feet. It was tucked up under the passenger seat pretty good, but a quick stop sent it sliding forward. An old composition notebook—it's worn out and has a coffee stain across the cover. It's been under that seat for months.

"This yours?" Jamie asks.

"Cleaning lady must've left it," Spence says.

"This your act?"

"Not really. Just some stuff I was working on. I haven't looked at it in a while."

"You mind?" Jamie asks.

"Knock yourself out." Spence nods. Anything to let him enjoy his tunes for a while.

Jamie reads from the notebook. Every minute or so he smiles. He flips through the pages, then back to the front, then toward the back. He laughs once, then twice. He smiles bigger and then flips randomly through the pages again. He keeps laughing over the sounds of Robert Palmer on the radio, bobbing his head to "Simply Irresistible."

"You don't do this stuff onstage at all?" Jamie asks after a while, his nose still in the notebook.

"Not yet," Spence says. "I haven't worked it out yet."

"It's great stuff, man," Jamie says.

"You like it?"

"Yeah, man. It's good. I mean, from what I can tell. I'd have to see how you deliver it onstage, but the writing is solid, yo."

"Thanks. That's cool."

"For real."

"I need to work it into my show," Spence says. "I just haven't been able to lately. Too many bar gigs, you know? Not the place to be trying untested material. I'd rather save it for an actual comedy club and not some saloon in Oklahoma."

"I heard that," Jamie says. "Do you normally write this clean?"

Spence laughs. "Not at all. I'm a dick joke comic."

Jamie laughs. "Shit, me too."

"Aren't we all?"

"This is all clean, man." Jamie closes the notebook and puts it back under the seat.

"That's what I was going for."

"You trying to go clean?" Jamie asks.

Spence thinks about this for a second. He never set out to be either clean or dirty. He never wrote a single joke because it did or did not have adult language in it. It just seemed that, especially after the divorce, that's where his head went every time he wrote something new. That's how he was feeling at that point in his life, and the crowd went with it. For the past month or two, he's found himself writing cleaner material. It's just what's been coming out of him when he writes.

Ever since Montreal, he thinks.

"I've been trying to get some TV spots," he says.

"*The Late Late Show* again?"

Spence shrugs. "Maybe. Or *The Tonight Show.* Or *Letterman.* Or *Good Morning, Albuquerque.* Anything, really."

"Yeah," Jamie says, "that'd be real cool, man."

"Maybe."

"I talked to the guy who books *The Tonight Show* once," Jamie says. "He came to a workshop at the Funny Bone. He knew that friend of mine who does the publicist shit. Gave me his card. He was cool. Greg something."

"Greg Saunders," Spence says. He's never met Greg Saunders, but he knows the name. Every comedian does.

"Yeah," Jamie says, "that was him."

"You ever send him a demo?"

"Nah, man," Jamie says, "I ain't near ready for that shit. I know I'm not clean enough, either."

"You have any jokes about shit that smells like pussy?" Spence asks.

"What the hell?" Jamie sits back and makes a disgusted face.

"Never mind."

"Well, this week we're at an actual comedy club," Jamie says, "not some bar gig."

"Right you are."

"So you should try out the new stuff."

"Maybe," Spence says. He tossed that notebook under the seat a couple of weeks ago and had forgotten all about it until Jamie reached down and picked it up. Lately his mind has been stuck on keeping the mediocre gigs he already has and not the possible TV work. Rodney never came through on showcases in New York, so the thought had left his mind.

"For real," Jamie says. "It's tight, man. You could get it on tape now and send it out to bookers if it works."

Spence shrugs. "I might just do that."

"I tape every show," Jamie says.

"You set a camera up in the back of the room?"

"Yeah, with a tripod and everything."

"I used to do that."

"You don't record your shows anymore?" Jamie asks.

Spence shrugs. "Sometimes."

"I can't help it," Jamie says. "I don't wanna screw up and not tape and then miss that perfect show and then be kicking myself."

"There will be other perfect shows," Spence says, "and a ton of bad shows."

"Little of both, huh?" Jamie says as he looks slightly right.

"That's the job," Spence says, hypnotized by the broken white line on the highway. Alphaville plays on the radio. Alphaville wasn't from Canada. Where the hell was Alphaville from? He can't remember. He watches the road flash by and thinks about the new material. It's clean, and that's exactly what he needs to be doing if he wants to get on TV anytime soon. Jamie thought it was funny. Spence wonders if a roomful of people from Ohio will agree with him.

He has always liked it at Connxtions Comedy Club in Toledo. The club is big enough to hold a large crowd but cramped enough to where the shows always feel intimate. The ceilings are low, the stage is just big enough, and Midwestern people tend to like to drink and laugh. Just the right amount of drunkenness encourages roaring laughter. Both are things he admires in his audiences.

Jamie is onstage and doing a great job, even though he's obviously new and hasn't been doing comedy for very long. The audience likes him, which is the most important part of being the opening act. His timing is good, but his presence onstage is sometimes awkward. He doesn't look out into the entire crowd and often only speaks directly to the front of the stage. And he's still not sure how to hold the microphone; it's common for newer comics to hold it too close to their mouths. Jamie has the writing down pat, but he's still learning how to deliver it onstage.

Spence stands in the back of the club as Jamie is onstage talking about what it's like to be the only kid in town with a pitbull piñata. He watches the crowd to see where the laughter seems the loudest. It's always part of his routine. He tries to get an idea of which direction the audience is going. Do they want it cleaner or dirtier? Are they old or a crowd of mostly college-aged kids? Is there one rowdy table that has been drinking since noon? He looks to make certain there isn't a regular customer leaning on a cane anywhere in the crowd.

"Here you go," a waitress says as she hands him his glass of Scotch. He thanks her and holds it but doesn't drink. He's saving it for when he walks onstage. If he's going to be in front of a drinking crowd, he's going to have a few drinks himself. It makes him feel as if he's one of them and not just their dancing monkey.

His phone vibrates in his pocket, and he looks at the screen. It's a text message from Sam:

Hey, handsome. Call me later? Stuff to tell.

He smiles and texts back:

You got it.

He can't help but notice that he's grinning like an idiot. It's been two months of this, ever since Montreal. He used to hardly ever text people with his cell phone. When he did, it was usually responding to Rodney about a gig or a payment or something. Now he finds himself typing with his thumbs like a teenage girl every time Sam's name flashes across the screen, which seems to be more every day. At this point, he's probably chatting with her more than he does with Rodney.

The club manager appears in the back of the room and pulls out a flashlight that she aims at the stage and clicks it on and off. Jamie sees the light and nods from the stage. He saw the signal and knows it's time for him to wrap it up.

"Which is what happens if you wind up at my house," Jamie says. "But only on Cinco de Mayo."

Spence waits in the darkness as Jamie bounces off the stage to the sound of the crowd laughing. He's going over different ideas he's been toying with in his head and little one-liners he just came up with. At some point in the show, he will pretend to improvise. He will tease a guy in the front row, and everyone will think it's ad-libbed. He wrote the entire schtick years ago but always tries to make it look like he's just winging it.

"That was fun," Jamie says and slaps him on the back as he walks past.

"Looked like it was," Spence says. "Nicely done."

"For real?" Jamie asks.

"For true."

Jamie extends a fist in the air, and Spence bumps it with his. He really likes the kid, and it's refreshing to work with someone like him. He can count on one hand the number of actual friends he has made in this business over the years.

"Ladies and gentlemen," the local MC says as the crowd settles down a bit, "it's time for your headliner."

Spence hears his name called and swaggers onstage, glass in hand. When he steps up to the microphone, the audience applauds as if they've already seen a great show. It feels more like an encore than his first set of the week. He always knows it's going to be a great show when the applause lasts long enough for him to make it to the microphone and set his drink down on the stool. They are warmed up and ready to go.

Thanks, Jamie, he thinks.

"Let's hear it one more time for Jamie Hernandez," he says. The audience explodes in more applause and cheers. They really liked the kid. Spence smiles and hopes Jamie is grinning in the back of the room somewhere.

"And that's why I only date Asian women." He wraps up his opening number, and the laughter is deafening. What a great crowd. He has nowhere to take them but down at this point. It is his audience to lose, and all he has to do is screw it up. All he has to do is say the wrong joke at the wrong time.

The feeling that rushes over him is rare. He often feels amazing onstage; that's nothing new. It's typical to stand under the lights and feel like a star. When laughter hits him, he can't help but smile thinking that he's responsible for it. It's the only thing he knows of that feels this good. Sex doesn't consume him the way laughter does when it explodes like this. There are days when the audience laughs, but then there are days when the audience simply adores him. This time is one of those infrequent moments when he feels adored.

They are ready for everything he throws at them. He smacks them again and again with an assortment of his greatest hits.

"I just figured he was masturbating," he says, "not that he was actually smacking a midget."

Huge laughs. One woman in the front row snorts when she laughs. Only women snort when they laugh. It's never a man.

"Then he hit her in the face with his penis," he says, "which was only impressive because it was possible."

They laugh some more. He feels he can say anything to them, and they will respond with love and applause. He wants to try routines he hasn't done in years. They seem like the perfect crowd. Why not go for broke? Why not try the new material Jamie read earlier in the day? Why not pepper this killer show with something he's never tried before? If there was ever a time to try it, this is it. The only thing he has to lose is the respect and laughter of a hundred people. That's nothing he hasn't done before.

"What I miss most about being married is the sex," he says, recalling a joke he scribbled in that notebook in the car. As he rattles off his new material, he tries to remember it all in his head. What was the follow-up to the divorce material? Where did he go after talking about being celibate? On the outside, he looks like he has done the bit a million times. He smiles and pauses at the right moment. He ends each sentence with the right inflection. It all seems rehearsed. In his head, a million equations and ideas fly by in seconds. He has to remember the jokes in that notebook. Wasn't there something about owning dogs?

After twenty minutes of nonstop laughter, it dawns on him that he did it; he actually pulled it off. He exhausted the new material, and yet it all went over just fine. There was no lull in the show and there were no moments of silence. There wasn't a point where the crowd could tell the bit was new and only smiled at him and nodded. Each joke went over just as it needed to.

I should play the lottery tonight, he thinks. *This never happens.*

Straight from the new material, he starts to round out the show with his usual closer. The profanity returns, but the audience goes right along. He switches right back into it without skipping a beat. They love it and don't seem at all weird about the fact that he went from talking about love and marriage to sex with watermelons. When he tells them they are a great crowd, he means it. He wants to take them on tour with him.

"Thank you, good night," he says and waves to them as he steps away from the microphone. The place explodes, and all he can hear is applause and cheering. Someone whistles. It's always cool when someone whistles. He's backstage by the time the applause dies down. Jamie stands there grinning like an idiot.

"Damn, man," Jamie says, "that was something."

"Yeah," Spence says. He hasn't killed like that in a long time.

"You totally brought that shit right to them, man," Jamie says.

"That felt really good."

"You did that new stuff, too," Jamie says.

"Yeah, can you believe it?"

"You really need to work that into the act for good."

"Yeah, I think you're right."

"You want the tape?"

"What?"

"The tape," Jamie says. "I told you, I record every show. I've got my camcorder hooked up in the back of the club. I taped the whole show."

"You're lucky that you're working with me"—Spence raises his eyebrows—"any other comedian would be pissed off that you taped the show without asking. Comics get paranoid about guys stealing their material."

"Whatever, man," Jamie says. "You want it or not?"

Spence thinks for a minute. He does want it. "Maybe. What kind of tape is it?"

"MiniDV."

"One of those little ones?"

"Yeah."

"Damn"—Spence winces—"I don't have anything I can do with it. I don't even have a camera right now."

He doesn't. He sold his camera last year to buy Christmas gifts for his parents. Now it's Gift of the Magi time, and he's screwed. Why did he sell his camera and not something he didn't need, like plasma or a kidney?

"Don't worry," Jamie says. "I'll burn it onto a DVD and give you a copy. I can edit it down to where it's just the clean stuff, if you want. Then maybe you can use it for TV or whatever."

"Yeah?" Spence asks. "You don't mind doing that?"

"Nah, man," Jamie says and smiles at him. "Consider it gas money."

Spence smiles, gives Jamie a pat on the shoulder, and turns to greet people as they file out of the showroom. People walk by and shake hands with both of them, telling Spence, "You were great," and telling Jamie, "You were funny, too." It's a great feeling and makes them both feel like celebrities for a few minutes more.

"You were sooo funny." A young brunette with an amazing body appears next to him, and Spence is suddenly at a loss for words. Women flirt with him from time to time; it especially happens after he's had killer shows. But this girl is sexy as hell.

He gives her a once-over, looking at amazing legs that start at the ground and go straight up into a perfect butt. Behind her, three other girls are standing, talking with Jamie and taking photos with their cell phones. One of them wears a sash that reads BIRTHDAY GIRL across it. Spence figures out instantly that his lovely brunette is part of the party.

"Hey, thanks," Spence says and shakes her hand. Her grip is aggressive, and she pulls him closer when she speaks.

"I mean," she purrs, "you. Were. Amazing."

Spence pretends to be cool as he glances over his shoulder to see if Jamie is catching this. "All in a day's work." He chuckles.

"The entire time you were onstage, I was laughing so hard. You had me in tears. I kept telling my friends you're, like, the funniest comic I've ever seen."

"What about Dane Cook," Spence says, "or Daniel Tosh?"

"They suck," she says, which makes his day. "You are way funnier than those assholes."

"Nah. Just doing my job."

"Yeah?" The brunette bites her bottom lip, still gripping his hand in hers. "Anything else you do that well?"

"I've been told I can sing pretty well," Spence says.

"Perfect! Then you're coming with us!"

"I am?"

"Both of you." She giggles like she's twelve and points to Jamie and the gaggle of women. "We're going to a karaoke bar!"

"And *you* are?" Spence asks, trying not to stare at what is an amazing pair of breasts.

"Kristy," she practically orgasms. She still hasn't let go of his hand. "And you. Were. Amazing."

"Heh, yeah, you said that."

"So you're coming with, right?" Kristy asks.

"I don't know—"

"Yes, we are." Jamie grins like a buffoon and holds up a single thumb toward Spence. "Definitely."

Kristy sticks out her bottom lip. "*Pweeze* come with us? I wanna get to know you better." She pulls Spence in closer and almost whispers, "I'll totally make it worth your while."

She lets go of Spence's hand and, making sure to show off every single curve in her body, slowly struts the ten feet over to her group of friends, who are all still laughing and taking photos of Jamie. Spence stands there for a second before he realizes his mouth is open.

"You cool, man?" Jamie says as he walks over and leans in to speak with Spence. "Going with the chicks to sing?"

"I dunno," Spence says, looking at Misty or Kristy—he's forgotten her name already—looking over at him.

"What do you mean you don't know?" Jamie slaps him lightly on the side of the head. "The girl might as well be throwing her vagina at you, man."

"Nah," Spence lies, "she just wants me to come out so I can make her laugh for three more hours."

"The friends say she's easy," Jamie says. "So I'd say your chances of getting laid are better than average. Besides, I need you."

"You what?"

"I need you. Without you there talking to Hot Pants, I've got no chance of getting laid with one of the other ones. You're the star of the show, and they want you there. Time to be my wingman, boss."

Spence shrugs and pretends not to be still staring at Kristy's breasts. "I've kinda got this girl I'm seeing."

"Oh, shit," Jamie says. "You got a girlfriend?"

"Not exactly. But we've been seeing each other."

"Is she here?"

"No," Spence says, "she lives in Canada."

"Aw, shit, man," Jamie says. "You're 'kinda' seeing a girl in Canada. So you can *absolutely* do this girl in Toledo."

"I don't know—"

"Damn. This girl is so hot, your chick in Canada would *want* you to do her."

Spence laughs and shakes his head. Two months ago, this wouldn't have even been a question. He'd already be at the karaoke bar with the girls, with or without Jamie. He'd be halfway into Misty or Krystal or whatever's pants within the hour. But something in him at this moment feels odd considering it. It's not like Sam is his girlfriend. They've never talked commitment. But still . . .

"Gimme a second," he says to Jamie.

"Take your time, boss," Jamie says. "I'll stay here and be charming."

Spence holds up his index finger to his hot admirer and mouths the words "be right back." She winks at him and bites her bottom lip again as he walks out into the parking lot. There is a cool breeze in the air. Toledo never felt so nice. He's normally there in the winter and can hardly stand outside for more than a few minutes at a time. Now he wants to just enjoy the night.

He even thinks about leaving his car there and walking the two miles back to the hotel, but he hates the idea of screwing Jamie out of a night with girls after a show. Every comic should experience the thrill of adoring women at least once in his career. Even if he didn't have sex with What's-Her-Name, Spence knows he could at least hang out and be a good friend to Jamie. Let the kid live large for one night.

Inside, the audience is still filing out of the showroom and talking about how great the show was. Spence still can't believe it himself. He puts his phone to his ear.

"Hey there," Sam's voice comes over the speaker. "I was just thinking about you."

"Something good, I hope," he says.

"Never," she says. He loves the sound of her voice.

"No?"

"No, you gave me the clap," she says. He regrets ever telling her about Rodney.

"Cute," he says.

"I thought so," she says. "How was tonight?"

"Absolutely amazing."

"Really? Better than when I saw you here?"

"Oh, yeah. I mean it was really something. I even tried new material."

"Very cool," she says. There's a pause. It's enough time for him to smile and wish he was with her. He loves talking to her, but it's not enough. This is one of those nights he wishes she had been with him. So many nights he winds up telling her bad news or complaining about an awful club. Just once, he'd love for her to see him like this, when he's a star.

"What are you doing?" he asks.

"Looking at apartments online," she says. He can hear the clicking of her fingers on a computer keyboard.

"You looking to move?"

"I have to," she says.

"Your lease almost finished?" he asks.

"Nope," she says. "You're not the only one who had an eventful day."

"Do tell," he says.

"A Canadian woman you know got a promotion today," she says.

"Really?" he says. "Tell Claudia I say congrats."

"Har, har," she says.

"That's great news," he says. "What's the gig?"

"Well, sir," she says, "the 'gig,' as you call it, is district manager, and it's in Toronto."

"Really? The capital?"

"Are you kidding me?" she asks.

"What?"

"Toronto's not the capital, you dumb American," she teases.

"It's not?" he asks.

"We've been over this before."

"It's Vancouver, right?"

She sighs. "I have so much to teach you."

He looks around at the people filing out of the club, at the cars in the parking lot. It was a great night. It all seems kind of simple now. It's been only a few minutes, but it might as well have been hours. He has forgotten the show and the new material. Now he's thinking about a bunch of girls on a birthday party outing, singing karaoke, and Jamie wanting to get laid. And Sam. He loves her voice.

"I can't wait," he says. "Teach me all about Toronto while you're at it. I've never been there, either."

He can hear her clicking the computer, and he tries to think about where Toronto is on a map. He knows it's not too far from Montreal. Is it? How far is she moving? Is Toronto the one way over above Washington State? That would suck. No, that's Vancouver. He thinks Toronto is closer.

"How about in three weeks?" she says.

"Three weeks what?" he asks.

"Come visit."

"In Toronto?"

"That will have given me a whole five days to settle in, and I know you're off then, right?"

"Nice memory," he says.

"Thanks," she says. There's a pause, and the sound of her clicking a mouse. "So what do you say?"

Inside the club, the sexy brunette is staring at him again. Spence realizes that there's nothing stopping him from going to the karaoke bar with Jamie and the group of women. And just going to the bar with them doesn't mean he'll sleep with anyone.

"A visit?" he asks.

"Yeah," she says, "I went to university in Toronto. I know it like the back of my hand. You'll have a blast."

He made up his mind when she asked the first time, but he takes a second to pretend to think about it. "I can do that," he says.

"Really?"

"Absolutely," he says.

"Sweet!" she says. "You visiting me and us spending time together. Almost like normal people do it."

He laughs. He's ten hours away from her at best. She's in another country, and he just got done talking to strangers about his penis. There's nothing normal about it. A couple of months ago, he figured she was a fun distraction for a weekend. Then she became texts and phone calls. Now he's getting ready to go spend a week with her all over again in another city in that country he barely knows anything about.

He looks over his shoulder and, not twenty feet away, Kristy the sex-bot is waving at him through the glass double doors to the club. Sam will never have a clue if he goes with her or not. Or if he sings karaoke or not. Or if he takes her to bed or not. They've never said that what they have is a committed relationship. It's just a thing they're doing.

But does this feel like it's just a thing? he thinks.

Spence turns away from the club and walks out into the parking lot. It's that nice, early spring where it's warm enough for him not to be shivering but cool enough to dry the sweat from the stage lights. He smiles as the night breeze hits his face, and he sits down on the curb. He imagines that Toronto is very nice right about now.

11

When he walks down the streets of Toronto, he feels as if he's in a nicer, cleaner version of New York City. All the things he used to love about that city he finds right here in this one. The buildings stand just as tall, although not as crammed up against each other. Traffic is everywhere and so are people, but they shove him around a lot less than New Yorkers do. For a guy who loves city life but often not city people, it's the perfect fit for him.

After having spent several days here with Sam, he now realizes that the rest of Canada is not nearly as European-looking as Montreal. That almost disappoints him. He enjoyed trying to figure out what the French writing on certain signs and billboards meant. There's a lot of French writing in Ontario, too, but English is obviously the dominant language. Everyone in Toronto knows as little French as he does.

Walking around the city relaxes him. After weeks of being in either a car or a hotel, it's comforting just to be able to go where his feet take him. Most days, while Sam is at work, he walks until he feels he has gone far enough, then turns around and walks back to her apartment. Midtown is just crowded enough to catch his eye and satisfy his people-watching needs without making him feel claustrophobic. He didn't realize until now how much he took for granted this freedom to just get up and walk until he was tired of it.

When he's not out walking, he's with Sam. The plan was to

see the city, explore the sights, and visit all the major landmarks. He wanted to see the museums and local haunts. He planned to visit the CN Tower, which is always looming off in the distance whenever he goes for his daily stroll. So far, the most sights he has seen with Sam are the places where they eat and her small one-bedroom apartment. It somehow manages to be enough, and they're both plenty happy with the arrangement.

"Who needs museums when we have the sofa and popcorn?" Sam tells him. He thinks she makes a good point.

Lying in bed reading a magazine while she reads some chick lit—he can't remember the last time he did this. It's odd not to have housekeeping banging on the door at some point or Rodney on the phone or the TV on making noise to clear his head from something else. He doesn't feel the need to check his e-mail or even deal with work. When he's on the road, he feels as if he's constantly having to network, promote, or just keep up with his schedule. Right now, he's happy to do absolutely nothing.

"How's the book?" he asks, putting down his copy of *Entertainment Weekly*. He needs to buy something different. Maybe *Details* or *Esquire*. Entertainment magazines threaten to make him think about work. He wants nothing to do with that.

"Sucks," she says but keeps reading. "How's Johnny Depp?"

"Sucks," he says.

"You don't like Johnny Depp?" She gasps and covers her mouth with her right hand. "It's over between us."

"He's fine. The magazine sucks."

"Wanna trade?" she asks and holds up her book about a woman living in a city who can't find a decent man despite her glowing smile and fabulous shoes.

"I'm good, thanks."

"Blah," she says and puts her book down. She's lying about thinking that it sucks. He can tell by the way she carefully puts a bookmark in before she tosses it aside.

They lie above the covers and stare at the ceiling for a few minutes. He can't remember the last time he lounged around like this and sex wasn't the main ingredient. Yes, they've had sex. Yes, he enjoys it. But this is different. He's had plenty of sex. He hasn't had a lot of . . . nothing. Nothing feels pretty good; sex is just the bonus.

"TV?" she suggests and hands him the remote. He nods and flicks on the small flat-screen that sits at the end of the bed on a tiny stand. Her bedroom is a quarter the size of most hotel rooms he stays in, but neither of them seems to mind. He flips through the channels and comes across a rerun of *Royal Canadian Air Farce,* a sketch show he's been randomly watching all week.

"Ugh," Sam says and rolls over to put her head on his chest.

"What?" he asks.

"You like this?"

"It's entertaining."

"Really?"

"Sure," he says, "the parts that I get. A lot of it goes over my head."

"It's just that it's so"—she pauses—"Canadian."

"Right," he says. "This is Canada."

"Right," she says. "And you're the only person I know who watches Canadian TV shows."

"Really?"

She shrugs. "Pretty much."

"That makes no sense to me."

"Canadians don't really watch Canadian TV that much."

"Apparently not," he says. "What's that all about?"

"Because it tries so hard to be"—she pauses again—"Canadian."

A full thirty seconds goes by with her looking right at him and him looking right into her eyes. Her eyes are beautiful. Even though he loves it when she wears her glasses, he really loves to be able to look right into her very green eyes without the lenses getting in the way.

"That makes absolutely no sense," he finally says.

"But that's how it is," she says.

"Canadians don't like Canadian TV because it tries too hard to be Canadian?"

"You got it."

"I think it's funny."

"Just you," she says. "And maybe twelve other people."

"Wow," he says, "remind me not to become a TV star in Canada. No love."

"Good luck with that," she says and runs her hand across his chest while trying to make him into a more suitable pillow. He watches the TV show and tries to figure out exactly how Parliament works based on the sketch that's on. The prime minister is some guy he has never heard of before. The studio audience is laughing, so whatever they are talking about must be funny. It has something to do with the GST, whatever that is.

"So what are you going to do?" she asks after a few minutes.

"I'll change it if you want," he says. "We can watch something else."

"No." She sits up and leans on her elbow. "I mean, what are you going to do next? After this week?"

"Oh," he says. He was enjoying not thinking about work. "I've got to go to Minneapolis."

"And then what?"

"Then Indianapolis."

"That's it, huh?"

"I think San Antonio at some point."

"No, I mean that's your routine," she says. "Different city, different week."

"That's the job."

"When are you off again?"

"I dunno," he says. "Two months. Maybe ten weeks. I'm not sure."

She puts her head back down on his chest.

"You want me to come back and visit again?"

"Of course," she says. "I'd like it to be sooner than ten weeks, though. But I'll take what I can get."

"You and me both."

She sits back on her elbow and looks at him. He knows a talk is coming so he turns the TV off. It's okay. He doesn't mind. When Beth used to have these talks with him, it was never good;

it was always bad news or he did something wrong. With Sam, it feels okay. She doesn't make him feel like she wants him to tell her what she's already thought up in her head. She can take the truth when she hears it.

"Is this what you want to keep doing?" she asks.

He leans in and kisses her. It's not to distract from the conversation, but just because he wants to. "I like doing this, yeah," he says.

"Not us, weirdo," she says. "I mean your touring. The traveling."

He sighs. "Well, I do like making people laugh."

"Yes, you do."

"And I seem to be good at it."

"Yes, you are," she agrees.

He sits there for a minute. Ten years ago this question was an easy one. He wanted to travel constantly and see the country. He wanted to entertain tens of thousands of people every year. He wanted to live in hotels and party like a low-paid rock star. Ten years ago, he thought and felt exactly like Jamie Hernandez. Fast-forward to now and all that glitters is not gold. It's not even gold-plated.

"Honestly," he says, "up until now, I've never made any real plans. I mean, sure I have my schedule and I fill my calendar with gigs. But I haven't thought about anything else but that in a long time. Once I fill up the first half of the year, I work on filling the second half of the year. By the time the second half is done, I have to start working on the first part of the next year. Between that and just doing the gigs, I haven't had time to think about much else."

"Do you want to keep doing it? Keep traveling like you are every week?"

"I don't know. I've been just kind of living one day at a time."

"Like an alcoholic."

He laughs. "Sure."

"One day at a time," she says.

He smiles at her and kisses her again. She actually nailed it. He never thought of it that way, but that's exactly what he's been doing. It's what most comedians do. One day at a time, one gig at a time, week after week, year after year.

"I guess I am, you know, addicted to it," he says, "and I'm not really sure how to quit. It goes back to that 'what-if' scenario I told you about before."

"What if you're always close to something bigger?" she says quietly.

"Yeah."

"Yeah, but have you ever wondered if you could love something else, too?"

"I could love you," he says before he even realizes it. What the hell was that all about? He's been trying not to think too much about falling in love with Sam, let alone telling her.

Idiot.

"Right back atcha," she says. "But I mean work-wise. Do you ever think that maybe there's something else you'd love as much as performing?"

How many times has he thought about this? Every week at least, maybe several times a week. How many careers has he considered? How many did he try before he finally wrestled up the balls to try this one?

"There were a lot of bad jobs before this one," he groans.

"Yeah?"

"You have no idea. So many jobs I took just because the money was good. Because I always needed something to fall back on."

"Like what?"

"Like the year in pharmaceutical sales. Jesus."

Her eyes go wide, and she laughs through her closed mouth, a silly choking sound accompanied by a ridiculous grin. "You?" she asks. "Sales?"

"You have no idea." He rolls his eyes. "I didn't even get to sell the good stuff, like boner pills or anything like that. I sold antianxiety meds. And not the ones you've heard of."

"That bad?"

He shrugs. "Not terrible. The money wasn't that bad. But it was boring as all hell. And I wasn't very good at it."

"I find that surprising," she says. "I figured you could sell ice to an Eskimo."

"Hardly," he says. "I didn't even show up most of the time. I lied to my boss and told him I was meeting with accounts when I was really out of town, doing gigs and auditions."

"How'd that work out for you?"

"Got promoted."

"Really?"

"No." He lowers his head in mock shame. "Got fired."

She playfully punches him in the arm, and he laughs. He shrugs it off these days, but he remembers when it used to sting a bit. There were many jobs he lost over the years. Even as a kid, he got fired more than anyone else he knew. The mouth that gets him in trouble all the time now was the same one he spoke with back then.

"There have always been 'what-ifs,' " he says as he rubs the back of his neck. "I was a substitute teacher for a while. That almost led to a full-time teaching job."

"Wow." Sam smiles. "What happened there?"

"Nothing. Someone else got the job, and the contract ended. So I moved on to another thing for a while. And then another something after that. Until I started piecing together enough gigs to go full-time on the road."

"And that was it?"

"Then I met Rodney," he says. "I haven't had a day job since."

"Is that why you keep him around?" she asks while fidgeting with her hands. Spence thinks she wants to bite her nails but won't do it around him.

"Having an agent is kind of like having a job," he says, dead serious. "The only thing worse than having one is looking for one."

"And you're done looking for jobs," she says. It's not a question.

"I know one thing," he says and rolls over on his side, leaning on his elbow the same way she is leaning on hers. "I can't work in a cubicle. I can't go to an office and sit at the same desk day after day, doing the same job that never changes."

She chuckles and kisses him.

"What?" he asks.

"Nothing."

"What is it?" he asks again and pinches her thigh. She squeals and pinches back.

"You're already working in a cubicle, you just move it around. It is the same job, day after day. It's just in a different city every week."

He sighs. He never really looked at it that way.

"And your commute is longer," she says and kisses him again.

"Good point."

She gets up and stretches, then looks around the tiny room. There's barely enough room for her to stand up, let alone really move around. "I'm not telling you not to do it," she says. "I would never even think of doing something like that. You obviously love performing, and you're obviously good at it."

"But . . ." he starts.

"But I think you're exhausted."

"Probably," he says. "Maybe all I need is a good vacation. I do know that I don't want to be one of these road-worn dinosaurs I used to work with. I used to open for them all the time. Sixty years old and still doing the same awful gigs, the same awful act. They're all on autopilot."

"Fuck that noise," she says, and it makes him laugh. Every once in a while she talks like a truck driver. It just doesn't fit. She looks like a porcelain doll and talks like a sailor.

"So I'm not too old," he says, "and I'm not too bitter."

"Not yet," she says.

Right now, if he could spend forever in this little bedroom, he would. Everything seems just fine right in this moment. But he knows that, for it to always be perfect, he'd have to freeze time.

No matter how great things are with Sam today, he'll always be steps away from walking down the same road he did with Beth.

He knew things were over with Beth long before she finally served him with papers. She simply couldn't take him being gone all the time and couldn't wait around to see if his career was ever going to lead to something bigger and better. He didn't blame her when she left him. He didn't fight her or scream at her or argue or cry. When she told him she was dating Evan, he just nodded and said "okay." She was surprised. She either thought she had done a great job of hiding it or that she somehow should have given her a different reaction. She wanted him to be more upset. She wanted him to be angry, but he never was. He just took the papers and signed his name. The best thing he ever did for her was walk away.

To be with Sam, he knows he'll eventually face the exact same questions he did before. This time around it'll be worse because he doesn't even live in Canada. He doesn't live anywhere. That should make everything easier, but it just leaves him clueless. He has no idea what he is going to do with his life in his own country. What the hell is he going to do in one he's barely visited?

"I know this much," he says as he gets up off the bed and walks over to her. "I don't like the fact that I have to leave you in a few days."

"Me neither," she says. "I don't like the fact that when I say good night to you it's on the phone every night."

Déjà vu sucks, he thinks.

"That's the job," he says. He says it a lot, for various reasons. And he's beginning to wonder who he is actually saying it to.

"I really do love this," she says, "but don't think that I can do this forever."

There it is. He's been waiting for it, and she finally threw it out there. He nods slowly. "I understand."

"I don't want months or years to go by, never knowing when I'll see you next. Or for how long. I would never ask you to quit what you do, but I don't think I could live like that. Not for long, anyway. It's like being a military wife."

A comedy bride, he thinks and almost smiles.

"I'm just thinking right now, right now," he says. "It's as far in the future as I can go. It's all I can promise."

"One day at a time," she says.

Beth gave him plenty of warning signs. He noticed them right away and pretended that he was oblivious to each one that was dropped right into his lap. Whether she realizes it or not, Sam just gave him her first one. He caught it, but he smiles, puts his arms around her waist, and kisses her. Then he gives her a raspberry on her neck and tickles her. Laughing, they both fall onto the bed together.

12

After driving for the better part of two days, his legs feel as if they are bent backward. He hears his knees pop as he gets out of his car. He slept in the backseat last night, and his back still hasn't recovered. At the time it seemed silly to pay for a motel since he was only planning on sleeping for a few hours anyway. But now, hobbled over like an old man, he kind of regrets spending the night in a rest area.

He stands in the parking lot at Doane College in Nebraska. He parked as far away from the main building as possible so that no one would see him stumble out of his car. Making sure no one is looking, he reaches down into the floorboard and grabs the urine-filled Diet Coke bottle. He quickly throws it in a nearby trash can. He really doesn't like to pull over any more than he has to, and that bottle came in handy along the way.

Doane College is always a good gig. He has to drive to the middle of nowhere in Nebraska to get to it, but it pays him for one show what he normally makes in a week. It's one of the few college gigs he still likes to do. He doesn't relate to the kids the way he used to; he knows that some of his material just doesn't fly with them. In his early thirties, back when he could still pass for being in his late twenties, he used to do a lot of college gigs and was making very good money doing them. Now he only does a few every year. The money is still good, but the gigs aren't nearly as much fun.

He's done this gig so many times he can probably just do the same show he did last year. Every summer, the Doane College Student Activities Division brings him there as part of their "End of Final Exam Week" celebration, just as the school year is ending. Each year the gig is the same, but the money gets better. The first time he did it, he got paid six hundred bucks. Then it went up to eight hundred, then a grand. This time around, he asked for twelve hundred and they went for it. Twelve hundred bucks for one gig, he must be doing something right. If only it were always that simple.

He's surprised every time he comes here how the halls of this building remind him not of college life, but high school instead. Banners and signs made with Magic Marker advertising the comedy show or the next baseball game. Silly posters that are obviously handmade proclaim the Doane Tigers as the "Bestest Ever." He doesn't know if college kids are maturing slower or if he's just getting older faster than he realizes. He looks at the faces of some of the students he passes. They're supposed to be adults, but they look like children. Eighteen now looks twelve.

He walks through two sets of double doors at the main building and makes his way up the first staircase. He has walked this way enough times now that he doesn't need to ask anyone where to go. At the top of the stairs, he turns right and goes immediately toward a set of administrative offices. Sitting at her desk, with the door open, is Emma Simpson. Her face buried in her computer screen, she doesn't notice him when he steps into her doorway.

"You look like you're trying to figure out calculus," he says as he softly raps on her open door with his knuckles.

"No, Facebook," she says and laughs. Her laugh is so loud, it fills the room and the hallway. A large, fiftysomething black woman, Emma has been at Doane for almost fifteen years. She has stayed in the student activities department that entire time. She must not make much money, but she obviously loves her job to have been there so long. That and it's probably the most interesting thing to do there. Her size does not slow her down, and she's on her feet shaking his hand in less than three seconds.

"How are you, Spence?" she says as she grips his hand warmly.

"Can't complain," he lies and smiles like an idiot. He almost wants to hug her. He likes her better than ninety percent of the club managers and bookers he normally deals with. She pays him better than all of them do, and still manages to treat him great. "How are things here?"

"The same," she says. "How has your career been going?"

"Great," he lies again. If his career were any different, he probably wouldn't be in the middle of Nebraska in the first place. "Still touring. Working new places all the time."

"That's wonderful," she says. "You must absolutely love it."

"How can I not?"

"You are living the dream," she says. Spence nods and remembers that he was just pissing in a bottle an hour ago. "We're all set for tonight," she says. "You ready to roll?"

"Of course," he says. "Ready to do my thing like I always do."

She laughs even though it wasn't remotely funny or intended to be. She's good like that. "I bet you are," she says and walks over to her desk. It's the most organized desk Spence has ever seen. There's an in-box and an out-box, and the wires on her computer are all clamped down and tucked neatly away. Even the pens on her desk are color-coordinated in separate jars. He should fire Rodney and hire her to be his personal manager. She'd probably make him rich.

She picks up a manila envelope and hands it to him. "There's everything you need. Directions to the hotel are on top. But you probably don't need them at this point, do you?"

"Nah, I think I can find my way," he says. The Starlight Motel is the only hotel within five miles of the school and straight down the road. It isn't hard to find. The hand-drawn directions in the envelope seem silly—one arrow pointing straight from point A to point B.

He looks at the other contents in the envelope. As usual, this includes a sheet detailing the history of the college, a list of cafeterias on campus where he's allowed to eat for free, and the standard warning to not incite "hate speech" on campus. Every college has these rules. Apparently every school is afraid that every comedian might incite a race war or political riot. Luckily, he just tells dick jokes. He remembers back when he went to college. He saw Dennis Miller once, George Carlin another time. He wonders if they got the same waivers back then.

"Showtime is at eight," Emma says, "but if you can be here by seven forty-five, that'd be great."

"No problem," he says, remembering the tiny cafeteria where he always performs. "Same place, right? The Tiger Inn?"

"Look at you. Good memory."

"Sometimes. It's slipping as I get older."

She scoffs at him. "Old? Honey, I'm old. You don't have to worry about a thing. What are you? Twenty-nine?"

He knew there was a reason he liked her so much. "Yep," he says, "just turned twenty-nine again this year."

She laughs again. He wishes he could clone her.

"Oh," she says as she turns back to her desk and he starts to make his way out of the office, "did you talk to your agent? What's his name? Ricky?"

"Rodney."

"Oh, yes, Rodney," she says. "Did you speak with him about the pay?"

He raises his hand and shakes his head. He likes her too much to talk with her about money. That always ruins everything. Besides, that's what Rodney gets paid to deal with.

"I'm not worried about it," he says. "I'm sure it's fine."

"I'm sure. Just wanted to make sure you were okay with it."

"I'm always okay. I get to come here every year and entertain you guys. What's not to like?"

Emma laughs again, and he gives her a salute as he walks out the door. If every single club booker acted the way she does, The Boom never would have ended. And if he got paid as much for every gig as what she was giving him, he wouldn't have slept in his car in Iowa.

He's at the Starlight Motel five minutes later and ready to collapse on the bed for a while. As he walks up to the front desk, an old man steps out from a room in the back. Looking like the love interest from an old episode of *The Golden Girls,* the old-timer walks over and, without saying a word or even nodding hello, places a piece of paper and room key on the counter.

"Name and vehicle info," the old man says while apparently still chewing something he was eating. He smells like peanut butter and pain cream. His plaid button-up shirt has a frayed alligator that has seen better days sewn over the left breast. His pants are pulled up right below his armpits. If he were wearing a hooded cloak, he could easily pass for Death.

"Alrighty," Spence says as he writes his name and info about his Camry into the blanks on the page.

The old man takes the sheet and puts it behind the counter. "Checkout is eleven," he says. Tiny motels always have checkout at eleven. Most national chains moved it to noon years ago. The smaller and cheaper the hotel, the earlier the checkout. Spence remembers once staying in a run-down motel that had a ten a.m. checkout time.

"Can I get a wake-up call for seven?" Spence asks.

"In the morning?" the old man asks.

"Tonight," Spence says. The old man looks at him like no one ever takes naps.

"I'll come knock on your door around then," the old man says.

"Thanks." Spence smiles at him and turns to leave the lobby.

"Welcome back," the old man says. "Always good to have you."

Five minutes later, Spence puts his luggage down and realizes immediately that he's in the same room he's always in and is once again the only person in the entire motel. He thinks that's why the old man recognized him: He's apparently the only guest they ever get. He wonders how it stays in business the other three hundred sixty-four days of the year.

In the room, he falls down on the bed and waits for sleep to hit him. He always tells himself that he's going to pass right out when he gets to the hotel, but it never happens. Some song is in his head and he can't seem to let it go enough to relax. This time is no exception, and the beat rages on in his skull. He tries to remember if it's a Canadian song. This makes him think of Sam, and he fires off a quick text message to her.

Just thinking about you, lady.

When there's no response ten minutes later, he figures she's at work and doesn't have her cell phone on her. He tries getting to sleep again. His mind wanders to his material. The new stuff did so well in Toledo. He's going to try it again tonight. It's more universal than what he's been doing; the college kids will like that. They never go with his stuff about divorce, so he might as well just forget even trying it. What do eighteen-year-olds know about losing their favorite chair? It only makes him look even older.

He feels his eyelids getting heavier and his foot stops tapping whatever song by Finger Eleven popped into his head. Lying fully clothed in the middle of the hotel bed with his arms folded across his chest, he must look like a corpse. If he died in this position, it would be very easy to just toss him in a coffin and throw him into the ground. As he drifts to sleep, he wonders what his tombstone would read. He'd like maybe "I'll be here all week."

His cell phone rings and pulls him back from a dream he was having that he has already forgotten. Sometimes he dreams he is onstage and unprepared. He never dreams he is naked, although he does often dream he's in his underwear or whatever he fell asleep wearing. That's when he usually wakes up the middle of the room, standing in front of the mirror and holding an imaginary microphone. This time he's still lying in coffin position on the bed. His phone is to his ear before he's even awake.

"Sam?" he says.

"Who?" Rodney is on the other end.

Damn it, Spence thinks.

"Nothing," he says. "What's up?"

"You in Nebraska?" Rodney asks.

"Key West, remember?" Spence says and puts his feet on the floor. He looks at the clock. He's been asleep for only forty-five minutes. It feels like days.

"Very funny, asshole," Rodney says. "You in the hotel or what?"

"Yeah"—Spence rubs his eyes—"I'm all checked in at the lovely Starlight Motel, truck stop, and delicatessen."

"Sounds scenic."

"Come visit. You'll never leave."

"I'm sure."

"What's the bad news?"

"Why do you always say that?" Rodney asks.

"Because that's the only time you call me."

"That's not true."

Spence scratches the back of his head and sighs. "Then what's the good news?"

"Actually, it is kinda bad news," Rodney says.

"See?"

"It's not that bad."

"What is it?"

"The college won't do twelve hundred," Rodney says.

"Aw, cripes," Spence says, and puts his feet on the floor, "are you kidding me?"

"Sorry," Rodney says, "I tried."

"You're telling me this now?"

"I just found out about it myself," Rodney says, which is most likely a lie. This is probably what Emma was alluding to earlier. Rodney probably knew weeks ago. Spence knows what happened. Waiting until this late to tell him assures Rodney that he takes the gig and that Rodney gets his cut.

"So how much am I getting?" he asks Rodney.

"A grand."

"Is that before or after your commission?"

"Before," Rodney says. "So you'll net eight hundred total."

"What? That's twenty percent. You get fifteen percent."

"For clubs. I get twenty for colleges, remember?"

He doesn't remember, but he says yes anyway. It's an argument that'd he'd lose, and he doesn't have the patience to deal with it right now.

"I thought the twelve hundred was a done deal," he says.

"I thought so, too," Rodney says. "It's still good money."

"Whatever."

"It is."

"It was *great* money."

"It's still not bad."

"If you say so."

"You gonna take it or not?"

"You know I'm going to take it," Spence says. "I'm already here. You knew I was going to take it weeks ago when you first found this out."

"You're being paranoid," Rodney says. "I just found out myself. Why would I not want to make you as much money as possible when I'm making a cut of it?"

"Yeah."

"Yeah," Rodney says. "So take the cash and be happy. They love you there, and you should be glad to have it."

"I am," Spence says. "When do I get paid?"

"As soon as I get the check, I'll cut one for you," Rodney says.

"Fine," Spence says. "Any news on Cleveland?"

"What about Cleveland?" Rodney asks.

Spence is back at the school before seven forty-five and finds Emma waiting with a huge smile on her face. There are two hundred college students waiting to see the show, which is always a good sign. Comedy clubs are hit or miss, but the colleges always have a great turnout for their shows. They are almost always free for the students and early enough in the evening where there's plenty of time left to drink or study or masturbate or do any of the things college kids do on a Thursday night.

"Ready to knock 'em dead?" Emma asks him as he stands behind the curtain in the makeshift showroom. It's actually a section of the cafeteria that has been converted into a comedy club for one night only. This is exactly how a lot of colleges do their shows—risers in the middle of a room with black curtains all around them. The bigger schools have the comedians perform in a theater, while the smaller ones have people telling jokes next to a soda fountain.

"I'm ready," he says and takes the wireless microphone that she hands him. He wants to ask her what the hell happened to the pay raise he was expecting, but he smiles instead. He likes her and doesn't want the money situation to sour it. He would have taken the gig regardless of the pay increase, and it's Rodney who screwed up the deal. He's sure of it.

"Go to it," Emma says and gestures toward what is supposed to be a stage for the next hour. At some schools, there is someone to introduce him or music to play. At Doane, the lights go down and he walks into a single spotlight. It's simple, but it's enough. The freshmen are silent the instant he steps out.

"And that's why I only date Asian women." The opening bit hits right away, and he knows it's going to be a good show. He smiles and takes them where he wants them to go.

The new material works just as well in front of the eighteen-year-olds as it did in front of the roomful of drunks in Toledo. He's two for two, which tells him that the new bits will become a permanent part of the act. Once is never enough to know whether or not a new routine is going to always work. It could just be a fluke—one great crowd that is willing to laugh at anything. If the bits work twice and in front of everything from teens to senior citizens, it's probably safe.

He wonders if maybe he's been going about this all wrong. Maybe the cleaner material is what he should've been writing all along. It's not that people don't like the dirty jokes; he's been killing with that same material for years. But he thinks maybe people like *him* more when he's keeping the humor light. For years he wrote what he thought was funny. Then he wrote what he thought audiences would like. This is the first time in a while he thinks he found a combination of the two.

He likes the feeling that he now has material that he can do for both club audiences and college crowds alike. He's always had to have two different acts. One for the middle-aged drinkers and one for the horny teenagers. Having one set he can do everywhere seems like a great idea.

He never minded clean comedy, but he never cared for clean comedians themselves. Clean comics are always smug. They think they write on a higher playing field. Someone a long time ago decided that adults speaking like adults to other adults is somehow childish. When he was a kid, the word *fuck* was reserved for adults. Now he's an adult and people are telling him it's a word for children. Grown adults who use the word *poop* are telling him that it's somehow classier than saying *shit*. He thinks they're full of both.

"Thank you, good night," he says and leaves the stage to a nice, healthy applause. College audiences tend to applaud nicely but don't have the rowdiness of a roomful of drinkers. It's good enough. He's rocked another crowd at Doane and ensured himself another gig for next year. In the end, that's all that matters.

He steps off the makeshift stage and hands the microphone back to Emma. She smiles like a pumpkin and yells into the microphone as if she's at a pep rally.

"Keep it going for him!" she screams. The applause response stays about the same. At least they are consistent.

Spence waves one last time to the crowd and steps around the corner to what is supposed to be considered "backstage." There, Emma greets him and hugs him so tightly he feels as if she cracked his ribs.

"That was wonderful," she says, beaming. "Just wonderful!"

"Thanks." Spence almost blushes. He's never seen her this receptive.

"I love the new jokes you did," Emma tells him and claps her hands together.

"Yeah, I've been trying different stuff."

"Well, it's great."

"I'm glad you liked it," he says. "Can we do it again next year?"

"Of course," she says. "We always love having you. You know that."

She holds up her index finger and disappears for a minute. A few students walk up to him and shake his hand. A few more tell him that he was "amazing." One of them has him sign a handmade poster that she has pulled off one of the walls. Signing autographs is still one of the best parts of the job. It always makes him feel like he's a celebrity even when he knows he isn't one.

"Here you go." Emma reappears with an envelope in her hand. She hands it to him and points to a few students nearby to start disassembling the stage. They waste no time. In twenty minutes, there will be no evidence he was even there.

"What's this?" Spence asks, holding up the envelope. He hopes it's a bonus. Miracles are known to happen.

"That's your check," she says.

"Oh? You're not mailing it to Rodney?"

"No, I thought you knew that," she tells him. "That's what I was going to tell you earlier. The school made out the check to you by mistake. So instead of having them reprint another one, I figured you'd be okay with just cashing it yourself and sending your agent his share."

"No problem," Spence says. This sort of thing happens from time to time. In fact, he prefers it. He knows it's quicker for him to send Rodney his two hundred bucks than it is to wait for Rodney to get around to sending him eight hundred.

"You sure?" Emma asks. She's way too nice to be in charge of booking entertainers.

"Absolutely," Spence says. "This works just fine."

He opens the envelope and looks at the check. Immediately, he feels the hairs on the back of his neck stand up.

Fifteen hundred dollars.

Printed in black ink, made out to him from Doane College in Nebraska, is a check for fifteen hundred dollars. Spence feels his blood starting to boil the second he reads the numbers. Just a few hours earlier, Rodney told him that the pay would be eight hundred bucks after two hundred for commission. Now he's holding a check for almost twice that amount.

"Is this amount correct?" he asks Emma, wondering if he really got that bonus after all.

"I hope so," Emma says and looks at the check. "Yep, looks right. Fifteen hundred. That's what your agent told us you wanted."

"Oh, yeah?"

"Yep, he said your price came up and we agreed to it. We always love having you here. I told him you were worth it."

"Oh, I was just making sure," Spence says. "I never handle the money stuff. I let him do that."

"That's a good idea," Emma says. "Let some other guy deal with the money. You deal with the funny!"

She laughs and puts a soft hand on his shoulder as if she's exhausted. Maybe the constant laughing is finally taking a toll on her heart. Spence reaches up and pats the hand she put on his shoulder.

"Well, I love being here." He smiles. "Thanks for having me."

"Anytime," Emma says and goes back to overseeing the dismantling of the stage. A student walks over and hands him a bottle of water. He thanks the kid and continues shaking hands and thanking people for coming to the show. After thirty more minutes, he says good-bye to Emma and walks out to the parking lot.

Don't think about this, he tells himself. *You'll never get to sleep tonight if you do. This will keep you up all night.*

But he can't help it. He has a million numbers adding up in his head. He's asking all sorts of questions and answering them at the same time. He thinks about picking up the phone and calling his agent right then and there. Rodney probably sleeps in that office. He's probably there right now, sitting next to the phone. This is probably the best time to reach him.

Almost as if he willed it to happen, Spence feels his cell phone vibrate in his pocket and he answers it without even looking to see who it is.

"Yeah?" he says, putting the check in his pocket and fumbling for his car keys.

"Hey," a familiar voice comes over the phone and it takes Spence a second to realize it's Beth.

"Oh," he says slowly, "hey."

"Don't sound so thrilled to hear from me or anything," she says. It must be after ten where she is, which makes the phone call even weirder. Beth is almost always asleep before eleven and never calls this late.

"Just surprised," Spence says. "What's up? Everything okay?"

"Yeah," Beth says, although she doesn't sound convincing. Evan is likely standing a few feet away, which would make most people uneasy. "Everything is fine."

"Great. So . . . what's up?"

"You're still getting mail here."

"Aw, hell," he says. "Sorry about that. I honestly forgot to change my address."

"S'okay," Beth says. "I just wanted to make sure you knew. Needed to see what the deal was."

"I'll change it tomorrow, I promise."

"No, it's okay. Don't worry about it."

"Then I'll do it soon. Really."

"It's okay," Beth says. "I can wait. It's not a big deal, really."

"What about Evan?" Spence asks. "He going to lose his mind?"

"It's fine. I said don't worry about it."

"Alright," Spence says. "Thanks for that." A few seconds pass, and it feels like an eternity. When the silence is enough, Spence clears his throat. "So I've got stuff I'm doing, so . . ."

"Yeah, that's cool," Beth says. "I'll talk to you later."

"Okay. Thanks again."

"Are you coming through here again anytime soon?" she asks just as he was about to hang up the phone.

"I dunno," he says, "maybe. Depends upon how angry I get at Rodney."

"What happened this time?"

"Nothing," he lies. "Just saying."

"Okay, well let me know," Beth says.

"You got it," Spence assures her and, seconds later, hangs up the phone. He knows something is wrong with Beth, but he doesn't know that he cares enough to stay on the phone and ask what it is. He imagines Evan on the other end, fuming and throwing his mail into the fireplace. He doesn't remotely look forward to going back there again, especially not for more worthless mail. He also knows it's only a matter of time before Beth and Evan give him the "great news" that they're having kids or buying a mansion.

When he hangs up the phone and looks down at it, a text message from Sam is waiting:

Hope you had a great night. Miss you.

A nice breeze blows past him, and he stands for a minute, leaning against his car. Before he picks up the phone to call Sam, he pulls the envelope out of his pocket and looks at the paycheck one more time. Fifteen hundred dollars.

Fuck you, Rodney.

13

The weather is perfect in Syracuse, and Spence is feeling perfectly fine as he pulls into the parking lot at the Funny Farm Comedy Club. He's only a stone's throw away from the airport and wonders if he should have just flown here and left his car in Nebraska. But the two days of driving aren't so bad when he recalls just how nice the weather was. The surprisingly cool summer feels just right. It's one thing he loves about being this far north.

He's still angry about Rodney screwing him over, but Spence finds himself surprisingly stress-free today. Since his plan is to keep it all to himself, the money from the Doane College gig was nice enough for him to relax a bit. The Funny Farm is actually paying him pretty well, too. The fact that they've put him up in a nice hotel is just gravy. It takes him a few steps away from firing Rodney, which has been his plan B for the past two days. When he sees his name in lights on the marquee outside the club, he grants Rodney yet another stay of execution.

Must be that time of year, he thinks to himself.

It seems that it's always right around now that he considers firing Rodney. A last-minute cancellation here, a questionable commission there. One disagreement leads to a fight, which leads to a day or two of both of them not answering each other's calls. Eventually, a new gig comes along that convinces Spence to stick it out. And, as much as Rodney pretends he is just another in a long line of comics he represents, Spence knows he brings in more money than most of the guys on the roster. He's the only one living in his car. He says yes to every gig.

It feels almost like a marriage that is trying hard not to fall apart. For all the clubs he hates or gigs that turn out to be awful, Spence knows there will be weeks of great shows. There are times when the pay is good. And, unlike a lot of comedians he knows, Spence has his calendar booked solid for months. Firing Rodney would mean those dates would instantly disappear. The bad gigs would go away, and the good ones would be gone with them. Just like with his ex-wife, Spence would be replaced by some other guy.

"Look who it is," a familiar voice calls to Spence as he steps into the lobby of the club. He turns to see Ashley standing behind the box office, just underneath a sign that reads NOW SHOWING. Ashley has been managing the Funny Farm for at least four years. Easily in her forties, she's still trying hard to be the sex kitten. She talks like a sailor and smokes like one, too. Her voice sounds like gravel in a washing machine. She and Spence have been close to having sex several times, but fate and clear thinking have always intervened.

"You still here?" Spence says as he accepts Ashley's hug that lasts too long and cheek kiss that feels too soft. "I thought you married some comedian and hit the road."

"Are you kidding?" Ashley blurts, her voice sounding like she's choking. "I wouldn't bang a comedian, let alone marry one."

"You expect me to believe you've never slept with a comic?"

"Ah, shit. I can't promise anything I didn't do when I was drunk."

"I rest my case."

"But I wouldn't marry a goddamned comic," she says. "Give me credit that I'd at least marry for money. And no comic I know has any."

"Ah," Spence says, "now I know why it never worked between us."

"Not for lack of you trying," Ashley says and winks. Spence can't help but notice one too many buttons are unbuttoned on her blouse.

"I think your memory is fuzzy," he says.

"I think I'm already drunk," Ashley says and lets out a long laugh. She's wearing a tight skirt that is probably too tight for a woman with a butt her size. Somehow, she makes it work. There is something slutty and sexy about her at the same time.

"How we looking for tonight?" Spence asks, peeking his head into the showroom around the corner. The room seats about two hundred and is usually packed in nice and tight.

"Almost full," Ashley says, still standing a bit closer than people normally do when they talk to others. "Not fucking bad for a Thursday, right?"

"Not bad at all," Spence says, thinking about his nearly empty Friday night show in Peoria. Occasionally he winds up in towns where the comedy clubs are almost full every single week. He never knows why some clubs are always packed while some are always empty. He can't imagine opening up his own comedy club, even though every comic secretly dreams about it. He's too afraid of being one of the many that fail and not one of the few that succeeds.

"I'm glad you're here," Ashley says. "I finally broke down and did it."

"Did what?" Spence asks.

"I got your name tattooed on my ass."

"Get the hell outta here."

"It's true, goddamnit." She practically hacks up a pack of smokes when she speaks. "I did it."

"I don't believe you."

Without missing the opportunity, Ashley turns around, raises her skirt, and shows Spence her bare behind. At first, he doesn't notice the tattoo, but only how nice her butt is for one its size. He also can't help but notice the very tiny, red thong underwear that matches her blouse. When his eyes move slightly left, he sees the tattoo in question. Printed in black letters, right across the cheek, are two words: YOUR NAME.

"Clever." Spence chuckles and rolls his eyes at the same time.

"Thought you might like it," Ashley says, slowly tugging the skirt back down over her large hips.

"Getting a lot of mileage out of that joke, are you?"

"You have no idea."

"I have a feeling that you got the ink just as an excuse to show people your ass."

"You complaining, asshole?" She mock-slaps him on the face. It's a polite touching and might as well be followed with her tongue down his throat. She has always laid it on thick, but Spence is beginning to wonder if they both could use a cold shower.

"Not at all." He smiles and steps toward the showroom. "I'm gonna hang backstage until showtime. You guys still serve food here?"

"Yeah, and you still get a meal on the house every night," Ashley says. Spence lets out an inner sigh of relief. He hasn't eaten all day. Ashley reaches underneath the counter and pulls out a menu, which she hands him. "There's some slut here to see you, too."

"What?" Spence asks. For a split-second he figures out the mileage in his head and wonders how far away he is from Toronto. Would Sam be crazy enough to surprise him? The thought leaves his head almost as quickly as it entered. He knows it's just wishful thinking.

"What do you mean 'what'?" Ashley scoffs. "One of your whores actually came back to see you again. All by herself. Said she knows you."

Spence feels a weird tingling on the back of his neck. When women show up by themselves at his show, it can either be golden or terrifying. Sometimes it's just a fan who has seen his show before and wants to see it again. But sometimes it's women he slept with years ago and never called, waiting for their chance to enact revenge. He's had his share of women throwing themselves at him, and he's had his share of drinks thrown at him, too. The odds aren't in his favor, and it makes him uneasy.

"Can I sneak into the back without seeing her?" he asks. "I don't like talking to people before the show."

"You wanna sneak out the back door when you're done,

too?" Ashley says. "Or should I go see if she's holding a paternity suit?"

"Hilarious."

"That's what you get for using your dick like a divining rod, you hound."

"Some would call me a hopeless romantic," Spence says.

"I call you a whore," Ashley says and points him through the kitchen. He walks all the way around the back of the club, behind the waitresses' area, and quickly backstage into the green room. Throwing himself down on the old, dirty sofa, he thumbs through the menu and tries not to think about how many times Ashley has had sex right where he's sitting.

When he's onstage, all he can see is the stage lights shining in his eyes. There is no audience—just a void into which he speaks and from which laughter comes back at him. He feels as if he is floating in space, surrounded by nothing but darkness on all sides and the sun beating down onto his face. There is no one here but him, and so he speaks into the void and waits for the laughter to return. There is no audience to imagine naked. There is no interaction that he needs. He simply puts out the act as he always has and, just as he hopes they will, the voices from within the void laugh back.

"That's why I only date Asian women," he says and awaits the thunderous laughter he knows will return. When it does, he hears it as a "screw you" to the Electric Pony in Oklahoma. The next wave of laughter is a "screw you" directly at Frank in Peoria, and the one after that is a sledgehammer taken to the roof of Frank's new Corvette. Everyone in Peoria was wrong, and everyone in Syracuse is right. He's a star. And this is right where he belongs.

Offstage an hour later, the ego has subsided a bit, even if the swagger still remains. He stands in the lobby, shaking hands with customers as they walk out the door. They beam as they walk past him, smiling and telling him how hilarious he was.

They loved the show, and they gush all over him as he stands there and soaks it in.

"My sides hurt from laughter," an old man says and pats him on the shoulder.

"Oh, my God, that was so funny," a girl young enough to be his daughter says.

"Why aren't you famous yet?" more than one person wants to know, leading him to wonder the exact same thing.

Spence spies Ashley giving him the once-over from around the corner, and he knows that he can do anything he wants with her if he only pursues it. Part of him wants to, being so caught up in the rush of having just killed it onstage. The other part of him just wants to get back to the hotel and call Sam.

He has shaken almost one hundred hands of the two hundred people who were at the show, it seems, when a drink magically appears in front of him. Held by a very small, very feminine hand, the tall glass of Scotch is exactly what he was craving.

"Thanks, Ashley," he says, still nodding at the last handful of audience members making their way out the door.

"Who?" a voice says that stops him in his tracks and makes him almost drop the drink now in his hand. Standing in front of him is a very young, very attractive redhead. No older than twenty-five or so, she's holding a drink above the cleavage popping out of a very revealing dress. Spence wonders if she and Ashley are somehow related.

"I'm sorry," he says. "I thought you were someone else."

"You don't remember me, do you?" The redhead smiles, and Spence realizes this is the woman Ashley was talking about when he first got to the club.

"Of course I do," he lies. "I wouldn't forget. Trust me."

"I would hope not." She raises her eyebrows and laughs. Spence starts to wonder if he slept with her, but he has no memory of it, which is odd. He forgets names and faces all the time, but remembers women he sleeps with. Regardless, he leans over and gives her a big hug, as if they've been friends for years.

"Marcy," she says, and Spence nods as if that sounds familiar. It does not.

"Yeah, I remember," he lies again. "Good to see you again. You come out just to see my show?"

"Of course," she says, "wouldn't have missed it."

"That makes one of us," he says, at which Marcy laughs and smiles. At least she didn't hit him with the paternity suit Ashley mentioned. It's flattering when you're thirty-seven and a woman more than ten years younger than you are finds you attractive. Spence immediately feels his guard drop and every ounce of charm he has in him begs for attention.

"You gonna let me buy you a drink?" Marcy says and bounces back and forth from one foot to the other. The flirting is not remotely subtle, which Spence likes even more. He's suddenly reminded of Toledo and his night with Jamie. Never in one year has he had so many women attempting to put booze into him and maybe get him into bed. Not since he was married, anyway.

"Didn't you just do that?" he says, pointing to the glass of Scotch she already handed him.

"Not here," she says, "somewhere else. You know, we'll have some tequila shots and some laughs."

"I don't know about that. I'm allergic to tequila."

"Really?"

"Yeah, I break out in handcuffs."

Marcy laughs big, tossing her hair over her shoulder as she does. Spence smiles, completely oblivious to how cheesy it looks. In the background, he sees Ashley make an exaggerated face and pretend to choke herself in disgust. Spence gives her his best "kiss my ass" look over Marcy's shoulder. Ashley mimics a blow job with her hand and rolls her eyes.

"Come on," Marcy says, "you didn't let me take advantage of you last time. Let me at least try it now."

So I didn't have sex with you? Spence thinks. *How did I mess that up?*

"I don't know," he says. "I'm getting kinda old to be hanging around with young girls."

"Maybe I like my men old," Marcy says, which almost makes Spence blush until he realizes that the compliment involves her calling him old. "You're not married anymore, right?"

"No, not anymore." Spence starts to realize why he never slept with her in the first place. He thinks of Sam and starts to say he has a girlfriend. Just as he opens his mouth, he stops himself and takes a sip of his Scotch instead.

"Then it sounds like you owe me for breaking my heart last time," Marcy says. "You led me on only to leave me hot and bothered. I'm not going to let that happen again."

"Sounds like you should bang her," Ashley calls from twenty feet away. Instantly, Spence feels his face turn pink. Marcy's eyes go wide, and she stifles a laugh without bothering to look back at Ashley.

"Thank you very much," Spence says to Ashley before turning back to Marcy. "I'm sorry about that. She's kind of bitter about having to walk around with two enormous balls."

Marcy laughs again. "No problem. But you could just have those drinks with me. I won't bite."

"You talked me into it," Spence says. "Just anywhere but here, okay?"

"Anywhere you want," Marcy says. "I'll get my coat and be right back."

She bounces off around the corner, and Spence promises himself he will only have one drink with her and nothing more. No sex. Not even a kiss. If he's going to make anything work with Sam, the first thing he has to do is not sleep with the hot, young girl with the stupidly nice body. He promises himself nothing will happen, even as he tries to remember whether or not he has any condoms in his suitcase.

"She looks like a Barbie doll," Ashley says from behind him and scares him half out of his wits. "A fire crotch. You gonna nail that?"

"Cripes," Spence says. "What is it with you? I'm just gonna have a drink with her. Calm down."

"A drink, sure."

"I'm serious."

"You'd let that piece of ass go just like that? Why aren't you in that car right now getting a hummer?"

"Not interested."

"She's smoking."

"She's a pretty girl, yes. But I'm not trying to sleep with her," Spence says, not sure who he's trying to convince, Ashley or himself.

"You don't have to try," Ashley says. "She's making the move for you."

"I'm behaving tonight, thanks."

"I'll still do you," Ashley says, standing suddenly closer.

"Rain check?" Spence asks, stepping a few feet backward and reaching for his cell phone to text Sam. Thinking of her makes him feel like behaving. He ignores Ashley's cleavage and reminds himself that Shania Twain is Canadian.

Ashley shrugs and starts to walk back into her office. Spence looks around the club now that the lights are all out and can't help but notice how nice it is. He likes working here, and has for years, but he never really stopped to notice how much money has been invested in the place. The furniture is leather and shiny. The carpet is always clean. There is expensive neon all over the place.

One thousand dollars, Spence thinks, remembering how much pay he's picking up from Rodney for this gig.

"Hey, Ash," he calls before Ashley can get into her office. "What am I making this week, anyway?"

"Two grand," she says. "Same as always."

Fuck you, Rodney.

"Meet me in the middle," Marcy says as she lines up the shot glasses on the bar and picks up one on the end. Spence doesn't bother to count how many glasses are there or how many he puts down as he picks them up and quickly shoots them back. The taste of Jägermeister hits his tongue and immediately causes him to wince. He moves slow enough that he doesn't have to drink many. The taste is awful, and he'd just as soon have stopped at one.

Marcy drinks like a champ. For every shot Spence has had, Marcy has had one, too. All the while, she's been sipping on a cocktail in her hand. She can't weigh enough to not be completely smashed, but she seems to not even be slurring.

"Come on, lightweight," she says to Spence. "You gotta be quicker than that."

"You're lucky I'm still standing," Spence says. Truthfully, he's not doing too badly, all things considered. He's been pretty good at pacing himself up until now. In between drinks, he's managed to put down a few glasses of water whenever Marcy has gone to the bathroom.

"I don't want you getting too drunk on me," she says. "You're no good to me if you pass out."

"My ex-wife would disagree with that statement."

Marcy laughs and rolls her tongue over her cocktail straw. Spence feels the buzz from the liquor hitting him full-on and knows he probably won't be able to resist her much longer if he keeps drinking like this. In the background, "Paradise by the Dashboard Light" is playing on the jukebox. Meat Loaf is not Canadian.

"So how long has it been since I saw you?" Spence says, his liquid courage making him more confident about the fact he still doesn't remember Marcy at all.

"About five years," she says and motions to the bartender to bring more shots. "I was an undergrad then. You don't remember, do you?"

"Sure I do," he lies. "Just not when exactly. After a while, it's hard to keep track of when I've been somewhere."

"And who you sleep with?"

"But we didn't sleep together."

"No," she says and sips her drink, "no, we did not. Not once I found out you were married, anyway."

"Yeah, that put a damper on my sex life back then."

"Didn't stop you from trying, though."

"Can you blame me?"

"For being an asshole?" Marcy says, and her face looks serious for a second. "Sure I can."

"Damn," Spence says and feels the pinch of sobriety hitting him a bit. "Harsh."

Marcy looks at him for a split-second and then winks. Her tongue rolls back over her straw, and she takes a long sip while smiling at him as seductively as she possibly can.

"I've always been attracted to assholes, if you must know," she says and winks again. Spence lets out a small sigh of relief that he hopes she doesn't notice. A second later, another set of shot glasses appears on the table in front of them.

"No way," Spence says. "I can't do any more."

"Just one," Marcy says. "And then we can get out of here."

Spence sighs and looks at his watch. If he leaves right now, he can go to bed, sleep off most of the hangover that is sure to come, and still wake up without feeling too guilty. If he stays, he knows that it will only lead to him in bed with Marcy and feeling like an utter cad in the morning.

This girl is so hot, your chick in Canada would want you to do her. Spence hears Jamie's voice ringing in his head.

"One more shot," Spence says, "and that's final."

"Ooh, you got it, sir," Marcy says and salutes him as she picks up her own shot glass. Spence downs the Jägermeister and slaps the shot glass back down on the table with a flip of his wrist. The sound it makes against the table is a defiant "quitting time" signal. The buzz in his head is just right, but feels as if it could lead to puking in a hotel toilet all night if he's not too careful.

"Well done." Marcy gives him sarcastic applause as she polishes off her drink. "You feeling good still?"

"Absolutely," Spence says and stands up from the table. His bladder feels like it could use some relieving, and he looks around for the restroom. Spotting it, he tosses a few bucks down on the table and smiles at Marcy. "I'll be right back."

There is a pause. Then nothing. Then blackness. Then a bright light in one eye. Then a bright light in the other eye.

Spence feels a pounding in his head and all down the side of his face. He closes his eyes for just a minute. His head hurts, and he feels dizzy. He hears a woman's voice and shakes his head for a second, trying to clear his mind and get rid of the headache. A second later, he opens his eyes and looks straight ahead. The bar is gone, Marcy is gone, and two women he doesn't recognize are looking straight at him. One of them holds a pen-sized flashlight in her hand, and she's shining it right in Spence's eyes.

"He's awake," the woman with the flashlight says to the other.

"You coming around?" the other woman asks Spence.

"What?" Spence says, his head pounding.

"You're in the hospital," the woman with the flashlight says. "Can you tell us your name?"

14

"What the hell happened?" Spence sits up in the hospital bed, staring wide-eyed at the two nurses looking right back at him the same way.

"We were hoping you could tell us that," the bigger and older of the two nurses, a rough-looking woman in her early fifties, stops shining the flashlight in his eyes and puts it into the pocket of her scrubs. She glances at the other nurse, a younger woman with long, black hair, who writes something on a clipboard she is holding.

"I just said I'll be right back," Spence says.

"When?" the older nurse asks.

"Just now."

"To whom?"

"The girl at the bar."

"When was that?"

"Just a few minutes ago," Spence says and closes his eyes for a second. His head hurts more than he can remember it ever hurting before.

"You've been unconscious for over nine hours," the older nurse says.

Holy shit, Spence thinks.

"Are you kidding me?" he asks.

"Do you know where you are?" the younger nurse says. "Do you know *who* you are?"

"I'm in the hospital," Spence says.

"We just told you that," the younger nurse says.

"I didn't need you to tell me that. I can see that."

"Calm down. Do you know why you're here, Spencer?"

Spence shakes his head, but it hurts worse when he does that. "I don't go by that."

"That's your name."

"My last name."

The younger nurse makes a note on the clipboard she's holding. Spence feels his eye twitching every time the fluorescent lights on the ceiling flicker, like hospital lights always seem to do. The twitch in his eye must make him look crazy, because both nurses look uneasy around him. The older one puts her hand on his chest and gently pushes him back down, easing his head into the pillow on the hospital bed.

"Alright, now, let's just take a deep breath and try to remember what happened, okay? Can you tell me where you were last night?"

"I just said that I would be right back," Spence says, feeling the pain in his head going all the way down the side of his face. "That was just a minute ago."

"Who did you tell that to?"

"The redhead."

"What redhead?"

"The redhead at the bar."

"What was the name?"

"Her name was Marcy."

"Not the redhead." The older nurse shakes her head. "The name of the bar."

Spence can't remember the name of the bar. Marcy drove him there, and he was too busy looking at her in the car along the way to pay much attention to anything else, let alone the name of the bar or even where it was. He remembers her red hair, several shots of Jägermeister, and then nothing else.

"I'm from out of town," he says. "I'm a comedian, here doing a show."

"You're a comedian?" the younger nurse repeats. "Well, this isn't some joke, you know."

Spence wants to take the clipboard out of her hands and slap her with it. People always seem to think that comedians find everything amusing, no matter the circumstance. He's just woken up from what feels like a coma and some nurse is acting like he just pulled a practical joke.

"No shit it's not funny," he says. "I'm not laughing, am I?"

"Alright," the older nurse says, "just calm down."

"Calm down? I've just woken up in a hospital with no idea how I got here and you think that because I'm a comedian I think this is funny? And now you want me to calm down?"

"You got here in an ambulance. They found you and brought you here."

"Found me?" Spence asks.

"You were lying in a ditch in the middle of the median on the highway. The ambulance was driving by and thought you were dead. They put you in the back and brought you here."

Jesus Christ, Spence thinks, *how much did I drink?*

The bigger nurse tells him that, best as they can tell, it looks as if he stumbled out of the bar, down the highway, and fell down onto the median. Or, at least, that's what it looks like might have happened. No one can tell, and he obviously has no memory of any of it.

"My head really hurts," Spence says, reaching up to touch it. The bigger nurse reaches over and takes his hand. She holds it politely and shakes her head. Spence knows her not letting him touch his head is not a good sign.

"You'll be okay," she says to him, "but you should prepare yourself."

Prepare myself for what? Spence thinks, but the words don't come out. His mouth just hangs open.

The younger nurse puts down her clipboard, picks up a small handheld mirror, and holds it up so Spence can look at himself. He immediately sees why she didn't let him touch it. The entire left side of his face is smashed and bruised. He has a thick, black eye, and his cheek and forehead are both terribly scraped up. It looks as if someone has hit him in the face with a crowbar.

"Jesus," Spence says, feeling his eyes welling up, but choking it back. "Did someone beat me up?"

"It looks like you fell," the older nurse says.

"You broke your fall with your face," the younger nurse says.

"Holy shit," Spence says, still staring at his awful reflection. "And no one kicked my ass?"

"Your wallet was on you," the younger nurse says. "That's how we knew your name. It was full. Money, credit cards. No one robbed you."

"But I didn't even drink that much."

The older nurse sighs and shakes her head. "Well, your blood-alcohol level was incredibly high. You're lucky to be alive right now."

Meet me in the middle, Spence thinks.

"I've been drunk before," he says. "I've never blacked out. Not once. Not ever."

The nurses both look at each other for a second. Spence can't tell if the look is concern or disbelief. They think he's lying. He's seen that look on enough women's faces to know what it means. The younger nurse puts down the mirror and picks up her clipboard again. Spence suddenly smells the hospital. It's an awful smell and reminds him of being around sick people, which he has always been uncomfortable with.

"Have you ever heard of Flunitrazepam?" she asks.

"No," Spence says. "Should I have?"

"Rohypnol?"

"I don't think so."

"Roofies," the older nurse says. Now Spence knows what she's talking about.

"The date rape drug," he says.

"Right," the older nurse says.

Just one more shot of Jägermeister, Spence thinks.

"You mean that someone drugged me?" he asks.

"Looks like it," the older nurse says. "Unless it was intended for someone else."

"Like who?"

"Who were you drinking with?"

"The redhead."

"Did she buy the drinks?"

Spence suddenly feels sick to his stomach. Marcy did buy all the drinks. She kept putting them in front of him. He remembers the first round of shots she bought after he got back from the restroom. They were already on the table. He doesn't know what to think yet and is still trying to clear his head. He knows that none of this is going to make him happy even when it does finally start to make sense. He suddenly realizes that her name probably isn't even Marcy.

"But I didn't sleep with her," he says.

"When?" the younger nurse asks.

"Ever," Spence says. "She said we never slept together."

"I hate to put it this way," the older nurse says, "but I think someone really wanted to hurt you."

Spence feels the pain in his face burning and moving its way down his entire body, through his stomach, and into his intestines. He feels as if he's going to throw up all over the bed right there in the hospital. The tears in his eyes start to well up again, but he shakes them away. He always knew that it was only a matter of time before his house of cards fell down.

Why would she do this to me? Spence thinks.

"I've got to get out of here," he says.

"Not yet," the older nurse says.

"Yes. Now."

Spence starts to get out of the bed when a throbbing pain shoots up his left arm. He winces and snaps his head around to find the source of the pain. Sticking out of his arm is a long IV, hooked up to a bag of clear liquid.

"Take this out of me," he says.

"You should lie back down," the younger nurse says.

"I don't care. You can't keep me here, and I want to leave. Please, take this out of me."

The older nurse calmly reaches over and, with an amazingly gentle touch, removes the small needle from Spence's arm. He barely feels it, even as she covers the small wound with a cotton swab and a Band-Aid. Spence looks around the small hospital room for the first time and realizes that it's not just the three of them in there. There is another patient, thankfully asleep, in a bed just a few feet away. Spence notices the other patient wearing a hospital gown and then realizes that's all he's wearing as well.

"Where are my clothes?" he asks, standing up and feeling the cold hospital air down his bare backside.

"That's a problem," the older nurse says. "We cut them off you."

"You did what?"

"When you were brought in, we had no idea what condition you were in. We didn't even know if you were alive. We had to cut them off you before we had your body X-rayed."

"You had me X-rayed?"

"To make sure you hadn't broken anything, yes."

I don't remember any of this, Spence thinks. It is only one of a million thoughts racing through his head.

The younger nurse reaches over to the small table beside the bed, picks up a large, brown paper bag, and hands it to Spence. He looks inside and finds his jeans, underwear, and shirt, all cut to pieces. He suddenly realizes that, if he's going to leave, he has to walk out of there wearing nothing but that hospital gown.

"Did you cut my shoes off me, too?" he asks.

"Of course not." The older nurse points at Spence's black boots on the floor. Spence puts them on and tries to ignore the pounding in his head and face. He feels like he could fall into that hospital bed and sleep for nine more hours. Or nine more days. He doesn't want to leave, and yet he can't stomach the thought of staying there, either. He wishes he could be nowhere.

"We have to talk to you before you go," the younger nurse says, giving a quick, scared look over at her boss.

"I don't have insurance," Spence says. "You'll have to send me a bill."

"Not about that," the older nurse says. "But we know you don't have insurance."

"What about, then?"

"The law requires us to talk with you about the dangers of alcohol. Anyone admitted to the hospital for alcohol-related injuries has to have counseling before they can check out."

"I'm fine, thanks." He's not sure if that's completely true.

"It's standard procedure. We just need to ask you about your alcohol consumption and habits."

Spence sighs and sits back down on the edge of the bed. "What do you need?"

The younger nurse flips the page on her clipboard and starts writing. "Do you ever drink or get drunk alone?"

"Yeah, so?"

"Well, that's a common sign of alcoholism."

"I also drink and get drunk with friends."

"Also a sign of being an alcoholic. Do you drink when you're upset or to avoid thinking of your troubles?"

"Yeah, sometimes. Is that a sign of being an alcoholic?"

"Yes, it is."

"Is it also a sign of not being one?"

The younger nurse looks up from her clipboard. "Well, yes."

Spence stands up again. "I'd like to leave now."

Both nurses let out an exasperated sigh at the same time and step aside as Spence gets up off the bed and wiggles his bare feet into his shoes. He looks ridiculous and he knows it. He is wearing nothing but his ankle boots and the hospital gown, tied loosely in the back and just barely exposing his ass to the world. It comes down to just above his knees, looking as if he's wearing a very ugly dress.

"So this is how I leave, huh?" he says and tries to smile. Neither nurse returns the gesture. Spence shrugs and feels the pain in his face again as if he's just been punched across the jaw. He wonders how long he'll look like this and if he'll be able to come up with a funny enough joke to explain it to the audience. He's got a full week of shows ahead of him and now has to do it with a broken face. He knows Ashley is going to give him hell about this for years to come. At least his busted look will keep her from trying to sleep with him the rest of the week.

"You're still legally drunk, you know," the older nurse says, "so you can't drive anywhere. You need to sober up before you get behind the wheel."

"I'm still drunk?" he asks.

"Legally, yes."

Spence realizes he came there in an ambulance and, at the very least, needs to get back to the hotel. He has no intention of driving. He just wants to curl up into a ball and stay there until showtime. And then go back into that ball immediately afterward.

"Can you call me a cab?" Spence says. He waits for one of the nurses to yell "You're a cab" at him, but is pretty sure that neither of them has a sense of humor.

"Your wife is here," the younger nurse says. "She'll drive you home."

"My wife?" Spence asks.

"We found her number in your cell phone," the older nurse says. "We thought you were going to die. We had to call someone, so we called her and she came here to get you. She's been in the waiting room for the past hour or so."

Jesus, Spence thinks to himself. *Beth drove from Jersey to Syracuse, New York?*

He doesn't bother to tell the nurses that he's not married. He's too busy trying to think of what to say to Beth when he walks into the next room. He is instantly flattered and scared out of his mind. It's nice that she came up to get him, but he knows that he's in for a world of hurt when she gets her hands on him. He's going to get an earful. And Evan is probably sitting right next to her. He hopes the bruises will elicit some sympathy.

"Try not to tell her about the redhead." The younger nurse drips sarcasm as she hands the clipboard over to the older nurse and then walks away. Spence wants to throw up all over the floor. The older nurse actually smiles for a second and then shrugs at Spence.

"You might want to consider slowing down a bit, okay?" she warns.

"What do you mean?" Spence asks.

"I mean the partying," she says. "I get that you work in show business. But the lifestyle is going to kill you. Is that clear enough for you?"

"I'm not an alcoholic."

"Probably not. But you're too old to be trying to live like this."

"I'm only thirty-seven."

"No, you're almost forty-two," the nurse says and hands Spence a plastic bag containing his wallet and car keys and ID. It suddenly hits him that she's right. He's been lying about his age for so long, he started to believe it himself. He suddenly feels very exhausted and very ashamed.

"This wasn't my fault," Spence says.

"No, but that won't make you feel better if it kills you."

With that, the older nurse gives a sympathetic smile and opens the door. She extends her hand and leads Spence around the corner and down the hallway. He sees hospital staff looking at him as he walks by. They stare at his face, then his hospital gown, then his boots. It's the worst walk of shame he's ever had to do.

He quickly and quietly checks himself out of the hospital as the woman behind the desk tries not to look him in the eye or stare at his face. After giving them Rodney's address so they can send him his very expensive bill, Spence bows his head as he steps out into the waiting room to get scolded by Beth. As he opens the door and tries not to make eye contact with the other people in the room, he sees her sitting across the room. She gets up from her seat and walks over to him.

It's Sam.

At first, Spence wonders if he's just still drunk and maybe

hallucinating. He has no idea what Marcy or whatever her name really is put in his drink. He could be having acid flashbacks for all he knows. As Sam steps closer, however, Spence realizes he's not dreaming. She looks exhausted and like maybe she has been crying. He realizes she must have driven through the night from Toronto to be here. It makes him feel about three inches tall. He wants to run back into the hospital and see if they'll put him down.

"I'm sorry," Spence says. It's all he can say, and he just stands there and looks at her. Sam looks at his face, and there are tears starting to form in her eyes. She looks him up and down, at his black boots and his hospital gown. She cocks her head to the side and looks at the bruises on his face, his black eye, and swollen lip. Slowly, she raises a gentle hand and touches him. He flinches as she lightly touches the cuts and scrapes and bruises and softly caresses the left side of his face.

Then she slaps him hard across the other side.

15

An hour later, Spence is wishing that Marcy or whatever her name is had poisoned him to death. After listening to everything he put Sam through, he isn't sure that even *he* would want to be around him at the moment. So it wouldn't surprise him if she pushed him out of the car and back onto the median where the ambulance found him hours earlier.

The hospital called Sam since she was the woman who appeared most often in his cell phone call history. Since it was the middle of the night and since it was a hospital calling, she knew that her being married to Spence was the only way they would tell her anything. But they had nothing much to tell at the time except that he was still alive and unconscious. Sam drove five hours through the night to be there, not knowing until she got to the hospital what the hell was going on.

Spence told her everything as best he could. He tried to make the relationship with Marcy sound as innocent as possible, especially considering he still wasn't sure what that relationship even was. He was certain now that her name wasn't Marcy and that odds were good he'd never see her again. Still, the story made him look like a complete and utter jackass, even though it was he who wound up beaten up. He figured this was the first time Sam has seen him as such an asshole. He really had hoped it would never happen at all, let alone like this. For the past hour, she hasn't smiled at him once.

"I had no idea they would call you," he says and touches her right hand, which rests on the gearshift of her car. Sitting in her Honda in the hotel parking lot, Spence feels the cold leather seat beneath him sending a chill up his bare back. Still in nothing but the hospital gown, he suddenly doesn't love the cool breeze so much anymore.

"I know," Sam says, looking straight ahead. She has barely looked at him for a while now. "You said that, and I under-stand."

"It does mean the world to me that you came down here, you know."

"I know."

Spence looks out the passenger window at the hotel and wishes he were inside, curled up on the bed, sleeping off the past twenty-four hours and forgetting them. "I can only tell you I'm sorry so many times before it starts to sound pathetic."

"I don't want you to apologize," she says. "I'm not mad at you. You didn't do anything wrong. You don't owe me any-thing."

"Sure I do."

"Why?" She turns and looks at him, but he's still looking out the other window. "We've never said this is anything more than it is, right? 'One day at a time'? I don't have any right to expect anything else from you. Not now."

She's right, but Spence knows she doesn't really mean it. As casual as they said the relationship was and as easygoing as Sam pretended to be, she wouldn't have driven to Syracuse if that was really the case. And Spence knows he wouldn't feel as guilty as he does right now if she was just a port in the storm. "Yeah, but this was stupid," he says.

"Yes, it was."

"I mean, I wasn't trying to sleep with her or anything like that."

"That doesn't exactly make me feel better, you know?"

Spence wants to look at her, but he keeps looking out the window instead. Syracuse is beautiful this time of year. Any other day, under any other circumstances, he'd be going for a walk in whatever park he could find. He wishes they were in Toronto, walking down Yonge Street together and holding hands. He doubts she'll ever do that with him again.

"For future reference," Sam says after what seems like five minutes but is only about thirty seconds, "people tell women all the time not to take drinks from strangers. You might do well to take the same advice."

"Point taken," Spence says. He turns his head and looks at her. She doesn't look so sad anymore. Her eyes aren't puffy, and she isn't crying. But there's something behind her glasses that makes him feel so guilty and awful. It's not anger. She hasn't raised her voice once. But the disappointed look she gives Spence feels worse than the bruises and scrapes down his face.

"You should probably take a shower," she says. "It'll make you feel better."

"You're probably right," he says and opens the car door. At first, he wonders if Sam is going to stay in her car and drive away the minute he steps out. He breathes a sigh of relief when she gets out of the car and starts to follow him into the hotel.

The breeze runs up his legs, and Spence is suddenly aware of the fact that his bare ass is pretty much exposed to the world. It's another situation he thinks would be comical if not for the fact that he's so depressed and feeling completely ashamed.

"I'm not going to be able to keep doing this," Sam says quietly, a few steps behind him. Spence doesn't look back at her, and he hears her perfectly fine.

"I know," he says. "But I don't know what else to tell you."

"I would never give you an ultimatum."

But you kind of are, Spence thinks.

"I know you wouldn't," he says. He stops walking and turns to look at her. "But I don't know what to tell you, and I don't know what else to do. In a perfect world, I could quit my job and go find another one. But I can't do that."

"I wouldn't ask you to," she says. "This is what you were

doing when I met you. I don't have some right to ask you to change your career for me. It's been a great four months or so, but we're not married. We don't live together. You don't owe me a career change."

Spence wonders who she is trying to convince. "And I don't think you're asking me to make one."

"But I won't do this again." She points to the ground with both of her index fingers. "If this is what you're used to, I hope you know I won't be a part of it."

"You think this is typical for me?"

"I don't know," she says and then catches herself. "No. But I can tell you that it will never be typical for me. I love being with you, and you mean a lot to me. But this isn't a life I can live. And it can only go on for so long."

Spence realizes that she isn't just talking about his drinking habits. Until right this moment, he thought she was upset at him for being poisoned, or for partying too hard, or for Marcy. Right at this moment he realizes that she's talking about all of it. She doesn't like any part of this.

"It's not always like this," Spence says. "I'm just in a slump right now."

"I see that," she says, "but you're not doing any of us a favor if you just keep going through the motions and then trying to take a break from it every four to six weeks and then just jumping back headfirst into it all over again. This is the first time you've gotten drugged and thrown in the hospital. But it's not the first bender you've been on, is it?"

Spence doesn't say anything because she's right. He used to spend his nights writing and trying to come up with new material. Sometimes he'd just sit and watch TV and relax with a glass of wine. Too many nights over the past two years have been about trying to get drunk or laid or both. The fading highlights in his hair and biker boots suddenly make him feel a bit like a desperate old man trying to look half his age and failing.

"This isn't typical," he says again. "And I'm always happy when I'm with you. I hope you know that."

"But I can't be the only thing that makes you happy. Especially not when I hardly ever get to see you."

"I will come visit more often. I'll rearrange my schedule."

"It's not about that," she says. "I'm not interested in being an army wife. But that's not even the worst of it. I'm really not interested in seeing you miserable or watching you let yourself get beaten up. And I'm not talking about your face."

Spence winces. He wonders how bad his face actually looks. He wonders how crazy it must look to people walking through the hotel parking lot or looking out their windows. A woman in glasses is yelling at a beaten man in a hospital gown and black boots. He imagines someone, somewhere is laughing or, at the very least, really curious.

"You need to take a look at how much crap you can take before it's not worth taking anymore," Sam says and reaches over and takes his hand. Her hands are always so soft.

"I think you were right," he says and his throat hurts, "when you said that I have a cubicle I move from city to city. I just feel like I'm in the middle of a rut."

"Well, you're not going to get out of it by just living it and reliving it and waiting for a change. And not with this Rodney guy you keep talking about. Especially not if he keeps ripping you off like you say he is."

Spence grimaces and feels the pain in his face shoot down his neck. He forgot about Rodney. He forgot about Doane College and the overpayment and the lying. He was going to spend today reading Rodney the riot act and trying to get to the bottom of things. Now he's suddenly trying to figure out if he should check himself into a psychiatric clinic.

"You need to figure out what you want, babe," Sam says and lightly gives him a strange, sad smile.

He's never discussed the future with Sam. He's always been afraid to because he didn't want to lose her. Through the past few months, with all he's been through, she's been the one constant in his life that has made him feel a shred of happiness. But the word *love* hasn't really come up, even if it has been danced around a bit. And he doesn't even know if she can even think about getting really serious with him. He doesn't even live in Canada. He doesn't even know if he *can* live in Canada. How can he get serious with Sam if he doesn't even know if it's *legal*? And how long could she possibly put up with him? The fact that she drove through the night to get him out of the hospital baffles him.

"I want to be with you," Spence says. "But I'm not sure how to make that happen just yet."

Sam shrugs her shoulders. "I don't have any answers."

"What do you want?" Spence asks.

"I want you, too," she says. "But I'm not going to wait years to get you. And I don't want the stress of what you deal with. I would never put up with it at my job, and I work at the Gap, for Chrissakes."

Spence laughs, which oddly hurts his face more than when he frowns.

"And I gotta be honest with you, guy, but only because you asked," Sam says. "I want a little honesty and a lot of monogamy."

Spence stops smiling and feels the clean side of his face suddenly getting red. He always wondered if Sam suspected that there were still other women. Realizing she probably knew it all along makes him feel very tiny.

"I haven't been with anyone else," he says. It's true, but he's hardly been a saint.

She looks up at him, narrows her eyes, and starts to speak. Then she stops herself and doesn't say anything else. Instead, she exhales deeply and takes his hand and leads him into the hotel. They walk in the front door and up to the registration desk. Spence is surprised when the hotel clerk doesn't even blink when he steps up to the counter in nothing but his hospital gown.

"Can I help you?" the clerk says as if it's completely natural to see a man covered in bruises standing almost naked in the lobby.

"I was in room two forty-two," Spence says, "but I obviously have misplaced my key." This makes Sam laugh.

"I see," the clerk says. "Do you have any ID?"

"Oddly enough, I do."

Spence reaches into the plastic bag and takes out his driver's license. The clerk looks it up and down, examines the bruise-free man in the photo, and compares it with the beaten slob standing in front of him. After he feels satisfied, he hands Spence back the ID.

"Let me get you another key, sir," the clerk says and begins to program a new plastic key card in front of them. Sam stands a few feet behind Spence, covering his exposed behind from the stares of people walking through the lobby. "And there's a message for you here."

"A message for me?" Spence asks.

"Yes, a woman called and left a message to give to you."

The hairs on the back of Spence's neck stand up as the clerk hands a slip of paper across the counter to him, along with the new key card. The clerk looks over at Sam, back at Spence, and then raises his eyebrow. Spence takes the key card and unfolds the message. He feels his stomach churning as he reads it:

HOPE YOU HAD AS MUCH FUN AS I DID—MARCY

Spence groans as he folds the paper back up and steps away from the front desk. Sam gives him a quizzical look, and he hands her the slip of paper. She rolls her eyes and makes a disgusted look as she balls it up and throws it in a nearby trash can. They don't speak again as they walk across the lobby, into the elevator, and up to Spence's hotel room.

"I'm gonna jump in the shower," Spence says as he tosses his plastic bag of belongings onto the hotel bed. "I think you were right, and it might make me feel better."

"Okay," Sam says, sounding distant again.

"I think maybe I could use a drink." Spence smiles broadly, hoping she will get that he's only joking. She doesn't laugh, but offers a small, forced grin. She walks across the room and looks out the window, into the parking lot. Spence watches her for a second as she stares outside. "You okay?"

"I'm fine," Sam lies, and Spence can easily see it.

"What is it?"

"Did you really not sleep with that woman?"

Spence sighs. "No, I didn't. I wasn't even trying to. I had no idea she was going to drug me."

"Not last night," she says. "Before. At some other point. Did you sleep with this woman and then never call her again or something? Was she a one-night stand you forgot about?"

Spence stands there for a second, thinking of what to say, and finally decides that there is no reason not to go with the truth. After all, she said she wanted honesty.

"I don't know," he says. "I don't think so. But I won't lie to you. I really don't remember."

"Okay," she says and looks back out the window.

"Look, there was a time—"

"You don't owe me an explanation." She raises her hand without turning around to look at him. That's the end of it.

Spence walks into the bathroom, shuts the door, and looks in the mirror. The florescent lights make the bruises and cuts look even worse, and he suddenly wants to cry. Nothing comes, and he just stands there instead, wincing at himself in the mirror and wondering how long it will be before his face heals. He tears off the hospital gown and looks at a body that is five years older than he's been telling everyone for years. He steps into the shower and lets the hot water wash the dirt and dried blood and shame out of his hair.

Forty-two, he thinks to himself. *When did that happen?*

After stepping out of the shower, Spence towels off and thinks of Sam in the next room. He wonders if she has makeup she can put on his face to make it look better. Or maybe younger. He wonders if she realizes how old he is. He wonders if she'll care when she finds out. He doesn't remember if he ever told her or if it has ever come up. He knows she is younger than he is, but doesn't know how much. He wonders if she'll freak out when he tells her, but figures he might as well keep the honesty going now that he's on a roll.

"I guess I should tell you," he says as he steps out of the bathroom, drying his hair with a towel. "I'm almost forty-two years old. There, I said it."

But when he looks out from behind the towel, he sees that Sam isn't there anymore.

16

"I've decided that I'm going to let you be my new agent," he says to Jamie while lying on his hotel bed. He kicked the comforter to the floor, which is usually the first thing he does when he gets into the room. Those things are hardly ever cleaned, and God knows what has been sleeping on them. He is lying on top of the sheets with his head propped up with all six of the pillows he was given.

"Yeah?" he asks. "Does this mean I can quit being an underpaid opening act?"

"Hardly." He laughs. His cell phone feels hot against his face, but he doesn't care. It's nice to hear a familiar voice. For the past ten days, he's felt like the loneliest person on the planet.

"Can I at least buy a car with the extra income?" Jamie asks.

"Not a chance."

"Shit, man. How about a scooter?"

"Now you're thinking," he says and looks around the room. This Holiday Inn in Des Moines is nicer than the Starlight Motel was in Crete, Nebraska, but not much. He likes Best Westerns the most. They always give him plenty of pillows, and the comforters feel clean.

"Why am I making this career change?" Jamie asks and knocks Spence out of his deep thoughts about important things like pillows.

"Think I'm a bit underpaid," Spence says.

"Join the club, my man," Jamie says. "Ain't that part of the gig?"

"It's worse than that," he says. "I think I'm actually paid pretty well. I'm just not seeing it. I think I'm being robbed."

"Really?"

"Yeah."

"What happened?" Jamie asks. Spence tells him the story of the overpayment and how it's quite possible this sort of thing has been going on for a while, maybe even for years.

"Shit," Jamie says. "You really think so?"

"Maybe."

"Damn." Jamie grunts. "I work for Rodney, too, man. You think he's skimming off the top of my cash?"

"What'd you get paid for Toledo?" Spence asks.

"Five hundred."

"Nah, that's standard feature act pay. You're getting scale." Spence switches the phone to his other ear. "He negotiates more for me because I'm a headliner with some TV credits."

"And you think this is typical?"

"I don't know," Spence says. "Maybe not. But if it's happened once, what are the odds it hasn't happened more times that I just don't know about? I've been asking for a raise everywhere, not just my college gigs. What if I got a raise at lots of places he never told me about?"

"So you're still getting paid."

"But the money isn't going up. Or is it?"

Spence starts doing the math in his head and trying to piece together all of the checks that he got from Rodney and not from the venues. It drives him crazy the more he starts adding it up, but he can't help but do it, over and over again. He has spent the past couple of days trying to figure out if all of the clubs he works have any idea how little money they're actually paying him and how much is going to his agent. He thinks of everything he could have bought and the bills that could have been paid.

"How many of your gigs are paid through Rodney?" Jamie asks.

"Most of them. Three quarters."

"God-*DAMN*."

"Yeah." Spence sighs. "Goddamn, indeed. This could be the reason everyone thinks I'm paid so well. I might just be."

"No wonder you're always on tour."

"No wonder everyone thinks I'm such an arrogant ass."

"Me too," Jamie says.

"Get ready for it," Spence says. "Your day is coming."

"For real?"

"Definitely. I was just like you when I started this business. Look at me now."

"Damn," Jamie says, "is that what I have to look forward to?"

"Only if you're lucky. It could be much worse."

"How do you figure?"

"Hell," Spence says, "I've been working nonstop for years. I'm considered a success in this business."

"But you're broke and pissed."

"Now you get it."

"Screw that," Jamie says.

"Screw that, indeed," Spence says. He rolls over onto his side and picks up the bottle of ibuprofen off the nightstand. He's been eating them like candy since waking up in Syracuse with a broken face. As the swelling in his face has gone down and the scratches have started to heal, his consumption of aspirin and any painkillers he can get his hands on has gone up. He chokes back four with a bottle of warm Diet Coke and rubs his forehead a bit.

"Maybe I'll just be a publicist," Jamie says. "No more of this dead-end comedy thing."

"If I thought you were serious, I'd tell you that's a good plan," Spence says. He wonders at what age he became too old for a career change, too old to suddenly go work in an office somewhere.

"I dunno," Jamie says. "I could at least do a little pimping you out. I've still got that demo of you from Toledo. I need to send you that thing. It was tight."

"Thanks," Spence says, "but I don't know what I would do

with it. Don't worry about me. I'm a middle-aged white guy doing stand-up comedy. I'm a dime a dozen. You're a half-black, half-Latino young guy. You're going to be hugely rich and famous. I just wanna be your assistant when it happens."

"True that," Jamie says. There's a pause on the line, and Spence can hear Jamie typing, probably sending an e-mail. The kid is an amazing multitasker, always doing a million things at once. Spence knows that, if he wanted to, Jamie could probably be a great manager or agent. Better than Rodney, for sure.

This thought makes him cringe for a second. He's avoiding the talk with Rodney and has been for almost two weeks. Every day in Syracuse was a chore. Between having to listen to Ashley make fun of his bruises to the nagging fear that Marcy would show up—this time with a gun—he hasn't made firing his agent a priority at all, let alone the top one. Having not spoken with Sam since she walked out of his hotel room that day, he's had other things on his mind.

"The only thing worse than having a shitty agent is not hav-ing one," Spence says and listens as Jamie grunts approval on the other line. That's what it really comes down to in the end. Rodney might not be the best agent in the business, but even a bad one is hard to get. There are plenty of comics who would trade places with Spence to be in his shoes.

Six months, Spence thinks to himself. That's how much work he has on his calendar. That's how many weeks worth of gigs he has lined up. Almost every single one of them is because of Rod-ney. Some money is good; some is not. But the second he fires Rodney, they all cease to exist. He can't afford to lose half a year's work.

"Hey, man," Jamie says, suddenly perked up. He must have finished typing his e-mail. "How're things going with that chick up in Canada?"

"Eh." Spence shrugs and feels his stomach hurt. "Don't ask."

"What? Damn, man, you'd better not tell me that ain't hap-pening anymore. Not after you kept me from getting laid in Toledo."

"It's a long story," Spence says and looks at his face in the hotel mirror. It's still healing, but the remnants of his battered face still linger. He wonders if it's been long enough for him to call or text message Sam. He wonders if she's forgiven him enough to at least speak with him.

"What kind of story is it?" Jamie asks. "Comedy or tragedy?"

"Heh," Spence says. "It's always the same story, pal. A little of both."

The phone on the nightstand rings, and it scares him half to death. It's a loud ring, reminding him of a phone his parents had in the mid-eighties. That was probably the last time the phones in this hotel were replaced. He's almost surprised it isn't a rotary dial.

"Hold on," he tells Jamie and, with his other hand, picks up the hotel phone. "Yeah?"

"Hey, Spence, this is Dustin, down at the club?" The voice on the other end sounds a little high-pitched for a man who is probably in his mid-forties. "You all checked in and ready for tonight?"

"All is well," Spence says to Dustin. A stocky guy, going bald but denying it, Dustin looks more like a trucker than a club owner. He's fond of denim shirts and dipping tobacco.

"Well, great," Dustin says. "Uh, listen, you know all about the charity tonight, right?"

"No, I do not."

"Oh, well, there's this charity function at the club tonight. The local Jaycees."

"Okay."

"Well, I just need you to dress real nice tonight, okay?"

"I always do."

"No, I mean *real* nice," Dustin says, "like in a suit. They really want the comedian dressed to the nines."

"I don't have a suit," Spence says. "I never wear one onstage. I don't even have one with me."

"Oh, that's a problem."

"Why? I'll wear a nice shirt and a blazer like I always do. Is that not nice enough?"

"Not this time," Dustin says. "I'm really going to need you to wear a suit."

Every so often, a ridiculous request like this comes from a club owner somewhere. Some guy has a ridiculous longing for the days of the supper clubs and thinks that comedians look official if they're dressed like The Rat Pack onstage. Spence thinks it's ridiculous, especially when you consider that most comedy clubs put up fake brick walls behind the stage and try to make the place look like it's a basement in New York City. Why would a guy in a three-piece suit be telling dirty jokes to drunks in the first place? Spence has overdressed before, and he remembers how ridiculous he looked doing it.

"Look," he says, "I don't even own a suit. If I'm dressed semi-casual and I'm funny, isn't that all that matters?"

"Not if you want to get paid."

Spence is about three seconds from losing his temper before he realizes that Jamie is still on hold. This isn't a fight he needs to be having, and this isn't the time to be having it. He's not going to win anyway and will only get himself fired before the show starts. He hopes Jamie is listening and getting an earful.

"What do you need me to do?" he asks Dustin.

"Whatever you got to do," Dustin says.

"A full suit?" Spence says. "Not just a jacket and tie?"

"Nope. This is a real nice function."

Go to hell, Spence thinks.

"Then I guess I've got to go shopping," he says.

"There's a Men's Wearhouse about five minutes from the hotel," Dustin says before he hangs up the phone.

Spence curses a few times before putting his cell phone back to his ear. "Sorry about that," he says to Jamie.

"What was that all about?" he asks. Spence tells him the situation.

"Damn," Jamie says. "Since when do comedians have a dress code?"

"Good question," he says. "I got into this business so I wouldn't have to wear a suit anymore."

"True that. What are you going to do?"

"I guess I'm off to buy a suit."

"Aw, man. That ain't so bad. Get some total pimp-daddy suit that will help you pick up a new chick and forget the Canadian who went and broke your heart."

"Thanks, Mister Glass-Is-Half-Full," he says.

"Damn straight."

He says good-bye to Jamie and hangs up the phone. Still lying on the bed, he feels a creepy feeling crawl over him and wishes he could just turn off the nightstand lamp and take a nap. He wishes he could sleep away the annoyance of having to go out and buy a suit.

There are worse things to have to go and buy, you know, he could hear Sam saying. He wishes her voice in his head could make him feel better. Jamie is right, and it won't kill him to own a new suit. But it's not like he has money to toss around on something he'll barely wear. He looks down at his worn-out shoes and is reminded of that very fact.

He gets up off the bed and starts collecting his things, looking around for his car keys. Before he gets to the door, his cell phone vibrates in his pocket, and he hopes that it's somehow Dustin calling to tell him to forget the suit. When he looks at his phone, there's no such luck: It's Beth.

"Yeah?" he says as he answers the phone.

"Nice to hear you too, grumpy," Beth says.

"I'm just annoyed and in the middle of something is all," he says. "What's up?"

"Everything okay?"

I've been robbed, beaten up, drugged, and dumped, Spence thinks.

"Just the usual stuff," he says.

"Alright," Beth says. "Well, if you wanna talk about it, let me know."

"Thanks, Dr. Freud," he says. "I'll be okay. But I do have to run out the door. So what's up?"

"Oh." Beth sounds quieter than usual. "Nothing, really. Was just wondering if you're coming through town like we talked about?"

We did? he thinks. It takes him a minute to realize that it's been weeks since he spoke with her. He got so caught up in his own soap opera that he forgot all about it. Slowly, the memory starts coming back to him.

He was always bad about it, forgetting conversations with Beth or putting them aside. Even though the split was amicable, and they got along pretty well even when the divorce went through, he never really got over the sting of it. He knows that now as much as he did then. Even though he wasn't happy, he wasn't that ready to call it off, either. Maybe it was comfort, familiarity, or just routine. But he'd gotten very used to Beth, even when things were rough. When she served him with the divorce papers, it felt like a gunshot. Right after that, he started doing everything he could to put her out of his head and at arm's length. That's how Evan made things easier for him. The sting of the loss was made easier when it was replaced with his distaste of the new guy in his home.

"I forgot about that," Spence says to Beth, being completely honest. "I've been dealing with some . . . other things. I don't know if I'm coming through there or not. I might, but I'm booked for another few weeks first."

"Oh, okay," Beth says, again talking slower than usual. Spence wonders if she's like Jamie and multitasking while talking to him. "Well, it would be cool if you could, alright?"

"Could what? Stop by?"

"Yeah."

"You want me to come over to the condo?"

"Yeah."

Spence feels the hairs on the back of his neck and wonders what he's setting himself up for. There is not good news coming, and he knows it. He spent enough years with Beth to read the sound of her voice, and this tone never ends with him laughing or getting a deposit in his bank account. If he had a dog, this is when she'd be telling him it was dead.

"What's going on here?" he asks.

"Nothing," Beth says.

"Don't give me that. What's going on? What aren't you telling me?"

There's a long pause, and Beth lets out a long sigh. "Evan moved out," she says at last.

"Really," Spence says. It's not a question. For a second, he wants to ask her if she's just messing with him. It hasn't even been that long since he saw them together, happy, having steaks on the grill. Everything seemed so perfect. When the hell did this happen? "I'm sorry to hear that," he says after a few seconds and realizes that he means it.

"Anyway," Beth says, "I just think maybe we could talk, you know? Maybe you could come by and we could figure things out."

"Figure what out?"

"I don't know. Things."

"What things? My mail?"

"No, not your mail." Beth snaps, and for a second, he hears the old her in her voice again. "I mean 'things.' You and me. Things like that."

"You and me?"

"Yeah, us."

The hairs on his neck stand up a little more, and now he's completely thrown off-balance. It has been years since Beth said anything about "us" to him, and it instantly becomes six years earlier. Everything fades away around him, and he suddenly feels as if a day hasn't gone by since he last spoke with her, lived with her, and had a conversation just like this one.

"I don't know," he says.

"I know you don't," Beth says. "Neither do I. That's why maybe we could talk, you know?"

The last time they spoke this way, Beth was talking about a trial separation that ended in a divorce and her marriage to some new friend she had been hanging out with. Now she's speaking that way to him again, and it's essentially about pressing "reverse" on the past six years. She's talking like she wants to do to Evan what she used Evan to do to him. Spence doesn't realize that the two of them are sitting in silence on the phone together for at least two minutes until Beth's voice startles him back to reality.

"Are you there?"

"I'm here," he answers. "I just don't think this is what you really want."

"I'm not sure yet. But I'm willing to try."

"But what about Evan?"

"What about him?" she says flatly. "You had to feel the tension when you were here. You had to know why."

"I didn't." Spence shrugs. "And I don't. Why would there be tension?"

"Why do you think?"

Pregnancy, bankruptcy, an affair with another woman, a secret meth lab, he thinks.

"I don't have a clue," he says.

Beth sighs. "Because of you."

"Me?"

"Yes, you. Evan said I've never really gotten over you. That you're this cloud always hanging over us."

Spence sits down on the edge of the hotel bed. This floors him. He's never gotten any vibe from Evan other than an air of superiority. If anything, he's always felt as if Evan treats Beth like a trophy he won in a battle against Spence. He certainly never got the feeling that Evan was insecure about how Beth feels toward him.

"Is that true?" he asks and scratches the back of his neck. His face suddenly hurts again.

"I don't know," Beth almost whispers. "Maybe. That's why I wanted you to maybe come here and talk. Maybe see how we feel."

"I have to be honest, this hits me out of left field."

She snorts. "You and me both."

Spence exhales deeply and rubs his temples with his right hand while holding the phone in his left. This was the furthest thing from his mind, but that doesn't mean he's not mulling it over. It's not that he's ever pined for Beth in the years since they split up. He hasn't sat around hating her guts, either. The biggest problem they've had over the past several years has been Evan.

"Just think about it?" she asks.

"Think about . . . ?"

"Just coming for a visit," she says. "A talk."

"I'll think about it," he says. He will at some point, but he wants to just shake it off and pretend the conversation never happened. He imagines that Beth is lonely. Maybe this doesn't really mean anything, and she'll move on to another Evan within the next month or two. After all, there was a man in her life before Spence came along, too.

Seconds later, he's off the phone and sitting in the hotel room, wondering what the hell just happened. Evan is gone, and Beth is apparently hoping to go back in time. Looking for some familiarity. A year after the divorce, he'd have easily taken her back as if nothing had happened. Six months after that, he would have probably gone back to her just to have his favorite recliner. Now, six years and about four hundred thousand miles later, he wonders if he'd be better off in that hospital bed dealing with alcohol poisoning.

And then there's Sam.

He wonders if Sam is going to speak to him again, let alone forgive him and take him back. Having not spoken to her in almost two weeks, he's not too optimistic. He deliberately hasn't tried to contact her, figuring she wanted to be left alone to either think things through or just plain move on. Every once in a while he wonders if Sam is just waiting for him to make the next move. At the very least, he knows what to expect from Beth, not that it makes him feel any better.

You're almost forty-two years old, he hears the voice of that old nurse ringing in his head. He wonders if she's right and he's too old to be living this way. The tips of his hair, still slightly frosted, hang into his eyes, and he wonders if they're going to go gray before too long.

He feels that mood hit him again, and he wants to wrap up in the filthy hotel comforter and sleep away the rest of the day.

He'd sleep right through the show, wake up tomorrow, and hopefully all of this would be behind him. Instead, he knows that he has to go find a suit and do so without bankrupting himself.

Maybe dressing in a suit would actually look good on a guy my age, Spence thinks to himself and, for the first time in at least a week, he genuinely makes himself smile. Somehow this thought gives him enough motivation to get in his car. Before he does, he looks down at his phone for a text message from Sam, even though it's not there. Feeling that pang in his stomach return, he texts her anyway:

I MISS YOU.

17

Several fitting rooms and a few hours later, he walks into the Comedy Café in Des Moines wearing a very stylish black suit, fresh blue shirt, and a bright blue tie. It all seems a bit silly considering his casual black boots, but he had to draw the line somewhere. It seems even sillier when thinking that he's about to walk onstage and talk about animals screwing while dressed like a maître d'. Why people think a comedian's attire matters is lost on him, but he does like to get paid.

He walks into the club and notices that the place is, indeed, packed for some local fund-raiser. He can't tell what the charity is, though. There are signs posted everywhere, but he's too busy noticing the people in the audience. Not only is no one else in a suit, no one is even wearing a tie. In fact, he's probably never seen such a lazy-looking group of people in one place in a long time. The double takes from the waitresses let him know how obviously out of place he looks.

"Whoa!" A familiar, high-pitched voice comes from behind the bar. Dustin is standing there with a bartender, pouring drinks and laughing. "Look at Mister Fancy Pants!"

"You dressed up for comedy or for a funeral?" the bartender says. A kid barely in his twenties and looking like he has had his fair share of crystal meth, he claps his skinny hands together every time he finishes speaking.

"Hell, I should have you seating people before you go onstage!" Dustin says, and his bartender laughs.

"I told you he'd fall for it!" the bartender says and extends his right hand forward for a high five. Dustin is more than happy to oblige, and the two of them giggle like hyenas.

"Shit, I thought for sure he wouldn't give in," Dustin says.

Spence loosens his tie while Dustin and the bartender laugh. This is not the first time he has seen this prank pulled, but it is the first time it has been pulled on him. It's normally done to new comics by headliners. It's considered a sort of initiation into the business to have your chops busted a little. It rarely involves forcing the comic to go out and buy an entire suit. Now he's out three hundred bucks. He thinks about how nice it would be to wear the suit to Dustin's funeral.

"Ha," he says flatly, "you got me. Ha."

Dustin laughs. "Shit, I should tell that to all the comics. I think it'd be nice to have y'all dressed that good."

"So I take it this isn't the Jaycees," Spence says.

"Nope," Dustin says. "Some bowling league or something."

"Hilarious," Spence lies.

"Yeah, I thought so," Dustin says.

"Do you have any idea how much money this cost me?"

"Hope you saved the receipts."

"I'm wearing it," Spence says. "I can't return it now."

"You shoulda tucked the tags in." The bartender laughs and high-fives Dustin again.

"You should reimburse me," Spence says to Dustin and ignores the bartender.

"Good luck with that," Dustin says and gives a long, shit-eating grin to the bartender. They laugh another time, keeping the joke alive way longer than it deserves. With one last snort of his nose, Dustin pats the bartender on the shoulder and walks back into his office.

Spence stands there and counts to ten before loosening his tie and following Dustin back behind the bar. In his office, Dustin sits down at his cluttered desk. All comedy club owners seem to have cluttered desks. Spence wonders why more of them don't have desks that look like the one Emma Simpson has in Nebraska. He thinks about how nicely arranged her computer cables were. If he had them right now, he'd strangle Dustin with them.

"Look on the bright side," Dustin says and reaches into his back pocket for a round can of Skoal. "At least you got a new suit, right?"

"Sure," Spence says and sits in front of the desk.

"Hey, what happened to your face?" Dustin says, finally noticing the healing scrapes and bruises.

"An accident in the changing room," Spence says.

"Really?"

Spence stares straight ahead at Dustin, who doesn't get the remark. After a second, he stops trying to understand it and just shakes his head. Then he thumps his index finger several times across the can of Skoal. "Listen," Dustin says, "I need you to keep the show clean tonight, okay?"

"Just like you needed me to wear a suit."

"I'm serious." Dustin puts a wad of tobacco under his bottom lip and stares straight ahead. "These people are good customers. This bowling group. I don't need nobody getting pissed off. We always try to keep it clean for them."

"No one told me this before."

"I'm telling you now," Dustin says and spits into a plastic cup he has sitting on the desk. Inside that cup is probably three inches of tobacco spit. It probably hasn't been emptied all day, maybe all week.

"I've never really been a clean comic," Spence says. He has plenty of clean material. He has written a ton of new stuff in the past month. Doing a clean show really wouldn't be hard for him at this point, but he's wearing a suit he didn't even want to buy.

"Well, I need you to be a clean comic tonight, whether you're used to it or not," Dustin says.

"Kind of short notice, don't you think?"

"A good comedian should be able to work clean or dirty, depending on what he's told to do," Dustin says.

"I always hear club owners say that," Spence says, "but never comedians."

"It's true." Dustin spits again.

"How long have you been a comedian?" Spence asks. He knows he should just let it go, but the pricey tie around his neck just makes him angrier.

"Just keep it clean," Dustin says. "Do someone else's routine if you don't have clean jokes of your own. I don't give a shit. But I don't want any complaints. It's that simple."

"Sure. It's easy."

"You can say 'damn,' you can say 'ass' or whatever. No f-bombs," Dustin says. Somewhere over the past few years, people in the business started referring to the word *fuck* as an *f-bomb*. All other words are simply called what they are, but the word *fuck* gets a special name for it, even offstage. Spence has always hated this and thinks it's childish. This doesn't help his temper a single bit.

"No f-bombs," he says to Dustin.

"Alrighty," Dustin says, "guess that's about it. Don't make fun of bowlers, I guess."

"Sure. Do I get free food?"

"Yeah," Dustin says and hands him a laminated sheet of paper. "You can order off the kids' menu. Everything else is full price."

"The kids' menu? Really?"

"Used to give a full comp on everything, but too many comedians abused it," Dustin says. "Ordering filet minon and halibut and whatever else."

"Okay," Spence says, "but can I just have a discount, then? Gimme whatever money you discount on the kids stuff and let me apply it to something on the regular menu."

"Do you want the chicken nuggets or not?" Dustin says and spits into the cup.

A half hour later, Spence stands backstage, listening to the host tell a few jokes before bringing him to the stage. The middle act just got done and did just fine with plenty of jokes that weren't very clean. No one seemed to mind. In fact, they seemed to enjoy it. These are bowlers, not a prayer group. They'd be happy with a dirty show.

Get over yourself, Spence, he thinks, *and just do what you were told.*

He has plenty of new material now. He knows he can go on-stage and do a clean show. This is no big deal for him. It's the perfect time to try his newest bits. He can be that comedian he watched on TV when he was a kid—that comedian who always wore a shirt and tie and told clever jokes that were considered PG-rated at worst. It's not that hard. He'll be just fine.

He looks down and notices that he's already starting to get sweat on his new suit. His pocket vibrates, and he pulls out his phone, hoping for a little encouragement from Sam, something to make him feel better before he does his monkey dance. Instead, it's a text message from Beth:

Hey, give me a call when you can, will you?

Cripes, he thinks, *like I don't have enough shit to think about.*

"Ladies and gentlemen"—the host onstage raises his voice—"are you ready for your headliner?"

The crowd applauds vigorously, and Spence waits for the sound of his name being called. When it is, he bounces out on-stage with the biggest smile he's ever had. He shakes hands with the host and takes the microphone. It doesn't matter what he's wearing. It doesn't matter what he had for dinner. All that matters now is that he is exactly where he loves to be. He is in charge, ready to take the audience where he wants to take them. They will go because they will love him. They will be his friends; they always are. They trust him because this is what he does.

"Hello, hello, hello," he says as the applause dies down and the crowd hangs on his opening words. "It is really fucking amazing to be here with all of you fuckers!"

He sits alone at the bar, waiting for Dustin to finish counting up all the money, finishing up his paperwork, masturbating, or whatever the hell he has been doing for almost two hours. The club is empty; everyone has gone home, including the staff. The bartender has gone somewhere to probably smoke meth.

Happy to be by himself, Spence sits in the dark with only the neon beer signs at the bar to keep him company. Sipping on a glass of whiskey, there's a very nice calmness to the empty club and the sound of nothing but neon humming in the air. His head still buzzes from the sounds of the night: laughter, applause, cheering. But, if he just concentrates on his glass of booze and the silence around him, it relaxes him just enough. He feels his phone vibrate and pulls it out of the pocket of his sweat-soaked, three-hundred-dollar suit. Everything around him stops when he realizes that it's a text message from Sam. He almost doesn't want to read it. If she hates his guts, it will ruin an otherwise great night. And maybe the rest of his year.

I MISS YOU, TOO.

He smiles. He hopes this means forgiveness and is not essentially another good-bye. Plenty of women missed him and still never spoke to him again. One girl apparently missed him enough to poison his drink.

"Yo," Dustin calls from inside his office.

Spence knows he killed tonight. He did it by doing the same act he's done a million times before in front of a million different audiences. If he wanted to offend them, they weren't buying it. If they weren't interested in hearing his dick jokes, their laughter betrayed them.

So much for the audience wanting a clean show, he thinks.

Spence puts his phone his pocket and walks into the office. He closes the door behind him, even though he and Dustin are the only two people left in the building. He knows that Dustin is pissed. That's the only reason he has been kept waiting for so long. He prepares himself for whatever is going to be thrown his way but promises himself not to lose his temper.

Just smile and nod, he tells himself, *and let Rodney earn his pay.*

Dustin counts a stack of bills in his hand. Then he counts it again. He whispers numbers out loud while he does it. Other than this, he doesn't say anything and he doesn't make eye contact at all.

"Here you go." He takes a stack of bills and puts them in his shirt pocket. Then he takes another stack of bills, paper clips them together, and tosses the wad across the desk. "Count it."

Spence picks up the bills and does a quick count.

"This is only half," he says.

"Right," Dustin says.

"And the other half?" Spence asks.

"I told you not to be dirty."

"You also told me I had to wear a suit."

"That was a joke," Dustin says.

"Sorry," Spence says, "I guess I just thought you were joking again when you told me not to be dirty."

Dustin picks up his Skoal can, thumps on it with his index finger, and says, "You know I wasn't joking."

"Seemed like it to me."

"I said no f-bombs."

"The audience loved the show," Spence says. "That's all that matters. It was a great set."

"That's beside the point. I told you to keep it clean," Dustin says.

"The point is to make the audience happy."

"The point is to do what I tell you."

"I'm not your dishwasher or your bartender," Spence says, and he sees Dustin's eyebrows furrow.

"No, but you're still my employee for the night, and you do what you're told."

"And the other comics?"

"What about them?"

"They weren't any cleaner than I was."

Dustin scoffs. "Don't worry about them. I'm talking to you. You're the headliner, and you should know better."

Spence takes a deep breath before speaking. "The audience liked what they got."

"A good comedian can do that and still be clean."

"With all due respect," Spence says, "how the hell would you know?"

Dustin sits there and finally makes eye contact. He glares over his dirty saliva-filled cup as he spits another mouthful of tobacco juice into it. Then he sets the cup back down on the desk and exhales. A full thirty seconds goes by with neither of them speaking. Dustin drums his fingers on the desk as if he's about to make a big proclamation and can't quite come out with it.

"We're done here," Dustin says finally.

"Pay me the other half," Spence says.

"You broke the rules. That's how it works."

"No, it's not. I did my job."

"And you're getting paid what I decide you deserve." Dustin spits.

"We have a contract."

"Tell Rodney about it."

"To hell with Rodney," Spence says. "You're going to pay me my money."

"Good luck with that."

It all happens so fast that Dustin has no hope of defending himself. It's not the force of the attack so much as the surprise. An entire body flies across the desk, hands reaching and feet kicking. Dustin is knocked out of his chair and to the floor so fast that he swallows the wad of tobacco that was in the cup.

Spence grabs Dustin by the shirt and hoists him up off the ground. He wants so much to punch Dustin in the face, to take his foot and bring it up as swiftly and as hard as possible into Dustin's crotch. Instead, he grabs him around the throat and pushes him hard against the filing cabinet. Still gagging from swallowing his tobacco, Dustin only gets up as far as his knees, flailing his arms around, trying to make contact.

"Gimme my money, asshole." Spence growls and slaps Dustin's hands down as if he's playing with a doll. He reaches into Dustin's shirt pocket and digs. He hits pay dirt and takes the wad of bills and stuffs them into the pocket of his new suit. He should just let Dustin go right here where he's got him. Instead he squeezes harder for just a second longer and shoves him back against the filing cabinet again. "How does it feel?" he screams into Dustin's ear as he tightens the grip around his neck. "You feel in charge now, asshole?"

After a few more seconds, he releases Dustin and backs away. Dustin drops to his knees and fumbles around on the floor, gasping for air and still choking on tobacco spit.

"Not so tough without your bartender here, are you?" Spence says, and starts to walk out of the office. "You shouldn't have waited so long to pay me. You might've had someone here to back you up."

"You son of a bitch," Dustin yells after him. "You're dead! You hear me? You're dead!"

Spence turns and looks back at Dustin. He straightens his tie and catches his breath. He'd probably laugh at the sight of himself if he weren't so angry. Dusting himself off like he's getting ready for a boardroom meeting.

"I'm going to ruin you, cocksucker!" Dustin yells, sliding around on papers that fell off the desk. If it had been as clean as Emma's desk, he would have been on his feet already. "You're finished!"

"Who the hell are you?" Spence says, even surprised himself at how calm he sounds. Dustin pulls back and almost falls down again as Spence steps toward him. "You're some nobody who took out a loan and opened a bar. You're nothing. You're not a comic. You're not even a good comedy club manager."

He lunges forward again with his fist cocked back, but stops short. Dustin flinches and puts his hands up in front of his face.

"Pussy," Spence says. He reaches down on the desk, takes the cup full of tobacco juice, and throws it across the room. It covers Dustin, running down his face and the top of his shirt. The sweet smell of spit and spearmint fills the room. Dustin curses in a voice even higher than his usual one and almost gags from the filth covering him.

"Son of a—" Dustin says as several days' worth of spit and old tobacco drips down his neck and chest.

"When you go trying to ruin me," Spence says, "remember what a little bitch you were just now. Make sure you don't leave that part out."

He knocks over a chair on his way out of the office and slams the door so hard it sounds as if it might come off the hinges. He's out the door and in his car seconds later. He half expects Dustin to come running outside with a shotgun. He doesn't wait to see what happens next. He peels out of the parking lot and drives as fast as he can in whatever direction he was pointed when he started the car. He doesn't even know if he's going toward his hotel. He's not looking at the road so much as looking at the distant horizon ahead.

The car accelerates, and he rolls down his windows. The breeze feels cold for this time of year. He likes it. He just keeps driving and puts his foot harder on the pedal. He's doing sixty, then seventy, then eighty. The car keeps going faster, the wind blowing up the sleeve of his new suit. He listens for sirens that never come. He looks for lights from other cars, but he's the only person on this stretch. He's going faster. How many miles has he gone?

Faster now, barreling into the darkness and down this long country road. He feels the wheel vibrate and the road coming up through the car and into the gas pedal. He can feel the asphalt underneath his shoe as if he is running and not just pushing the pedal to the floor. He punches the steering wheel once, then again. Then he punches the roof above his head. Then the wheel again. He wants to scream and curse, but instead just glares silently at the road ahead of him. The darkness gets lighter as he accelerates.

Up ahead, he sees lights coming from a tiny gas station. He's doing over ninety now. His car is just a ball of light that comes barreling up to a Shell station in the middle of the night. He doesn't brake; he just takes his foot off the gas pedal and listens to the engine get quiet as the car slows down. He steers into the parking lot faster than he should and looks around. No one is there; the station is closed. He opens the door to the car and steps out. The air isn't as cool now, and he can feel sweat soaking through the back of his shirt. He stands in the tiny parking lot and looks back down the country road he was just on. How far did he drive?

His heart is racing. The thumping in his chest is so loud it's the only thing he can hear. He takes several deep breaths and waits for the pounding in his ears to settle down. Across the street is a big open field. He looks both ways, even though he's the only person around for miles. There is nothing but darkness and the after-hours lights coming from the Shell station.

What just happened? he thinks. *What did I just do?*

Silence. The only thing he hears is the sound of his car beeping to let him know the driver door is open. He hears it less the farther he walks into the big field. It's nothing but grass. This is Iowa. There should be corn.

What do they grow here if there's nothing but grass? he thinks. He looks around but still can't see any corn.

He reaches into his pocket and takes out his money. He didn't rob Dustin; he only took what he was owed. He reaches into his other pocket and takes out his cell phone. He never responded to Sam's text message. He doesn't know if she has forgiven him. He doesn't know if she'll even answer or if she'll be angry when she does.

"Hello?" Sam answers the phone, sounding as if she's been sleeping.

"Did I wake you?" he asks. He hates it when he wakes her.

"No," she says. He hopes she's not lying. "No, I was just reading."

"I hope you don't mind me calling."

"No," she says quietly, then clears her throat. "No, I wanted you to."

"I'm glad you're there," he says. Then, after a second, "I mean, I wish you were here. But I'm glad you're there when I call. Do you know what I mean?"

She actually chuckles slightly, and he can hear her smile a little bit through the phone.

"Yeah, I know. Did you have a show tonight?"

"Yeah, I did. That's why I'm calling so late. I'm sorry."

"It's okay," she says. "Was it good?"

"It really was, yeah," he says. He can still feel his heart thumping in his chest. It's getting slower now. Everything is clearing up, and the pounding in his head isn't hurting as much. The cell phone is rubbing against the leftover scrapes on his face, but he doesn't feel them. He feels oddly warm and comfortable. He wonders if it's the suit that brings it out of him.

"You still there?" she says, and he realizes that he's just been breathing heavily into the phone like a pervert.

"I screwed up tonight," he says.

"What do you mean?" she asks.

"The job," he says. "I think I really did it this time. I think I really . . . I really did it this time."

"What happened?" she asks. He imagines her sitting up on her bed, dropping her book to her side, and wondering if he's back in the hospital or—worse—in jail. "Is everything alright? Are you okay?"

"What?" he asks and looks around. His car door is ajar. The beeping sound drones on in the night.

"Are you okay?" she asks, her voice quieter than before.

He stands there for a minute and looks around. No lights; no other sounds. He's breathing okay now. His heart feels steady. Sam is listening.

He smiles.

"Yeah," he says. "Yeah, I feel great."

18

The air is cool in Toronto. Spence likes that about this city more than anything. He sweats easily and has always hated summer for that reason. This time last year he was in Arkansas and thought he was going to drown. Sitting in Sam's apartment with the window open, he is pleased with how nice it feels to just sit and let the wind hit him. It was worth the fourteen-hour drive from Iowa to get here.

Sitting on a barstool with his feet propped up on the window ledge, he hears a familiar buzzing noise and knows it's his cell phone vibrating on the end table next to the sofa. Sam is sitting there reading another chick lit novel. She doesn't look up but raises one eyebrow when the phone goes off. He's been ignoring it for the past couple of days because he knows who is calling. He has no interest in listening to Rodney scream at him. He hasn't even listened to any of his voice messages.

"That's five times today," Sam says without looking up.

"Yep," he says.

"He might be worried about you," she says. He looks at her and raises his eyebrows. "Probably not," she concedes.

He drove straight through the night, thinking about what he would say when Rodney called. The first call came mid-Sunday afternoon when he was trying to sleep off the drive. He thought he would eventually regret what he did in Iowa, but the regret never came. Over the next twenty-four hours, he simply let it ring every time that familiar number popped up on the screen.

He's been too content just being with Sam to bother with Rodney. He still has no idea what he wants to say, but he picks up the phone anyway.

"Here goes nothing," he says to Sam, who closes her book and gets up off the sofa. With a quick kiss to the cheek, she leaves the room. It's for the best. She has never met Rodney but already hates him. Besides Spence's onstage performance, she hasn't seen much about the business that she has ever found appealing. And that was before the Syracuse hospital debacle even happened.

"What?" Spence says as he puts the phone to his ear. He thinks that Rodney is going to scream at him the second he gets the chance, but he's surprised at how quiet Rodney is when he finally speaks.

"There you are," Rodney says. "Jesus, I've been trying to reach you for the past two days."

"I know," Spence says. "I was avoiding you."

"For God's sake," Rodney says, "I was worried. For all I knew you were wrapped around a telephone pole in Idaho."

"Iowa."

"Wherever," Rodney says. "I didn't know if you were dead or alive. You could've eaten a shotgun for all I knew, you idiot. I'm sitting here wondering if I should call a morgue or something."

"I'm fine."

"Christ, what the hell happened?" Rodney says.

"What did you hear?"

"I heard you're lucky you didn't get your ass kicked."

"You heard wrong," Spence says, "but I figured that's how he'd spin it."

"So what the hell happened?"

Spence sighs. In the past couple of days he has managed to calm down. He's even managed to enjoy himself doing absolutely nothing but just being with Sam. It's been a good couple of days of watching TV, making love, and not thinking about Rodney or Dustin or hotels or nightclubs. He knew he'd have to talk about it eventually. Now he's instantly just as annoyed as he was when he left.

"He tried to take half my money," Spence says, "so I took it back. It's that simple."

"Simple?" Rodney says. "Jesus, you are out of your mind. You're lucky you got out of town in one piece. You're probably lucky to be alive."

"I highly doubt that," Spence says. "When I left him, he was crying like a baby on the floor of his office."

"That's not the way I heard it."

"Yeah?" He looks around the corner. Sam is pretending not to listen, but he highly doubts that she has been reading the same page this entire time. She's tapping her foot nervously while lying on the bed. He's never noticed her doing that before. "Well, I got my money, so I don't know what you heard. Seems unlikely that he'd beat me up and then pay me for it."

"That's not the point," Rodney says. "You screwed this one up good. He's on a warpath. Guy wants your head on a platter."

"Tell him he can have my ass on his lips," Spence says and smiles. Big.

"Stop screwing around. I'm serious."

"You seem to think I'm kidding," Spence says. "I'm through with this crap, Rodney. I'm not going to have these idiot club managers throwing their weight around with me and thinking they aren't going to get taken down a few pegs for it. That guy got exactly what he deserved. I could not care less about him. To hell with him and his club. You got that?"

"Say what you want," Rodney says, "but that's yet another club you can't work. And you know he's got friends, genius. What do you think is going to happen when he tells other club owners about you?"

"I don't want to work for them, either," Spence says. "I really don't care."

"Well, you should care," Rodney says. "How do you expect to make a living as a stand-up comic when you can't get work in comedy clubs? Huh? You aren't cute or clean enough to do cruise ships, and I can't think of how you could possibly do corporate work."

Rodney is right about that one. Corporate comics are squeaky clean. Way more than the guys on *The Tonight Show* or *Letterman*. They make a ton of money, usually six figures per year. But to do corporate comedy, a guy has to be both clean and lovable. It's real cheerleader stuff, and Spence knows he would never make it. He has no interest in it anyway. At least on cruise ships he could get a tan.

"Like I said, to hell with Dustin," Spence says. "The guy is strictly C-list at best. Give me a break. He's not booking the Improv. We're talking about a C-room in godforsaken Iowa. I put him on his ass, and I'm glad I did it. He needed to be humbled."

"Are you out of your mind?" Rodney asks. "You wanna talk about pots and kettles? You've got the biggest goddamned ego I've ever seen! Only person who needs to be taken down a few pegs is you!"

"Oh, please," Spence says, "I'm sick of hearing that nonsense. Last I checked, the audiences don't come out to see Dustin and they don't come out to see Rodney. I'm sick of pretending like what I do is no big deal. You walk on that stage and do what I do every night, you can scream to me about how I need to act all humble and modest. Until then, let's just remember that there's no comedy business without comedians."

"And there are plenty of you," Rodney says without even pausing. "I've got dozens besides you that pay me, you know that?"

"That doesn't have a thing to do with me, and you know it."

"Not everything is about you."

Spence fakes a laugh. "Then who is it about, Rodney? Who is my career about if not me? If I don't put me first, who will? You?"

"I do that all the time."

"Oh, please, Rodney, you have never put me above one of those clubs. Not once. Not ever. If it comes down to the club versus me, you side with the clubs every single time."

"The clubs are usually right."

"Aren't you paid to fix this?" Spence ignores Rodney and keeps going. "I know I don't pay you to just set up these low-rent gigs. For Chrissakes, Rodney, do something other than mark my name in a calendar and then collect the checks."

"Screw you," Rodney says. He sounds angry now. "Those checks I get for booking you aren't nearly as nice as you think they are."

"Yeah?" Spence says, setting up the punch. "The check from Doane College was pretty nice, if you ask me."

"What?" Rodney says, oblivious. "You think that twenty percent from your college gig pays my rent, genius?"

"Seven hundred dollars," Spence says. There's a silence on the other end of the phone for about ten seconds. "Yeah. I know, Rodney. I know that you were going to make seven hundred bucks on that gig. The school made the full check out to me."

"What are you talking about?" Rodney dances around it but knows he's caught.

"You lied to me," Spence says. He is calm again, mostly because he's right where he wants to be. He's been thinking about this conversation for two days and finally has it right where he dreamed it would be. "You got greedy, and you lied to me. You told me they didn't agree to pay me twelve hundred. All the while you got the pay up to fifteen hundred so you could keep almost half."

"That's not how it happened."

"Oh, please," Spence says. "How long have you been lying to me, Rodney? Huh? How long have you been ripping me off?"

"Ripping you off?" Rodney says. "I work for my money, Mister Ungrateful. You've been working for years because of me."

Spence remembers the day he met Rodney. How exciting it was to have an agent who wanted to sign him onto his roster. There were so many promises. He was going to be on TV more, Rodney said. He was going to get some serious auditions, Rodney said. There would be movie offers and television sitcom pilots, Rodney said. He shook Rodney's hand and didn't look back. The future was bright, and he looked forward to years of fancy clubs and four-star hotels. A couple of years later he was performing in the backroom cafeteria of a Days Inn in West Virginia.

"Yeah," he says, "and look at that work you got me. Old biker bars and cowboy saloons. One-nighters in the middle of Mississippi. Karaoke bars. When I met you I was doing week-long clubs every week."

"You still do."

"Half as much as I used to. And now I don't even know how much money you're skimming off the top."

"Your money is typical for headliners at your level. If you're happy making your money, why do you care what I make?"

"If I was happy, we wouldn't be having this conversation, Rodney," he says. "If I was happy, I wouldn't have beaten the snot out of Dustin in his own club."

"You've got no one but yourself to blame on that one."

"Wrong," he says. "I blame you. If you had more respect for me and what I do, maybe these club owners would, too."

"Do you honestly think you're so damned special?" Rodney asks.

Spence laughs again. Special. That's exactly what Rodney told him he was the first night they met. Spence came offstage at Rascal's Comedy Club in New Jersey and Rodney was there. He gave Spence a business card and told him he was going places. Rodney told Spence he was different than the other comedians he represented. He was special.

"That's just it," he says. "I don't think I'm special. I think I'm pretty average. But even average deserves to be treated better. Average feels like shit."

"At least you realize it," Rodney says.

"What? That I'm average?"

"Yeah."

"Remember this, Rodney," Spence says. "Even the most average comedian is far more talented than the most phenomenal agent."

There is a pause. Spence doesn't know if Rodney is simply listening or trying to multitask as usual. He looks outside and watches people walking down the street in midtown Toronto. A couple walks by holding hands and makes him suddenly wish he could just leave and take a walk somewhere with Sam. It's sunny out. It would be the perfect day for a walk. The song "Sometimes When We Touch" suddenly pops into his head for no reason. Wasn't that by a Canadian guy?

"I've always believed in you," Rodney says.

"No, you believed you could get me some work."

"Same difference," Rodney says.

"You're fired." Spence hangs up the phone. He looks up and sees Sam standing in the bedroom doorway. "That went well," he says.

Sam chuckles quietly and crosses the room to where he is. She reaches out to put her arms around him. For the first time, he realizes that he's sweating. He feels fine, but his temples are wet and he can feel his shirt sticking to his back. He just now noticed that his hands are trembling a little bit. When she embraces him, he feels as if he hasn't touched her in weeks.

"Now what?" Sam asks him after he holds her for a couple of minutes.

"Sushi?" he asks.

He can't remember the last time he had sushi. He thinks it was two years ago in the middle of Kansas. Some club manager really liked it and recommended he try some place in town. The guy was right and, oddly enough, that place in the middle of the country had some pretty good California rolls. Suggesting it for lunch was a good idea. Spence doesn't know how that popped into his head or why he suddenly recommended it, but here he is shoving raw salmon into his mouth.

Sam smiles at him and tries to deflect the fact that she keeps fumbling with her chopsticks. Spence pretends not to notice when she drops food on her shirt, and she pretends not to notice when he occasionally just picks up the food with his hands. They would never be able to live in Japan. They'd be starving and covered in food within a week.

Spence and Sam, he thinks. It sounds corny, but he likes it.

He hasn't been unemployed in years. Not since before he started doing stand-up comedy. He's not exactly sure how to handle it. He hasn't even had a vacation in ten years, so the idea of not working is something he can't wrap his head around. He has a couple of gigs coming up next month that he lined up without Rodney, but he knows everything else was canceled the minute he hung up the phone. Six months' worth of work, instantly gone. There might be an e-mail from Rodney confirming the lost work, but probably not. In a week, he'll check club websites to see his photo replaced by some other guy.

"How about Second Cup?" Sam asks as she drops rice in her lap.

"What the hell is that?" he asks.

"It's like Canada's Starbucks."

"But Canada has Starbucks." He points across Yonge Street from the little sushi restaurant they are sitting in directly to a Starbucks on the corner.

"But we also have Second Cup," Sam says. "And Second Cup is better."

"Maybe."

"Maybe you'll work there?"

"Maybe it's better than Starbucks."

"What about waiting tables?" she asks.

"I've done that before, as you know," he says. "I'm not against it. It's been a while, though. Something like twelve years."

"They'll still hire you," she says. "What about bartending?"

"I think I wanna stay out of bars if I'm not doing comedy. I don't want to just work a different job in the same place."

"Good point."

Spence doesn't tell her, but he thinks about caving in. It's only Monday. He could take a couple of days off and then start making phone calls. He could rebook some of the dates he lost from Rodney himself. Plenty of clubs will hire him anyway, especially if they get to pay him a little less without an agent stepping in. He could call the clubs he likes and stay away from the dives and saloons. Maybe offer to work cheaper if he has to. He could try and find another agent. There's some lady in Brooklyn who is just about as low-rent as Rodney. She'd probably sign him to-morrow if he called her.

Maybe Jamie wants the job? he thinks and almost smiles.

He looks out the window and watches the people walking down Yonge Street. The idea of not moving feels good, too. Just staying in one place for a while and going nowhere. If he could afford it, he'd take the entire month off and just sit in Toronto. Wait and see if anyone misses him. In the back of his mind, however, he's scared to death because he's pretty sure no one would.

He also thinks about calling Rodney. He doesn't tell Sam because he knows she'd think he's crazy. But he hasn't had to really book himself for several years. He doesn't remember how to do it every single day. He knows that he hated it, which is why he hired and kept Rodney in the first place. He never really liked Rodney all that much, but he absolutely hated making all of those phone calls to club owners.

And he doesn't really know what else to do with his life.

"What are you thinking?" Sam asks. He realizes that he's been staring straight ahead with the same piece of sashimi wedged between his chopsticks in front of his face for at least a couple of minutes.

"Thinking about working at Banana Republic," he lies.

"I could teach you how to fold pants," she says and grins like a clown.

"Perfect."

This is not the first time he has fired Rodney. That's probably why it didn't seem like such a big deal at first. For a while it was a yearly thing. The most recent was that time a few years ago when Rodney booked him to open for some TV star that turned out to be a complete jerk. It was some fourth banana on a sit-com who constantly complained about how he hated that his opening act got more attention from the audience. The TV star demanded Spence be fired, and Rodney did it without hesitation. Spence swore that was the end of their business together. He hired Rodney back three days later.

"No regrets," Sam says to him. It's not a question.

"I'm fine," he lies.

Rodney hasn't tried to call. He usually doesn't for at least a couple of days every time he's fired. If the guy is smart, he won't call at all. He should know that this time it's serious. If Rodney is smart, he'll stay away for good. But if there's a paycheck to be had, Rodney will likely try to make a comeback. Spence has given Rodney more second chances than he's ever been given in his life. In the past, he's always thrown his hands up and gone right back to business as usual. But he won't do it this time. Today is about starting over. With his life, his career, and Sam. He won't go back to Rodney.

But he could.

Spence watches Sam as she eats more sushi. He secretly hopes that Rodney isn't smart.

"How about selling cars?" Sam asks. He grimaces and re-members that year in pharmaceutical sales. His friends all made a mint selling Viagra while he barely got by because he had to peddle the world's least popular antianxiety pill. Sam sees the look on his face and changes the subject back to waiting tables and being a substitute teacher.

You'd better grovel, Rodney, Spence thinks. *You'd better beg me for forgiveness.*

It's every few minutes that he thinks that maybe he'll take Rodney back again. But only if Rodney is the one who apolo-gizes this time. If Rodney admits that he was wrong and has been screwing things up, Spence can take him back. He can work things out. He'll take a couple of weeks off here in Toronto and recharge his batteries. He'll spend time with Sam and then hit the road again with a fresh new outlook on it all. He'll make better money once Rodney is really on his side and not taking such a high cut. If he makes more money, he can tour less anyway and spend more time with Sam. They both want that anyway. That's the deal.

"Or you can just keep doing what you've been doing," Sam says, and he wonders if he was thinking out loud. He smiles at her and shoves the sashimi in his mouth. It seems a bit warm. How long was he holding it?

"I don't know," Spence says. "Maybe."

"You're leaning toward it, aren't you?"

"Sometimes it scares me that you know me so well."

Sam shrugs and looks out the window at the people walking by. For a split-second, her smile seems to fade away. They've been joking around and enjoying the conversation for a while, but she suddenly looks serious, even if she is trying to hide it.

"I know you love to be on that stage," she says. "There is no taking the performer out of you, is there?"

He grimaces. "Probably not. It's the thing I've done the longest. The thing I know best. The thing I always wanted to be."

"What about part-time?" she asks, twiddling her chopsticks into her little dish of soy sauce. "What if you did something else and just did comedy on the side again?"

"It doesn't really work that way," Spence says. "It's a demanding job, even part-time. There's only so much local work before a comic has to hit the road again."

"I know."

"And you hate it, right?"

She shrugs. "Why wouldn't I? Who wants to be with someone that is never home? Or the stress of worrying all the time?"

He feels a pain in the back of his neck, and the throbbing starts to grow a bit. He doesn't answer her immediately, but looks at her and raises his shoulders a bit. He knows that there is no way Sam can think about him being on the road and not think about Syracuse and his night in the hospital. Chances are good she'll think about it every time he leaves and goes back on the road. And he'll always be wondering what's next. If he stays with her and stays on the road, he'll always be making up for that night. But he knows she'll never stick around long enough for him to find out.

For a second, he wonders if she's ever seen the good parts of his business or only the worst of it. He wishes he could show her the parts of being a comedian that are so addictive. He wishes he could share with her the intense rush of applause and laughter. He wishes she knew that kind of addiction and that there was some way of sharing it with her.

"You know how I feel," she says. "I won't beat you over the head with it. I promised you that after the last time that I would never tell you what to do."

"When a comedian gets famous, he can tour less and make three times the money," he says. "But . . ."

"You're not famous," she says.

"And I have no idea how to get that way."

"Right."

"And if I knew something else that would keep me entertaining people and keep me happy and keep me here with you, I'd do it in a second," he says. "The problem is, I can't think of any such thing."

"I know," she says. "Neither can I." She takes another bite of sushi and smiles at him. She looks guilty for a second, as if she feels bad for changing the tone of the conversation. They promised each other a nice day and to put the past behind them. No more talk of Syracuse. No looking back at those awful weeks when they didn't speak. But he's not angry with her anyway. He knows she's right.

"Whatever you do," she says, "don't go back to Rodney."

Spence winces and wonders if she's been reading his mind. Every minute he tries to talk himself out of calling Rodney he feels a pain grow in his stomach. He had such amazing balls with Dustin in Iowa. Now he needs to have them again when it comes to Rodney. After all, that's why he felt so alive and amazing just hours ago. Sticking up for himself was a shot in the arm that he needed. Now he needs to follow through by putting that same shot into the rest of his life.

"Maybe Second Cup is a good idea," he says. She rolls her eyes and smiles and then touches his hand across the table.

And I wanna tell you that I love—

His cell phone vibrates on the small café table, and he looks down at it.

"You gonna talk to him?" Sam asks. She looks a little disappointed. He looks down at the phone. It's not Rodney. He doesn't recognize the number at all. If it is Rodney, he's calling from a completely different area code.

"This is Spence," he answers as he puts the phone to his ear.

"Hi there. This is Diane Perez," a woman's voice comes from the other end. "Is this Mr. Spencer?"

"Yes?" Spence says. He's not familiar with the name or the voice, but it's not a wrong number.

"I'm Greg Saunders's assistant," she says.

"Greg Saunders?"

"With *The Tonight Show*?" Ms. Perez's voice seems to say "duh."

"Oh, yeah," he says, "of course." He holds up his index finger to Sam and walks out of the restaurant. Sam looks at him with an eyebrow up but doesn't move. He steps out onto the sidewalk and is surprised by how quiet it is on a rather clear summer Monday evening in the middle of the city. "What can I do for you?" he asks and crosses his fingers.

"Mr. Saunders wanted me to call you to see if you're available to be on the show."

"The Tonight Show?" Spence asks.

"Of course."

"I'm sorry, but . . . is this a joke?" he asks. He wonders if Rodney is just being a sadistic fuck. Or if Dustin is getting even.

"I assure you it's not, although everyone always asks that," she says.

He laughs. "Go figure."

"So does that mean you're interested?" she asks. He wants to be the one who says "duh" this time. *The Tonight Show.* Here's Johnny. Hello, Ed. Ladies and gentlemen, Jay Leno. *The freaking Tonight Show.*

"Of course," Spence says and wants to do a backflip. "I'm just curious. How did you find me?"

"Your publicist sent us a tape," she says.

"My publicist?"

She pauses and sounds as if she's reading something. "Jamie Hernandez," she says. "He sent us a press kit a few weeks ago. I assumed you knew about it."

Damn, Spence thinks, *I didn't think the kid had it in him.*

"Oh yeah," he says. "Sorry, I forgot. Been on the road a lot."

"Well, Greg—Mr. Saunders—liked what he saw. So he wants to know if you can do it on the show," she says and then tosses in, "The material on the tape, of course."

The clean stuff. The new stuff. Everyone likes the new stuff. *The freaking Tonight Show* loves the new stuff. He's going to do his new stuff on *The Tonight Show.*

Fuck you, Rodney, he thinks.

"Absolutely," he says.

Spence looks back at Sam through the restaurant window. She shrugs her shoulders and mouths the word *what.* He gives her a big thumbs-up and realizes that he's bouncing up and down like an idiot in the street. "Sure. I can do anything you want," he says into the phone.

"Have you done TV before?" Ms. Perez asks.

"Yeah, I did *The Late Late Show* once," he says.

"Oh," she says, "with Craig Ferguson."

"No, with Craig Kilborn."

"Oh," she says, then does the math in her head. "Oh. Wow."

"Yeah."

"Well, great," she says. "Can you be in LA two weeks from Thursday?"

19

He has only been to LA once before. That was almost ten years ago, when he did the Kilborn show. Nothing has changed, really. The same gorgeous people everywhere. The same sunny weather. Seeing the underwear models everywhere he goes reminds him that he has spent the past decade entertaining the flyover states. He thought he looked old and tired when he was in Toronto. A day later and he looks like a zombie compared to everyone he sees in southern California.

He hasn't seen much of the city, except from different types of windows. The airplane window, the windows in the taxi, the windows of the hotel. Just like being on the road, he shows up to get work done and leave. There is no time for sightseeing, but he wouldn't enjoy it even if he had the time to do it. He's too busy thinking about what he's going to say on TV and trying to keep the churning in his stomach from making him sick.

The Tonight Show, he keeps saying to himself. He says it over and over again in his head just to make it seem more real. More than two weeks after he got the phone call from Diane Perez and he still wonders if the whole thing is a big joke. He's waiting for someone to yell "gotcha." This comes after several straight months of some truly awful gigs and some truly awful blowouts, being inches away from taking a job at McDonald's. All of that seems way more real than anything happening right now.

In the hotel, there's a gift basket from the show. Random

fruits, muffins, a nice welcome card. He looks out the window and lets the sun hit him as he goes over his set in his head. He's got four and a half minutes he's got to pull off. Just less than five minutes to entertain millions of people. Two hundred and seventy seconds to turn his career around. It usually takes him twice as long just to get warmed up onstage. Now that's all the time he's got to change everything.

His cell phone vibrates in his pocket. He pulls his phone out and looks at it. A text message from Jamie has come through.

Kick ass, man. Make us both rich.

He smiles. Out of all the people he has met in the past several years, Jamie is the last person he expected to suddenly be his angel. The kid somehow did in a matter of weeks what both he and Rodney weren't able to do in years. Maybe all this time all that was needed was a fresh set of eyeballs. Spence texts back to Jamie:

I can't believe you pulled this off.

A moment later, a text comes back from Jamie:

I shouldn't have, the way you screwed me out of getting laid in Toledo! You're a terrible wingman. ;)

Spence tosses the cell phone on the bed and smiles. He tries to remember the name of the girl in Toledo with the amazing body, but he can't. He doesn't even want to. He wants to think of his four and a half minutes and hope to God he doesn't fall flat on his face. He wants to walk into that studio a nobody and walk out a star. Others have done it. Why not him?

The phone on the nightstand rings, and he answers it.

"The car is here, sir," the hotel clerk says on the other end. He can't remember the last time a car was sent to get him and bring him anywhere. Most clubs he works tell him to find a way there and make sure he's on time. Sometimes they reimburse him for cab fare. Waiting for him outside is a town car. He can't remember the last time he was in one of those.

Crunch time, he thinks to himself as the car leaves the hotel parking lot and heads toward the TV studio. He can already feel the butterflies in his stomach. He reaches in his jacket pocket and takes out the small flask. A little Johnnie Walker. Just a snort. Just enough to take the edge off. A friend who did *Letterman* years ago gave him this advice. Have at least one drink. Don't overdo it, but toss back at least one to keep you from going crazy. Taking a long pull off the flask, Spence believes his friend was right.

The past couple of days, he has been over his material a million times. He knows these four and a half minutes better than he knows his own name. He had to clear it with Diane Perez, who had to clear it with someone else, who had to clear it with Greg Saunders, who had to clear it with someone else. He then had to do all of that again. There was a list of things he was not allowed to say. No product names. No political comments. Nothing that could be deemed too vulgar for TV. They went over his material several times. Then they went over his material again.

The fucking Tonight Show, he thinks as he sees the building off in the distance.

The studio in Burbank is bigger than he expected. The entire place is huge. He checks in at one desk and then at another. He is cleared by one person and then another. There are signatures and forms and visitor badges. He is then led into a green room that is larger than any of the other ones he has ever been in. He has appeared on several local TV shows. He's been on *Good Morning, Cleveland* more than once. There wasn't even a green room for that show. He just sat in the lobby until they were ready to use him.

"This way," a kid with a headset says to him and points him toward another kid with a headset. Spence goes where he is pointed. One hallway, then another. He walks past picture frames on the wall of Jay Leno and random celebrities, framed posters of popular sitcoms and TV shows.

"Follow me." A random staffer all in black leads him into a room and puts him into a chair in front of a huge mirror. He's only had a couple of pulls off that flask but wonders if he's already drunk. It's all going by so fast. The place is like a machine. He smiles and shrugs and tries to act like it's all no big deal to him. He does this every day. He's used to this sort of thing. Legendary late-night talk shows are old hat, as far as he's concerned.

He's only in the building a few minutes before someone is applying makeup to him. The last time he did TV was some local news interview in Sioux Falls, South Dakota. There was no makeup. They just put him in front of the camera as is. The news anchor looked tan and healthy, while he sat next to her and looked like a heroin junkie. By the time *The Tonight Show* makeup woman is through with him, he looks like he lives there in California.

The makeup person is speaking to him, but Spence doesn't hear her. She's polite and friendly and asking him questions he somehow seems to be answering. But he's lost in his material. He's thinking of his act and what he wants to say. He's going over the bits in his head as if any of it has changed at all in the past two and a half weeks. He smiles and he talks to the people around him, but he's not really there.

"Is he ready?" a kid in a headset asks the makeup person who says that he is. The kid checks him out and then crooks a finger. "Follow me."

Spence follows the kid down the hallway and back into the green room. Wearing a *Tonight Show* T-shirt and blue jeans, the kid couldn't be older than twenty-one or so. But he rushes around with a serious look on his face as if he's twice that age. Looking at this kid, Spence doesn't feel quite as old as he did when he first got to LA. He wonders if working behind the scenes in TV ages a person faster. Maybe the kid is pushing forty but has years of California sun and Botox to thank for his youthful appearance.

Spence takes a seat in the green room and tries to look like he's not having an anxiety attack. He pretends to be reading *Va-*

riety magazine and acting as if he's just hanging out. This is completely normal. He always hangs out in the green room of *The Tonight Show*.

Two minutes feels like twenty. An Asian man ten years younger than he is walks in the room and sits down. The guy is a TV star. He's been all over the place. A year ago he was nobody, and now he's got some cop show that is a huge hit. *Kung Fu: Reborn* or something like that. Sitting across the green room, his legs folded and his sunglasses on, the celebrity nods his head toward Spence and smiles.

"How's it going?" the TV star says to him.

"Oh, you know," Spence answers and smiles. The TV star smiles back.

"Just another day at the office, right?" the TV star says and looks over the top of his sunglasses.

"Yeah." Spence laughs. "Sure."

"Comedian?"

"Yep."

"Cool," the star says. "I'm an actor. David Nguyen."

The TV star extends his hand. Spence smiles and shakes it. "Yeah, I know who you are. I'm Spence."

"Cool," David says. "I love stand-up."

"Cool."

"First time on the show?"

"This is it," Spence says and raises his eyebrows.

"Very cool," David says. "I'm sure you'll be great."

"Hope so."

"No worries, man," David says, "no worries."

Spence holds up his fingers and shows David that they are crossed. David laughs and pushes his sunglasses back up to the top of his nose.

"I was the same way my first time," David says and leans back on the sofa. "But they wouldn't have you on if they didn't have the cards stacked, you know what I'm saying?"

"Guess so," Spence says. "How many times have you been on?"

"Let me see." David thinks for a minute. "This would be . . . twice!"

They both laugh. David slaps his leg and seems to enjoy the joke for longer than it is funny.

"This is just the same ol' routine to you then, huh?" Spence says.

David smiles and nods. "Are you high?" he asks.

"No," Spence says. "Had a drink. But that's it. You?"

"As a fucking kite, bro," David says and laughs.

Spence smiles and leans back in his own chair, trying to look as cool as David does. A woman with a snake wrapped around her walks in the room, stares at the two of them for a minute and leaves. Spence looks over at David, who obviously thinks he was imagining it. His eyes are as big as the odd smile on his face. Spence decides not to tell him that she was really there. It would be too ridiculous to try and explain it.

"That's cool stuff, man," David says after a minute. "Stand-up comedy."

"Yeah," Spence says. Everyone who is way more successful than comedians always think comedians are cool. Millionaires in awe of people who barely make thirty grand per year and sometimes sleep in their cars. David probably drives a Porsche.

"Hey," David says, "you like Dane Cook?"

The kid with the headset walks in the green room and looks around. He's carrying a clipboard, and he flips through the sheets of paper on it. He speaks into the headset for a second and listens to someone on the other end. Then he looks at the clipboard again.

"We may have a problem," the kid says and looks at Spence. At first he thinks the kid is talking to someone on the other end of the microphone. When he realizes otherwise, he gets up from the chair and stands in front of it.

"What kind of problem?" Spence asks.

"We're looking a bit full today," the kid says. "Would you be available tomorrow if we had to bump you?"

"Sure," Spence says and nods with a smile. He wants to hang himself.

"We'd just keep you at the hotel and use you tomorrow or the next day," the kid says.

"That's fucked up, bro," David says from the sofa. No one pays attention to him.

"It's no big deal," Spence says to the kid with the headset. He wants to shoot himself in the face.

"It would only be another day or two," the kid says.

"No problem," Spence says. He knows that the kid is just being polite. When comics get bumped, they rarely get put on the show the next day. They normally have to wait weeks or even months before they get another shot. Sometimes it never happens. Sometimes you just get to sit in the green room and tell people you almost did the show.

"At least I got to ride in a town car," Spence says to the kid and laughs. The kid gives him a blank look and nods and walks out of the room.

"That's fucked up, bro," David says again.

"Nah." Spence tries to pretend he doesn't want to eat a bag of glass. "Shit happens."

"Damn, man," David says, "I'll just bring you out with me, yo. You can tell jokes, and I'll just sit there and laugh." He holds up his hand and high-fives Spence. He probably doesn't even know he's on *The Tonight Show*. In ten minutes, he'll walk outside and call Jay Leno "Conan."

Spence feels his pocket buzz and realizes that he forgot to turn off his phone. He pulls it out and reads a text message from Sam:

I LOVE YOU, TV STAR.

He smiles. He doesn't have to tell her yet. He'll enjoy the green room and the gift basket and the free baseball cap with *The Tonight Show* printed across it. He even gets paid to be here. He'll just come back and do the show tomorrow, right?

Right?

A second later the kid in the headset returns and practically carries David out of the room.

"Kick some ass, bro." David high-fives Spence again on his way out of the green room.

"You too." Spence smiles as David leaves to go onstage babbling like an idiot. In the green room, there is a large TV where he can watch the show being recorded. He turns up the volume and watches. Jay Leno looks smaller in person.

"My next guest is the star of a very popular program you can see right here on NBC," Leno says to the camera and introduces David Nguyen. David walks out with a smile on his face bigger than the rest of his head. He sits down next to Leno and begins his interview by giggling like a ten-year-old girl.

The phone buzzes again. This time it's a phone call from Rodney. First time Rodney has called him since the big blowout. The same blowout that ended in Rodney getting his walking papers. Spence winces and lets it go to voice mail. He's about to get bumped from his *Tonight Show* appearance. The last thing he needs is Rodney rubbing it in.

On the TV, Leno is obviously uncomfortable with the nonsense coming out of David's mouth. He is asking questions but getting back mostly giggles and "yeah, mans." The audience is laughing, but mostly because Leno is able to make a few cracks here and there.

"Ah, the youth of America," Leno says. David grins and tries to high-five Leno. Leno smiles, shakes his head, and introduces a clip of David's TV show.

"This is gonna run short," the kid with the headset has reappeared and is standing in the doorway, looking at the train wreck that is David Nguyen's interview unfold on the TV monitor. "We're gonna cut to a break and bring you on right after."

"I'm not bumped?" Spence says, looking more eager than he probably should.

"Not after watching that." The kid points at David being stared down by Jay Leno on the TV, trying his best to cover up the fact that his current guest is somewhere in Oz.

"Cool," Spence says out loud without realizing it.

"Congratulations." The kid practically winks at him and then holds the microphone on his headset close to his mouth. "Here we come."

With one hand, the kid gives him a "follow me" signal and leads Spence down a part of the hallway he hasn't been through yet. There are more framed posters on the wall, more pictures of Jay Leno, a few of Johnny Carson, at least one Ed McMahon photo. He's surprised how many people run this show. There are people all over the place, many of them wearing headsets, almost all of them dressed in black.

"Right this way." The kid motions him around another corner where yet more people are standing. The Kilborn show was so much smaller. There was no house band, no dozens of staff members everywhere. It seemed downright tiny compared to this operation. His walk seems to go on for miles before he steps through a doorway and to an area where he can hear the show. It takes him a minute before he realizes that he's standing behind the curtain. He's in the studio now. He's backstage at *The Tonight Show.*

"Holy shit," Spence says.

"Don't say that when you go out there, please." The kid in the headset smiles at him.

"Oh, I . . ."

"It's cool," the kid says. "You're gonna be great."

"Yeah?"

A young woman, who is also wearing a headset, runs over with a tiny microphone in her hand with a thin wire that runs from it to a little black battery pack.

"Clip this to your lapel," she says. "Run the cord down the inside of your shirt and then clip the battery pack to the back of your jeans."

Spence does what she says and adjusts his sports jacket so that the microphone seems hidden. He's done this many times before on local TV shows and on the Kilborn show. In the clubs, he always likes the feeling of the microphone in his hand. But every comic knows it's good to get used to performing with a wireless microphone.

"Say something," the kid says to him.

"What?" he stammers.

"Perfect," the girl says, "don't touch the mic."

"I—" he stutters as she walks away.

"Have fun, and remember where to stand," the kid in the headset says and steps back a few feet to give him some room. There was a brief moment earlier where they showed Spence where to stand. Now it seems as if that was four months ago. "Go straight through the curtain and right onto the mark. You know the drill."

"The drill, yeah," Spence says. He thinks Glass Tiger was a Canadian band. He tries to remember what Canada is. He thinks it's a country.

"And don't touch the mic," the kid says.

Everything is much cooler here. Spence wonders if the blood in his body is going cold and he's dying. Then he remembers that it's very cold on TV sets. He remembers that same feeling from when he did the Kilborn show. They have to keep all the equipment cool and make up for the fact that the lights are so hot. He's practically freezing. It will change when he steps out from behind the curtain. It will be warm. The lights will hit him, and he'll feel better.

Music is playing, and he knows that there's a commercial going on. The music starts to get louder. He hears commotion outside, behind the curtain. About ten feet away, people in headsets are watching TV monitors. He sees the title card for the *The Tonight Show* come on one of them. The audience begins applauding. The music comes to an end as the bands stops playing.

This is it.

"Welcome back," Jay Leno says to the camera.

Jay freaking Leno, he thinks.

"My next guest has appeared on numerous television programs," Leno embellishes, "and can be seen touring regularly all over the United States and in Canada. A very funny, talented young comedian. Please welcome: Michael Spencer."

He hears his name, and it sounds amazing. He just heard Jay Leno announce his name on *The Tonight Show*. In an instant, one of his biggest dreams just came true. With a huge smile on his face, he steps out from behind the curtain and onto the set. Applause surrounds him and cameras focus in as he steps up to his mark. The nervousness is gone. The anticipation is gone. The butterflies are dead.

He's ready.

20

Spence stands in his hotel room feeling triumphant. It has been hours and yet he still stands and looks out the window of the hotel as if he just walked off camera. It has taken several drinks to make his hands stop shaking, but he doesn't feel drunk. He feels great. He feels more alive than he has felt in years. He feels like he just conquered the world.

"Great stuff," Jay Leno said to him as he shook his hand and the show went to a commercial break. That was all he said, but it was all that mattered. It felt amazing to hear it, and it was only two words. The audience applauded as the "Applause" sign blinked on and off again, but it was obvious they would have applauded either way. His set was just that good.

HOW DID IT GO?

The text message is from Beth. He forgot that he even told her he was going to be there. He types back that it went great and takes a few moments to simply smile and dance around his hotel room. He hopes that Evan doesn't think that comedians on *The Tonight Show* are such deadbeats after all. He doesn't know why he cares. Evan is out of the picture anyway. Evan is a douche.

The phone buzzes again, and he rolls his eyes. He knows he's going to have to call Beth and splash cold water all over whatever nonsense is in her head. He has no intention of going back to her. He never really did. He considers defaulting on his storage space and letting all of his belongings sell to auction. He looks down at his phone at the new message that came through:

I LOVE YOU. I AM SO PROUD OF YOU.

This time the text message is from Sam. He deletes the message from Beth and dances around the room a little bit longer. He wants to call Sam right away and tell her all about it. In a few hours, she'll watch the whole thing on TV, but he wants to give her the details, line by line.

He thinks of going out to some jewelry store in LA and buying her a huge diamond ring, bigger than anything he can actually afford. He thinks of flying home and asking her to be with him forever. He knows it's crazy, but he enjoys the thought and dances around the hotel anyway. He never thought this about Beth. He thinks the word *forever* all of a sudden, and it doesn't make him puke. That has to count for something.

He puts down the booze and takes a deep breath. He might pass out before he gets to see himself on TV and wake up with a terrible hangover, which is exactly the opposite of what he wants right now. He tells Johnnie Walker to take a break and then gives the bad news to Jack Daniel's, too. Tonight, he's going to just enjoy life a little bit, watch himself on TV, and experience life with twenty-twenty vision.

Just like he does with Sam.

His phone rings, and he picks it up right away. He knows it's Sam, and he wants to tell her how everything seems right in the world. He gets down on one knee, prepared to propose over the phone if he has to.

"Hey, baby," Spence says and leans on his right leg as he kneels.

"Wassup, sweetums?" Rodney says on the other end. When he hears Rodney's voice, Spence bolts upright and stands looking at himself in the mirror on the wall. He wanted to talk to Sam.

"What do you want?" he says, instantly sober.

"Nice to hear from you, too," Rodney says.

"What is it?"

"What do you think?" Rodney says. "I'm calling to congratulate you."

"Congratulate me for what?" Spence asks, playing dumb.

"For what," Rodney scoffs. "What the hell do you think for?"

Spence pauses and looks over his right shoulder. It's still very bright outside, but he feels as if it's midnight. "For the show?" he asks.

"Damn right, for the show," Rodney says. "*The Tonight Show*. Way to go, buddy."

"How'd you find out about that?"

"I've got my sources, you know. I've got people working for me out there, too."

"Great."

"Yeah," Rodney says, "great. Listen, if you wanna talk about it, I think I can get you some really great work."

"Work? This the same work you were offering me before I fired you?"

"Yeah." Rodney tries to laugh. It comes off phony. "Better than that."

"You don't say."

"Listen, are you still pissed?" Rodney asks. "Because I can get you some really good gigs. All you've got to do is say so and they're yours. You stop being pissed, and we can do some real business here. Or you can take everything personal and miss out on some sweet work."

"What kind of gigs?"

"Good gigs," Rodney says. "Some good stuff. Funny Bones. Improvs. All the good places. Top clubs."

"Yeah?"

"Absolutely."

"You offering me this because I'm that good?" Spence says. "Or because I just did *The Tonight Show* and you can make some money off me?"

"Does it matter? You just did *The Tonight Show,* baby. Your ticket up that ladder."

Spence thinks for a minute and wonders if Rodney has a very good point. That A-list work has always been the goal. Does it really matter how he finally got it, or even why? As long as it's keeping him from being the late-shift manager at Second Cup, isn't that the point? And if Rodney is the enemy, isn't it better to keep him close?

"What does that mean? What kind of touring are we talking about?"

"Well, a lot of the same stuff," Rodney says. "I won't lie to you. But a lot of really good gigs. I can get you some casinos, too. Just like I said."

"What about the money?"

"Good money."

"Like what?"

"Like more than what you were making before," Rodney says. "Not TV star cash. But a little more here and there."

Spence looks in the minibar and thinks about a little bottle of Hennessey. Or, better yet, nothing. Room service would be great. He could get a nice steak and then call Sam and talk about when he's flying back to Toronto. Maybe she'll go on the road with him. If he made more money, she could quit her job and travel with him. But what Rodney is offering sounds like a *lot* of travel.

More money, less touring, Spence thinks.

"I've gotta be honest with you," he says. "That doesn't sound so great."

"What are you talking about?" Rodney says. "That's the best deal going for you. That's the best thing out there. Top clubs. Top pay—"

"It's not top pay," Spence interrupts.

"It's good pay."

"Fine," Spence says, "but it ain't great."

"Better than what you've had."

Spence takes a deep breath and sighs loudly into the phone. He likes the idea of making Rodney wait the way he always had to when Rodney was multitasking. "You know what I didn't hear?" he says. "I didn't hear the words 'A-list' come out of your mouth."

Rodney chuckles. "It ain't that easy, kid."

"What does that mean?"

"It means you did one spot on *The Tonight Show*. That's great. But that doesn't change things overnight."

"It used to."

"And there used to be three channels on the TV," Rodney says. "But things are different now. You've definitely shown your chops, pal. But I've got guys that have done *Letterman* a few times who still aren't at the top of that ladder."

"Then what's the point?" Spence asks.

"To keep climbing it," Rodney says.

Spence feels the skip in his step turning into more of a dragging of his feet. He wanted the high of what he just did to last longer before the reality of his career came barreling up like a Toyota in the middle of Iowa.

"You wanted to prove me wrong, and you did," Rodney says. "You want me to show you I believe in you? Look at the gigs I can get you. That's your proof, my friend."

"Better gigs," Spence says.

"It's work," Rodney says. There's a long pause after this, and Spence sits there for a minute and takes it in. Rodney is right; it is work. After tonight, there's probably plenty of work in plenty of clubs. He'll probably get more gigs in places way better than the Electric Pony. He might even get a full calendar of nothing but weeklong gigs in nice clubs like the Improv in Hollywood or Carolines in New York City. But one appearance on *The Tonight Show* isn't going to make him a star overnight. Now, more than ever, Spence wishes it were 1987. He wishes he'd just had this TV spot during The Boom.

"How much work do you think?" he asks Rodney while he does a little math in his head.

"I dunno," Rodney says. "Probably as much as fifty weeks. Whatever you want. However much you wanna work."

"On the road. Doing club gigs."

"Yeah," Rodney says. It almost sounds like a question. "That's the job, remember?"

"Fifty weeks."

"That's being a comedian."

"I guess it is, yeah," Spence says. He hears a beep on the phone and knows it's Sam sending him another text message. He wants to see what she's writing, but he has to hang up on Rodney to do so. On the other end of the phone, he can hear Rodney tapping a pen on the desk. He looks around the hotel room and at the familiar setup. He looks down at his suitcase on the floor.

Tour less, make more, he thinks.

"So," Rodney asks after a minute of silence, "what do you say?"

Spence sits for a few seconds that feels like a half hour. Then he says, "I have to call you back."

"What?" Rodney asks.

"I have to call you back," Spence repeats. "Just give me a minute."

"Okay. You know where to find me."

"I do," Spence says and hangs up the phone. He doesn't sit down. He doesn't move an inch from here he's standing. He dials Sam, and she answers almost immediately.

"Hey, you." Her voice sounds amazing. She sounds happy and sultry and quirky and sexy. Everything Spence thinks about her is how she sounds in just two words. It's just what he needed to hear.

"I love you," he says. A stupid grin instantly appears on his face.

"I love you, too." Sam giggles. "That all you had to say?"

"No." Spence turns around and faces the other wall. He feels like walking somewhere or pacing the room or jumping up and down. Instead he just stands there and changes direction. "But I did need to say it. I haven't yet, and I needed to. I needed you to hear it. To know it."

There's a pause before Sam speaks again. "Well, I do know it. But it is nice to hear."

"And you'd hate living on the road."

"I'd hate what?"

"Living on the road, like I do. Town to town. Going to shows all over the country."

"Is this a trick question?" Sam asks.

"It's not a question at all," Spence says. "If I went on tour and brought you with me, you'd probably hate it."

"Well, I have always wanted to see Chicago."

"How about the other fifty-one weeks in a year?"

"No, thanks."

"That's what I figured." Spence looks down at his feet. He could use that new pair of shoes now. He sits down on the edge of the hotel bed. "I don't think I'd want that, either."

"What brought this on?" Sam asks. "Shouldn't you be getting ready to watch yourself on TV and bask in all its glory? Everyone at work can't wait to see it."

"Me too." Spence nods, even though Sam can't see him do it. "But it took doing that show today to make me realize a few things."

"Yeah? Like what?"

"I'm good at it," he says. "Being a comedian."

"Yes, you are."

"But I don't know that I care anymore. I mean, it's great to make people laugh. But that might just be the only part that matters at all to me anymore. The only part I remotely like."

Sam chuckles quietly into the phone. "And you realized this after performing stand-up comedy on *The Tonight Show*?"

"Is it ironic?" Spence asks, not sure why he's smiling.

"A little," Sam says. "But not surprising to anyone who knows you."

"That's just it," Spence says, leaning forward. "No one knows me but you. I'm not sure anyone ever really did."

"Have you been drinking?"

"Yes."

"Well, bring me back a bottle of whatever you're having," Sam says. "Because I like the effect it has on you better than whatever you normally drink."

Spence laughs and lies back on the bed. The hotel is so nice, he thinks nothing of being on top of the comforter. He never wants to have to throw a dirty hotel comforter on the floor again. "It's true, you know," he says. "All of it."

"I know," Sam says quietly. Spence can tell she's blushing a little bit just from the sound of her voice.

"And I think what happened today made me realize that I've been reaching for the wrong goal all along," he says. "I was trying to get something that was never going to make me as happy as something I already have."

"And that something is . . . ?"

"A district manager for the Gap."

"I see," Sam teases. "Think you got me, do you?"

"I can only hope."

"You're crazy."

"Does this mean you'll have me?" Spence asks.

"Silly. I'm already yours." She laughs. "You had me at dick jokes."

This makes Spence laugh out loud, and he runs his hand through his hair. He's almost forty-two years old. This is probably the worst time for a career change, immigration to another country, and relationship with a woman he spends more time with on the phone than in person. A woman he met in another city while doing the job he's now considering leaving right a time when everyone he knows would think he was crazy for doing it.

"I've got some ideas." Spence exhales deeply and shakes his head at himself.

"I'm listening."

"First thing's first," he says and sits up on the bed again, his feet feeling the cushy carpet between his toes. "Just know that I love you."

"I love you, too. You're my TV star."

"For one night, at least."

"That's good enough for me," she says. "I hope you know that. I never fell for you because you're an entertainer. Or because you were that guy on the stage that night. Or because you're so funny and can make everyone laugh like you do."

"I thought that women always wanted a man who can make them laugh." Spence grins. He always thought that was the silliest line. If women want funny men so much, how come Brad Pitt is always on the cover of *People* magazine's "Sexiest Man Alive" and not Drew Carey?

"But it's easy to make me laugh," Sam says. "I love you because you know how to make me smile."

It's at that moment that Spence realizes exactly what he wants and where he wants to be. He stands up again and walks over to the window. A million crazy thoughts are running through his head, but one of them seems like it might just work. He smiles and crosses his fingers.

"I have to make a phone call," he says to Sam. "Let me call you back?"

"Always." She makes a kiss noise through the phone and hangs up. Spence feels like he's seventeen again as he immediately starts dialing the phone again.

"Yo," Rodney answers on the second ring. It's the first time he's ever done that.

"Let me ask you a question," Spence asks without bothering to introduce himself. "You get fifteen percent, correct?"

"Yep," Rodney says. "Depending on the gig, of course."

"Let's call it fifteen percent," Spence says. "But I'm looking for a specific gig."

"Where?"

"Toronto."

"For when?"

"For good," Spence says.

"What the hell are you talking about?" Rodney asks.

"I'm talking about I have an idea," Spence says and paces the hotel room. "And if I know you and the million pies you always have your fingers in, I think it's possible that you might be able to help me help both of us. The right phone calls, the right demo, the right auditions. I think it could work out well for everyone. If you're willing to try something different."

"Yeah?" Rodney says, and it sounds as if he's actually sitting on the edge of his seat. "What'd you have in mind?"

21

Spence's headphones feel a little loose, so he tightens the top of them during the commercial break. Going over his notes, he quickly rereads the asides he came up with earlier in the day but hasn't had a chance to use yet. He can probably get off a few quick one-liners here and there before the show wraps for the day. Across the desk, Skip is checking the time left on whatever song is playing and gives him a nod that there's less than thirty seconds to go.

"Just another weekday morning with Mad Man Skip and the Gang," a prerecorded voice plays over the airwaves, "on Toronto's hit music station, the Wolf."

The sound of a wolf howling at the moon is heard, followed by a crazy scream and the sound of a guitar thrashing a hard rock chord. Skip nods his head and flips a switch on the soundboard. A red light goes on in the corner of the room to let everyone know that the show is now live on the air.

"Mad Man Skip in the morning," Skip says, a big smile on his face. There's an old saying in radio that, even if people can't see you, they can hear whether or not you are smiling. Skip firmly believes that and lives by the motto. "Wrapping up another long set of favorite hit tunes right here on Toronto's number one home for rock. This is the Wolf, and this is Thursday morning. Sitting across from me, my partner in crime. How you doing, Spence?"

"I'm still awake, so that's good news," Spence says as the

sound of a jackhammer plays in the background for no reason whatsoever but to make background noise. He follows Skip's lead and smiles as big as he can.

Skip and Spence, he thinks. It sounds corny, but he likes it.

Skip has been a great new boss and is quickly becoming a fast friend. In his fifties, he has been doing radio forever. He knows his days on the air are numbered, and he likes having a younger guy next to him to carry a lot of the heavy load. Spence doesn't mind it, either, since he plays well off his boss. Skip and Spence. It's a ridiculous-sounding combo, but at least he's not called "Monkey-Boy."

"Hey, Spence," Skip says while checking the digital clock on the wall, "I see you're gonna be doing a little stand-up this weekend, huh?"

"That's right," he says. "Everyone out there can come check me out tonight through Sunday at Absolute Comedy at Yonge and Eglinton. I'll be hosting the show all weekend."

"Nice," Skip says, "and while you're there checking out the show, be sure to pick yourself up an ice-cold Molson Canadian. The true Canadian beer, Molson is available at Absolute Comedy and all across the country. Truly Molson, truly Canadian."

"Nice plug," Spence says.

"That's why they pay me the big bucks," Skip says. The sound of a cash register is played and a loud "cha-ching" noise fills Spence's headphones. Presumably, somewhere in Toronto, morning commuters are hopefully at least cracking a smile.

"You get paid?" Spence says. "I need to renegotiate my contract. I've been doing this crap for free."

Skip laughs and makes a sweeping motion with his hand. "Counting Crows up next. It's Mad Man Skip with Spence in the Morning on the Wolf. But first? Here's Megan with traffic and weather."

Skip takes of his headphones and steps out from behind the desk. Slapping a hand on Spence's shoulder, he retrieves a pack of cigarettes from his shirt pocket. His long ponytail has gone gray. He looks like an aging hippie, which is pretty much what he is. He's also technically a liar. The radio station is actually not number one. Recent numbers say it comes in third out of six. Not half bad, really. But not first.

"Going for a smoke." Skip smiles. "See you in ten, okay?"

"You got it." Spence nods and takes off his headphones.

"I'm coming out to the gig tomorrow. Bringing the wife."

"I get to finally meet Mrs. Skip?" Spence says.

"Mrs. Skip number three," Skip corrects and coughs. His husky DJ voice is probably due in part to the smokes he's getting ready to inhale. He steps out of the booth and walks down the hall.

Spence takes a look at the digital clock and decides to grab a quick cup of coffee. There're a few songs left to play and then some commercials, but they're all lined up and automated. He gets up from his small corner in the booth and steps out into the hallway. There, staring him straight in the face, is his own photo. A poster of him and Skip smiling like idiots in some wacky pose. The framed poster is the same one he's seen recently on a couple of bus stop stands. He looks ridiculous, but Sam was right. He definitely looks better now that he has stopped highlighting his hair.

He smiles. He hasn't been behind the wheel of a car in months. He takes the subway to work every day and, when he can, walks as much as possible. He's been told that, when winter hits in a few weeks, he'll walk less. He wonders if that's true. He likes to think that he'll suck it up better than people think he will, but it doesn't matter. Whether it's on a bus or a streetcar or subway train, it sure as hell beats being behind the wheel for eight hours a day. He can't imagine driving across Iowa anymore.

"Time for a recharge?" A sales guy spots him in the break room and offers him a cup of coffee. Spence chuckles politely and takes the cup. The early hours took some getting used to at first, but he's doing okay now. He used to go to bed around four, so it's different for him to be getting up not long after that and making the trek downtown to be on the air by six. A year ago, he couldn't have imagined going to bed before eleven every night.

"Sounding good today," the sales guy says and raises his cup. He raises his back and thanks him, although he can't remember the guy's name. There are so many people that work at the Wolf, it can be pretty overwhelming. The hardest part has never been the early hours or the public promotions or even the silly, censored jokes over the airwaves; it's keeping up with the dozens of other employees and who the hell they all are. People randomly walk by him and pat his back.

"There's the funny man," some guy in a tie says as he walks down the hall.

"Here comes trouble," a receptionist will say when he walks through the lobby. It's always some remark about his role as second banana. He's "the funny guy" or "wacky dude" or some variation of comedic sidekick. And sometimes they just call him Spence.

He just hopes the people in their cars and offices are laughing. So far, the ratings say they are. Even if they aren't number one, they're not bad. He crosses his fingers every once in a while and hopes it stays that way. He likes the gig. That smiling that Skip insists he keep doing isn't fake.

It shouldn't have worked out this way, but it did. Oddly enough, for the first time in his life, everything went according to plans. The right phone calls, the right demos, and the right auditions. A little bit of wrangling for the right permits, a little rough start auditioning for the spot, and then, out of nowhere, everything just clicked. Turns out that Buzz in Peoria was right all along: Spence is pretty damn good at doing radio.

"Yo, Spence," a familiar voice calls from the hallway as he starts his way back to the booth. He turns to see Greta walking down the hall. A short twentysomething with long, dark hair that goes all the way down her back, Greta is a bit of a wonder woman at the Wolf. She does everything from answer phones to record commercials to set up live appearances. She has been

Spence's lifeline ever since he started a few months back, showing him around and helping him out whenever he felt lost.

"What's up, Greta?"

"Messages," she says and hands him a few little sheets of paper.

"Wow," he says, "I must be popular or something."

"Or something," Greta says. "Absolute Comedy wants you to confirm that you're performing this week."

"Just announced it on the air, so I hope so," he says.

"Alrighty," she says. "I'll e-mail them for you."

"Thanks," he says. He looks down at the scraps of paper. One is the message from Absolute Comedy. Another is from some other comedy club in the city. The local gigs keep coming, which he's always happy to take. The money is always good, and the commute is always short. Just the way he likes it.

A third message is from Sam:

Sushi tonight?

"You wanna bring the boyfriend and have sushi with me and Sam?" he asks Greta. "Maybe I'll bring Skip."

"Don't count on it," Greta says. "Skip doesn't eat raw anything. But I'll bring Tommy, sure. What time?"

"Seven," he says. "I've got that gig at nine."

"Look at the local celebrity." Greta smirks.

"Sure," he says, "keep thinking that."

"Not too shabby, if you ask me," Greta says. She's right. He gets more for his stand-up shows now than he ever did before. And that's not including random public appearances. The ironic part is that he gets the gigs more because he's popular on the radio than because he did *The Tonight Show*. But at least *The Tonight Show* got him through the door at the radio station in the first place. It also didn't hurt that the program director was a fan of Craig Kilborn.

"So? Dinner at seven?" Spence asks.

"You got it," she says and walks back down the hallway. He pulls out his phone and sends a text message to Sam.

Dinner with Greta and her guy at seven?

A second later, she replies:

Works for me. I love you.

He smiles and steps back into the booth. Skip has returned and is doing something on the computer screen; probably reviewing the music list for the next hour. Skip nods as Spence comes back in the room. They never talk too much during the breaks. It keeps it fresh when they go live. It works out very well and makes their timing better when they're on the air. It took getting used to, but Spence likes it now.

He looks at the scraps of paper in his hand and flips through them one more time. There, in the stack of reminders about meetings with network guys and appointments he needs to make, is a short note that Greta scrawled out for him.

RODNEY CALLED. SAYS KEEP UP THE GOOD
WORK. AND THAT YOU HAVE SYPHILIS.

He laughs to himself as he looks at the paper. Never in a million years did he think he'd smile when he got messages from that guy. For the first time in almost a decade, he thinks Rodney might just be worth every penny.

Fuck you, Rodney, he thinks, only now it's with a grin.

"What?" Skip says.

Spence jumps a bit in his seat. He didn't realize he was talking out loud. He clears his throat as he looks up at Skip and smiles.

"Nothing," he says. Skip gives him a smile right back and returns to what he was doing.

He looks at the note for a second and then looks up at Skip. Skip does the swirling motion with his hands, flips some switches, and puts his headphones on. The prerecorded intro plays again and welcomes the listeners back from a commercial break. Spence picks up his headphones and gets ready to go live again. Then he takes the message from Rodney and places it on the table in front of him, right next to the tiny photo he keeps there. The photo of Sam.

He smiles big and leans into the microphone.

Thank you, good night.

Acknowledgments

The author would like to thank The Andersons, The Gruniers, The Chaplicks, and Allison Dore. Also thanks to Eric Alper, Chris Baedorf, Bob Canter, Matt Dusk, Terry Fallis, Howard Glassman, Tina Gruver, Andrea Lakin, Jason Laurans, John Lewis, Brendan McKeigan, Victoria Makhnin, Terry Mercury, Ric Meyers, Larry Nichols, Tom Nowell, Pamela Ohberg, Fred Patterson, Aron Pepernick, Phil Perrier, Nathan Quinn, Chris Reil, Tracy Rideout, Robert Rosen, Davin Rosenblatt, Ritch Shydner, Ralph Tetta, Joe Thistel, Aisha Tyler, Cal Verduchi, Mike Wixson, Eric Yoder, and especially Peter Senftleben and everyone at Kensington Books.

A Conversation with Ward Anderson

There are a lot of highs and lows in *I'll Be Here All Week*. What is the worst part of being a stand-up comedian?

Without question, it's the travel. It's constant and can be quite exhausting, which I think you see in Spence's story. When you first start touring, it's an amazing feeling. It's what you've probably dreamed of for years. After several years of just weeks of constant driving from one place to another, sleeping in your car on long trips, and staying in cheap hotels, you long to be in one place for several weeks at a time. When you reach the point that you can afford to fly most places, it eases up a bit . . . until that becomes a chore as well. There's a joke in the comedy biz: "Comedians aren't paid to do comedy. They're paid to travel. Making people laugh is the reward."

Like Spence, you were a comedian and now you're a radio host. How much of *I'll Be Here All Week* is based on your life?

It's tough to say when you define it that way. Everything in the story is true in some form or another. Everything that happens in the book either happened to me in real life or to someone I know. But not necessarily in order or exactly the way it appears in the book. It's funny that I wound up working in radio, like Spence does, because that came after I'd written and sold the novel. That makes it look more like it's based on my life much more than it actually is. By the time I started working at SiriusXM, the novel was almost ready to go to print. For all the similarities between Spence and myself, that one happens to be a coincidence. But it's still not that much of a stretch. Many comedians wind up in radio at some point.

You're also an American who met (and married) a Canadian. In addition to your comedy background, is a lot of your relationship with your wife in the pages of *I'll Be Here All Week*?

One event in my life that is mirrored in the book is that I also met my wife while in a pub in Montreal, just like Spence meets

Sam, right after a show. But the similarities in the relationships pretty much ends there. By the time my wife and I met, much of the drama in my career was in the past. I would be lying, however, if I said that there is not a lot of my wife in the character of Sam. My wife is very quick-witted and clever, and her sense of humor is much like Sam's. Plus, like with many comedians and their spouses, my wife and I forged the early parts of our relationship through phone conversations. Comedians are like teenagers the way they wind up talking for hours over the phone with their significant others.

Spence puts up with a lot from his agent, Rodney. It seems like there has to be an easier way. Why doesn't he fire the guy sooner?

Well, Rodney's not really a villain so much as he's a product of his industry. Comedians don't make movie star money, as we see in the story. So the only way for them or their agents to make money is to constantly work. More than being selfish or evil, Rodney is swamped. He's overworked and chasing a bigger payday, just like Spence is chasing fame. Rodney doesn't skim from Spence because he's trying to sabotage his client; he feels he deserves the higher rate but isn't allowed to take it.

Spence is no angel, either. He seems to sabotage himself plenty.

That's the relationship, really. Spence and Rodney are in an abusive marriage that they are constantly trying to reconcile. Spence is like most comedians in that he is so stubborn and determined to do things his way, he never realizes that he'd do well to listen to some of the advice he gets from Rodney and others. He deliberately does things he knows will get him in trouble. It takes Sam coming along for him to realize the kind of person he's being. He's being his own worst enemy, which is common for comedians. It's what happens when you try to make a business out of your art. It's called show *business* for a reason, and too many comedians forget that fact.

Spence thinks his tombstone will read "I'll Be Here All Week." Why'd that wind up being the title of the book?

Spence thinks that'll be funny on his tombstone, but he doesn't realize that it's already his life. Sam tells him he already works in a cubicle. He just moves it from city to city every week. "I'll Be Here All Week" isn't just a catchphrase at this point in his career. It *is* his career. It's his life. One week to the next, he's going to be in the exact same place. Even if that place is geographically a thousand miles away from where it was last week. Nothing really changes. That's Spence's life when we meet him. So it became the title because it not only fits the book perfectly but because the phrase is so closely associated with stand-up comedy that readers will know what it's about.

The title might seem like it's all about stand-up comedy, but *I'll Be Here All Week* is really a love story between Spence and Sam, isn't it?

It's three love stories! It's a love story between Spence and Sam, and how that grows into what it does. But it's also a love story between Spence and Rodney, and how they are both struggling to make a failing relationship work. And it's also a love story between Spence and comedy. When we first see him, Spence is really struggling with his love for comedy but, by the end of the book, he has found that he still loves it. It just needed to evolve into something new.

There is also the relationship with Beth. Even though Spence refers to them as still being "friends," it doesn't seem like they've ever really recovered from their divorce.

Well, although some would call it good that he gets along with his ex, it's hardly a healthy relationship. For one thing, Spence has never really been okay with being replaced so soon, even if he pretends that it doesn't bother him. For another, it becomes obvious to him that he makes the mistake with Beth that he keeps making with the rest of his life: He keeps going in circles.

He has gone back to Beth in the past, and continues to rely on her when he should move on and get out of her life altogether. He knows this but, like with so much in his life, he's afraid to change.

There seem to be many women in his life between Beth and Sam. But Sam stands apart from the string of one-night stands Spence seems to be having.

For Spence, the best part about Sam is meeting her in that pub and not at a comedy club. He realizes that she actually likes the man she meets in person, not the man he can be onstage. All of those women that Spence has flings with see him as an entertainer, so that's all he tries to be to them. He has as little interest in getting to know them as they do getting to know him. Sam is different because, from the beginning, she wants to know the man in front of her, not the performer onstage. Spence isn't used to being himself with anyone. Sam changes that, which makes him treat everything about her differently than any other woman in his life.

There is a lot of talk in the book about Spence needing to get more TV exposure. Is that really so important to traveling comedians?

It's incredibly important, and becomes a bigger deal every passing year. Like the rest of the entertainment industry, this all comes down to advertising. Stand-up comedy has to compete with so many other forms of entertainment, from sporting events to popular movies to the time of year. And now Netflix, iTunes, and the Internet are also competition. You can see stand-up comedy cheap or free if you want to. Audiences see a guy who has been on TV as somehow being more legit than the guy who has not. Being able to advertise the act with "has been seen on *Late Night with David Letterman*" gives the comedy club something that stands out. The irony is that people are using TV to judge club quality, instead of the other way around. That comedian you see on *The Tonight Show* is doing five minutes of clean, non-offensive jokes. A headlining club comedian has to perform onstage for forty-five minutes to an hour. Still, that TV credit or logo looks good on a poster and in an advertisement. The more of those TV credits a comedian gets, the more his asking price can go up.

Do comedians have "groupies" like musicians and rock stars?

Sure. I imagine every single form of entertainment has people who are enamored with the performer onstage. Jugglers probably have groupies. There is something very attractive and powerful about a person who can command an audience. Couple that with someone who can make you laugh, and it's easy to see how some people would take a comedian home.

Spence seems to be working all the time, but complains about not having any money to show for it. Where does it all go?

And Spence is lucky! He has no mortgage or rent. He has no wife or kids to support. He's living his life out of his car, going from show to show. His money is spent on hotel rooms on his off-nights and gas in his car. But the honest truth of it all is that comedians don't make the money people think they do. Sure, you can make a fortune doing it. Get enough TV credits and A-list work and you can make a very respectable living by selling out larger theaters. But a comedian at Spence's level is happy when he gets that $1,500 per week payday. That's before agent commission, taxes and expenses. That means that, most weeks, he's earning far less. Since comedians only get paid when they work, the only real way to make money as a comedian is to be constantly touring. Do that enough, and a person can make a living doing nothing but stand-up comedy. The downside is that comics often wind up sacrificing relationships in order to do it. That's one reason Spence is so torn when Sam comes along. He has to constantly tour and is never in one place for very long. The promise of a bigger payday ("Tour less, make more") is always so enticing. But Spence isn't making big bucks at all. That's why he keeps hoping for a TV spot to raise his status and pay.

Spence really changes as he begins to fall for Sam. Is this all a comedian really needs? The love of the right woman?

Spence is never really a bad guy. He's in a bit of a funk when we meet him, so he's being self-destructive. But he's only involved with the people who will be involved with him. The thing about Sam is not that she changes him, but that she accepts him for who he really is, which makes the real Spence come out more. He doesn't really want to be the hard-partying entertainer, living life by the seat of his pants and moving on from town to town. He doesn't even want to be dying his hair and pretending to be younger than he is. By the end, he realizes that he's been what others have convinced him he should be. Now he can finally be himself. And Sam loves him for it.

The hardest part of his life is quitting stand-up comedy, even though he thinks about it all the time. Is it that addictive to most comedians?

Most comedians are probably even worse than Spence in that regard. He actually comes up with an idea to keep using his talent while getting off the road and improving his life and stability. But comedians quit the business all the time and then wind up back at it, one way or another. There are comedians from the '80s who were very popular and all over television. They quit doing the road so they could write for TV or produce or direct. Twenty years later, they start doing open-mic gigs in bowling alleys again just because they miss being onstage. The hardest part is walking away and being happy with it. Like Spence says, there's always a what-if in the back of their minds. When Spence tells Sam that he's good at stand-up comedy but doesn't know if he really cares anymore, that's a very big deal.

Where do you see Spence being in ten years?

He's still with Sam. Definitely married and probably with a kid by then. He's a local celebrity, the way a lot of radio show hosts become semi-famous in a certain market. He can show up to local events and people know his name. He hosts comedy shows in town for celebrity comics touring through. And he's in one place and making a good living. His radio cohost may have retired by now, and Spence is now the elder half of the morning show, with some Monkey-Boy kid working under him. Maybe Jamie Hernandez!